A PLACE CALLED PERFECT

Sometimes Violet liked silence, but not now. Blindness made silence scary. She pushed her hands under her thighs and swung her legs, trying to remember a happy song.

Suddenly she heard faint footsteps enter the shop at speed, growing louder as they paced towards her. She looked blindly in the direction of the sound.

"I need to speak to your dad," a voice whispered in her right ear.

"Who's there?" she gasped.

Then heavier footsteps entered the shop. "I've caught you now, you mangy orphan," a different voice panted.

To Mam, the original dreamer

First published in the UK in 2017 by Usborne Publishing Ltd., Usborne House, 83-85 Saffron Hill, London EC1N 8RT, England. www.usborne.com

A C IP catalogue record for this book is available from the British Library.

ISBN 9781474924160   04252-06 JFMAMJJ SOND/18

Printed in the UK.

A PLACE CALLED PERFECT

HELENA DUGGAN

USBORNE

CONTENTS

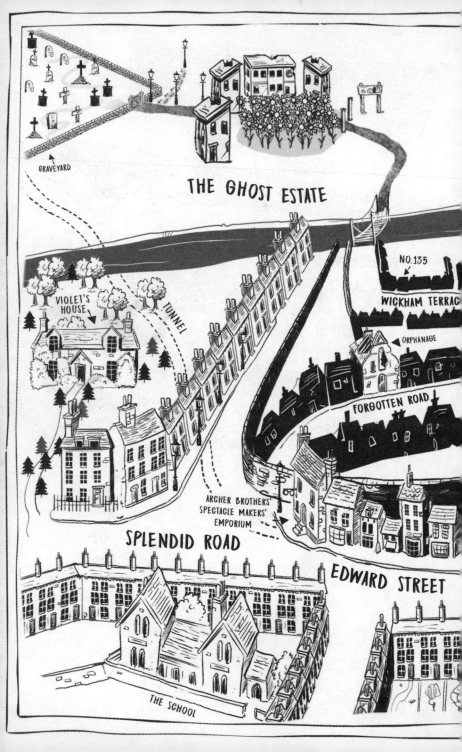

"Violet, is that you, pet?" her mother called from a room down the hallway. "Come in and say hello to our guests."

Violet shook the dark thoughts from her mind, putting all sounds down to the wind. *There goes your imagination again*, she scolded herself, getting up from the floor.

She pulled off her shoes and threw them down by the door. The hall was covered in shiny, cream tiles perfect for socks. She took a run and slid the whole way into the room straight ahead, coming to a stop against the kitchen table.

Four pairs of eyes stared at her, two in embarrassment, two in shock.

"Violet!" her father snapped. "We have guests."

Violet didn't respond.

She'd decided the night before that she wasn't going to talk to her dad for as long as it took him to change his mind and move them all back home again. She hated not talking to him because she loved him more than a billion pounds. But she didn't want the same things as her dad. Her mam didn't really either. Rose Brown was an accountant in a successful firm and had lots of friends in their old town – but she'd told Violet that sometimes you had to do what was right, even though it was hard and you might not want to do it, and that this move was right for their family.

Violet had thought about not talking to her mam either but as an only child that would mean she'd have no one to talk to at all, at least until she made some friends.

Quickly her dad covered the silence, introducing her to the strange men who sat round the kitchen table.

"Violet, this is Mr George Archer."

"Just George is fine," the tall man said, standing up to shake her hand.

She tried not to laugh. George Archer was so tall he couldn't stand straight in the low-ceilinged room. His head bent to one side almost touching his shoulder. Everything about him was long, from his snake-like arms and wormy fingers to his pencil-thin nose that almost divided his face in two. His head was completely bald and creamy white like a freshly laid egg. Clearly uncomfortable, he quickly sat back down.

"And I'm Edward. Pleased to meet you, Violet," the smaller of the Archers said, as he stood to shake her hand too.

Again she had to stop herself laughing. Violet wasn't even the tallest in her class, but she was the same height as Mr Edward Archer. What he lacked in height he made up for in width. He was square, like a loaf of bread. His head was attached straight to his shoulders as if he had forgotten to grow a neck and his eyes stuck out a little as though they were trying to escape from his face.

The two brothers wore the same brown suits and shiny brown shoes. Edward Archer had a funny bowler hat just like the one on her dad's favourite painting of a man with no face. Mr George Archer had the same hat but his rested on the table beside him – he probably wasn't wearing it because it would fall off every time he stood up indoors.

Both of them had weird reddish eyes hidden behind rectangular gold-framed glasses. They looked a little scary until George took his specs off.

"Oh, it's just the glasses. I thought there was something wrong with your eyes!" Violet smiled at the taller twin. "Why are the lenses red?"

George Archer pushed his glasses back onto his nose.

"They're rose-tinted." He scowled. "We—"

"Well, Violet dear –" Edward Archer quickly interrupted his brother – "it's a funny story really, one we hope your father will help us solve. You see this little town of ours is perfect except for one curious fact: every single inhabitant here wears glasses. After only a short time in Perfect, Violet, you and your family will find that your eyesight starts to get dusty, then the edges of your vision will blur. Eventually you will all go completely blind. We've had numerous scientists come to investigate our situation. They say it's because we're so close to the sun."

"Mam!" Violet quivered, trying not to cry. "I don't want to go blind. I like being able to see. I knew we shouldn't have moved here."

"Oh no, I didn't mean to frighten you, Violet dear," Edward Archer said, kindly. "I assure you the effects are only temporary. They wear off as soon as you leave this town of ours – although I'm quite sure you won't ever want to leave Perfect, nobody ever does." The stout man smiled. "In fact, we have found a clever way around our little problem. These glasses work a treat. You'll find everybody here is wearing them; they're quite in vogue as they say." He adjusted his own pair a little, resetting them on his nose.

"You'll have to visit our spectacle shop, dear, so we can fit you with a pair," George Archer smiled.

Violet grabbed her mother's pinstriped skirt.

"I don't want to wear glasses, Mam, there's nothing wrong with my eyes."

"That's why your father's here, dear." Edward smiled. "Hopefully soon nobody will need to wear them."

The Archers were her dad's new bosses. "Eugene was headhunted" her mam had said proudly to friends one evening. Violet didn't think that sounded like a good thing and tried hard *not* to imagine her dad without a head. He'd won an award for his research and had been on the cover of *Eye Spy* magazine. Her mam said the whole world was talking about it, or at least the part of the world that loved eyes too. She said the Archers had read the article in *Eye Spy* and searched him out for the job.

"It's only for a short time, Violet," her mother shushed, looking anxiously at her husband. "Your father will fix the problem."

"Don't worry, Violet," her dad said, reaching to rub her head.

She moved round her mother's back, away from his arms.

"She's tired," he sighed, his cheeks a little red. "It's been a long day, I think it's probably time for bed."

"Oh no, not yet," Edward Archer said quickly. "You must try our tea. It's a Perfect tradition."

"Oh yes." George Archer smiled, grabbing a teapot and cups from the worktop. "It's our custom, I assure you."

A small package sat on the table. Edward opened it, scooped out two large spoons of tea leaves and tipped them into the pot. The package was navy with 'Archers' Tea" printed in ornate gold letters under a brownish picture of the twins in their bowler hats and white aprons.

"It's you," Violet said, looking at Edward.

"Eagle-eyed I see." The smaller twin smiled, pouring boiling water into the pot. "Yes it's our tea. We own the factory that produces it; it's a big employer in the town. Something we're proud of."

"I don't like tea," Violet said, looking at her mother.

"You'll like this one," George Archer replied sharply.

"This tea is a speciality here. It's harvested daily and delivered fresh to every doorstep in Perfect each morning. It's made from the Chameleon plant, which is unique to our town. It's very good for your health and has the most unusual properties. You'll see what I mean. Most people here drink at least a cup a day. It's a tea-mad town." Edward smiled.

Violet didn't like tea and she wasn't sure about the Archers; there was something odd about them.

Eugene and Rose looked at each other as they sat down at the table; Violet sat between them. George Archer stared at her from his place opposite, as his brother poured the tea.

"Now imagine the nicest taste you can think of then take a sip," Edward said, raising his mug.

Violet did as she was told. She imagined her father's favourite drink, which was hers too – ice-cream sundae. Big chunks of cold vanilla ice cream dunked in fizzy orange. She pictured clouds of froth bubbling over the rim of a glass and could almost taste the burst of flavour. Her mouth watered as she raised the mug of tea. A waft of vanilla tingled her nose. She took a sip, careful not to burn her lips. The tea fizzed as she tasted orange and vanilla heaven. This couldn't be tea. She opened her eyes to check no one had swapped the cups, but sure enough, a dull milky brown liquid smiled back at her. She glanced either side at her mam and dad; their eyes were still shut and silly smiles played on their lips.

"I think I'll have another cup," her father said, a little later.

"We thought you might," the Archers replied in unison.

The Browns finished one pot and then had another as Edward told them all about their new home.

Edward was the chatty one and Violet warmed to him a little more than George, who just seemed to snarl and stare. Though, truth be told, she wasn't sure she liked either of them very much at all. Violet heard her mother say the same thing to her dad as they waved goodbye to the Archers from the steps of their new home a little later.

"They give me the creeps, Eugene," Rose whispered through a staged smile.

That night, Violet climbed beneath her new sheets in her new room. The town sounded nice enough from what Edward had said and the tea did weigh heavily in its favour. There were some strange things about the place though. Edward had told them about a curfew. He said it was so everyone got a good night's sleep in Perfect. "Sufficient sleep makes for a happy and healthy town."

She definitely didn't like the idea of a curfew or going blind. And anyway, how could she ever live in a place called Perfect? She'd have to be neat and tidy; she'd definitely have to brush her hair and probably even clean her shoes. It just wouldn't work.

Violet made up her mind: she didn't and wouldn't like Perfect. Then she turned over and slipped into a perfect night's sleep, oblivious to the troubles the morning would bring.

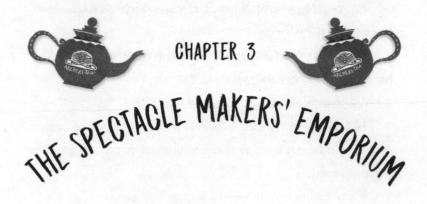

CHAPTER 3

THE SPECTACLE MAKERS' EMPORIUM

The sun warmed Violet's face, pulling her gently from her dreams as it shone in her bedroom window. She'd slept like a log in her new bed.

She'd already stretched and sat up before she realized something was wrong. She could faintly see the edges of her room but everything straight in front of her was covered by a big black blob, as if ink had leaked all over her eyes. She rubbed them but nothing changed – she still couldn't see.

Her heartbeat quickened. She stuck her foot out of the duvet and stretched for the floor.

"Ouch," she yelled, smacking her toe off something solid as she walked blindly towards the door. "Mam!"

"Violet, what is it?" croaked her dad's sleepy voice.

A sudden crash shook the house.

"Eugene!" her mother cried. "Eugene, what's happened, are you okay?"

Violet gingerly felt her way out the door and down the hall to her parents' room.

She stumbled inside. "Mam, I can't see!"

"Neither can I, pet," her father replied, his voice strangely cheerful, "but it's nothing to panic about, we were warned."

"They didn't say it would happen this soon, Eugene!" her mother called.

"No need to panic, girls," he repeated, his voice now a little high-pitched. "Violet, come over and get into bed with your mother. I'll go downstairs and see if I can get hold of the Archers. They'll know what to do."

"But how, Eugene? You can't see either," her mother sobbed.

"Don't worry about me," he replied, walking into Violet as she crawled across their bedroom carpet.

"Dad, watch out!" Violet shouted, breaking her vow of silence only because it was an emergency.

"Oh, what a good idea, pet!" her dad said, easing himself stiffly onto his knees. "I'll be back soon with help, trust me."

Violet's father crawled across the room and out into the hall.

Trust him? He didn't deserve her trust. This was all his fault.

"Ow," she cried, as she banged into the side of her parents' bed.

"You okay, pet?" her mother called from above.

Violet rubbed her forehead, searching for blood.

"Yes, I think so," she moaned, crawling into the empty space beside Rose.

The mattress was still warm and the sheets smelled like her dad; she wriggled over closer to her mam.

"Good morning!" a voice called from below her parents' window. "Isn't it a glorious day, family Brown?"

"Mam, there's someone outside."

"I know, pet, stay here," her mother whispered, getting up from the bed.

Rose stumbled across the room, then the window squeaked and cold air tickled Violet's toes where they stuck out from beneath the duvet.

"Hello?" Rose called.

"Oh, good morning, Mrs Brown. I just stopped by to see how your first day is going and to offer Eugene a lift to work."

"Oh, it's you, Mr Archer," her mother gasped, "what a godsend you are. I'm afraid we have all woken up a little worse for wear. The effects of the sun came on sooner than expected."

"Oh no, that's a pity. Sometimes it happens that way. Not to worry. We'll have you back to normal in no time."

In a few minutes, Mr Edward Archer – it was definitely him because he was almost the same height as Violet – led Eugene, Rose and Violet carefully out of the house and into the back of his car.

"Now on to our spectacle makers' emporium," he called, as the engine whistled into life.

Violet had always thought a "spectacle" meant she was doing something wrong, as her mam often told her to stop making a spectacle of herself. Now she discovered it meant glasses. Emporium was more difficult but she had a feeling it was just a posh word for shop. The Archers seemed to like posh words.

As Mr Edward Archer slowly led her by the arm out of the car, Violet decided she never wanted to be blind again. She liked seeing. Already she missed colour and longed for blue or purple or pinky yellow, or anything that wasn't black and fuzzy. Even brown would do.

"Mr Archer," she said, a thought suddenly hitting her, "we haven't been in the sun yet. So how could it affect our eyes?"

"It was streaming in your window all morning, dear," Edward Archer replied.

"But—"

"Some people are very sensitive to it, Violet," he

interrupted, squeezing her upper arm so tight she thought he might sever it off.

She squirmed away a little just as her toe hit something solid.

"Ouch," she squealed, lifting her foot off the ground.

"Oh, silly me, I forgot to mention the steps," Edward Archer said, easing his grip.

Holding Edward's elbow tight, she gingerly inched up five wide steps, then suddenly the black got blacker and she stumbled.

"Oh, don't worry, dear, we're just coming inside, that's why the light has changed a little." He laughed.

Violet smiled as politely as possible. She'd half decided already but his laughing made it fact: she hated Edward Archer almost as much as his brother.

"Now I'm just going to lower you into this chair," he said, grabbing her hands and easing her backwards.

She winced as the cold leather touched her bare legs. She was still wearing her short pyjamas, the furry love-heart pair. She blushed, picturing the pink and red pattern. She'd told her mam she was getting too old for love-hearts but parents never listen.

"I'm just going to get your mother and father, dear," Edward Archer called, his footsteps fading into the distance.

Silence filled the shop.

Sometimes Violet liked silence, but not now. Blindness made silence scary. She pushed her hands under her thighs and swung her legs, trying to remember a happy song.

Suddenly she heard faint footsteps enter the shop at speed, growing louder as they paced towards her. She looked blindly in the direction of the sound.

"I need to speak to your dad," a voice whispered in her right ear.

"Who's there?" she gasped.

Then heavier footsteps entered the shop. "I've caught you now, you mangy orphan," a different voice panted.

A chase ensued. Someone raced behind Violet's chair, hitting the wood and rocking it sideways, before both sets of footsteps ran back out the door and faded off into the distance.

"Who's there?" she cried, gripping tightly to the arms of her chair.

"Violet, what are you doing here?"

This voice she recognized. It was George Archer.

"Somebody was in the shop; there was a chase!"

"Really?" he replied, sounding worried. "Did you see them? What did they look like?"

"No," she said quickly. "I can't see but I heard them. One of them whispered in my ear!"

"Ah." George Archer laughed. "You've gone blind

already? Losing one's sight can play havoc with one's hearing, you know."

"No, there really was someone here, I didn't imagine it, I swear," Violet insisted.

"No, there wasn't, Violet," George snapped, stopping the conversation dead.

Other familiar voices entered the shop.

"Mam, is that you?" she said, leaning out of her chair.

Someone grabbed her shoulders, pulling her back.

"Lots of glass to be broken here, Violet dear," George Archer snarled behind her.

"Violet, don't worry – we're here, pet," her dad soothed from somewhere on her left.

She wanted to reply but couldn't. Silence hung in the air for a moment, then Edward Archer spoke. "Now, you're first, Violet," he said; it sounded like he was standing directly in front of her. "I do hope these fit. If not we can adjust them. You have a rather large head for someone so young."

Violet winced and closed her eyes as a pair of glasses were shoved roughly onto the bridge of her nose. Warm, sweaty hands cupped her face and adjusted the frames. The arms of the glasses felt a little chunky and uncomfortable behind her ears.

"Now," Edward said, "tell us what you see."

Violet held her breath. What if she was still blind?

Slowly she opened her eyes and gasped.

Colour filled her vision. Rich brown from the shining dark wood that panelled the walls of the shop, deep red from the thick carpet at her feet and bright gold from the rows of spectacles that rested inside sparkling glass cabinets. It was the poshest place she'd ever seen.

"Is something wrong?" Edward asked.

"No," Violet stammered, looking around. "It's just, I've never been anywhere quite like this before. It's amazing!"

A look of pride passed between the brothers.

"We try our best." Edward smirked.

She sat in her chair and watched the twins search the cabinets for glasses to fit her parents.

All the frames were the same, rectangular, gold-rimmed and delicate, with rose-tinted lenses. There was something unusual about the part where the arms of the glasses hooked in behind the ears. It was flat, boxy and rectangular, in contrast to the delicate frame. Violet adjusted hers. They were pinching the sides of her head.

"Try to leave them alone, will you?" George snarled as he caught her fiddling with her specs.

She sat on her hands and watched the Archers hover around her parents for a few minutes. Then, sure the twins were distracted, she slipped off the chair and looked round.

Everything in the shop was shiny. She could see herself in the gold handles of the glass cabinet doors that filled the wall in front of her, from floor to ceiling. Edward Archer, trying to reach a pair of glasses in the top cabinet, was perched on top of a huge wooden ladder with his back to her.

There was a panelled wall to her left and Violet noticed a thin thread of light leaking through a gap in the dark wood. She walked to the wall and gently pushed on the polished panel. It opened inwards to a secret room.

She stepped inside and found herself in a library, its dark wooden shelves lined with books. The books were old and some were so worn it was impossible to read their spines. They were the type her dad loved, the sort that he said told a story not just on the pages but about the people who owned them before. Her mam said that meant they were second-hand and smelly.

Violet pulled some books out, first *An Optical Illusion*, then *Blind Man's Bluff* and finally *Seeing Things*. All the books were the same, they were all about eyes. She was reaching for another when she heard a voice behind her.

"Don't even think about it."

She turned on the spot and froze. George Archer stood in front of her.

"Perfect kids must act perfectly!" he barked.

"There you are, George," Edward Archer said, peeping

his head round the panel door. "I see you found Violet. We were worried, dear."

Violet raced past Edward back into the shop and the safety of her mother's side. She studied the Archers from behind Rose's chair as the brothers carried on fitting her parents' glasses.

Oddly, Edward didn't seem as small as before; his head wasn't as large either and his eyes were hardly bulging. George too had changed. He didn't look overly long, his eyes fitted his face and his arms and legs weren't so spindly. He even stood tall without bending his head. They were small changes, but added together they meant the Archers didn't look quite so ugly. You could even say they looked nice. It didn't mean she was starting to like them though.

Her parents both wore gold-rimmed glasses now too. Rose looked lovely but she had always been beautiful, everybody said so and Violet hoped someday they'd say the same about her. Her dad looked handsome too – he even seemed to have more hair. They were the perfect couple, why hadn't she noticed it before?

"Violet," her mam said, as they left the shop, "those glasses really suit you, pet. You're beautiful!"

Perfect was sending them all a little mushy but Violet still wasn't falling for it. She didn't like the town for making her blind and she definitely didn't like the Archers, especially George who seemed pretty angry most of the time.

Standing on the steps outside the Archers' Emporium she lifted up her specs and looked around. Everything was a fuzzy, dark mess. She dropped her glasses back over her eyes and her sight returned.

She tried it a few more times and shivered. Without their glasses the three of them would see nothing at all. The same had to be true for everyone else who lived in the town. As far as Violet was concerned, this wasn't her idea of perfect.

CHAPTER 4

FIRST SONS OF PERFECT

The Archers had given Violet's dad the day off to settle in. So the family decided to head into the town and have a look around.

The best way to see Perfect was on foot, Edward Archer had said as he dropped them home, so that's what they decided to do. They changed out of their pyjamas and had a quick breakfast, then Violet led her parents down their driveway. Rose stopped at the bottom and gasped. "Isn't it beautiful, Eugene!"

They were surrounded by mountains. Greenish hills were to the front and blue mountain peaks loomed high behind them with nothing else for miles around. Perfect sat in the middle of the ranges, as if a scoop had been taken out of them leaving just enough space for the town. On the journey yesterday Violet had had the distinct feeling they were driving into the middle of nowhere – now she knew she was right.

After a few short hours she was already used to wearing her glasses. In a strange way it was like they'd been stuck on her face forever. Everything was now crystal clear and, she had to admit, the view was kind of nice.

Their house was on the edge of town, at the bottom of a long, tree-lined avenue. As they walked Violet noticed the trees were exactly the same distance apart – she measured them by counting her steps.

After walking for a few minutes they turned left off the avenue and the town centre came into view. A black iron plaque high on the wall of a building read "Splendid Road".

The road was narrow and lined with three-storey, red-brick buildings. It ran the whole way to the Archer brothers' optician's which stood out like a beacon ahead of them. As they walked towards it, Violet noticed that every door on the street was painted black and a window box of flowers decorated every sill.

They reached the optician's shop and the steps in front reminded Violet of where she'd bashed her toe earlier that morning. Now she saw the stone building in all its glory, sparkling gold letters proudly spelling out "Archer

Brothers' Spectacle Makers' Emporium" above their navy-painted door.

To the left of the emporium was a high stone wall, to the right was a street of stone buildings which seemed to be filled with shops. Another black iron plaque, high on a wall, read "Edward Street".

"Isn't it beautiful, Violet?" her father smiled. "I love these old walled towns, lots of history."

Violet held her silence. History was her least favourite subject in school.

The family continued on to Edward Street.

They walked past the Hatchet Family Butcher's three doors down from the optician's, and received a big hello from a man in a white hat, with a red-striped apron and gold-rimmed specs. He greeted them by name, which was odd, because they definitely hadn't been introduced.

"It's a small town, Rose, something we'll have to get used to," her father said, when her mother questioned the friendliness of the locals.

"Oh, I think I'm used to it already, Eugene. This place feels like home, it's what we've been searching for. I'm so glad you brought us here."

What? Violet's mother hadn't liked the thought of moving. She'd said loads of times that she was only doing it for the good of the family. She'd changed her mind quickly.

"I think we've made the right choice, Eugene." Her mother smiled, squeezing her husband's hand.

Her dad beamed and kissed her mam's forehead outside "Sweet Patisserie", the baker's shop. Violet cringed.

Things were strange in the town. Firstly *everyone* wore glasses, the same rectangular, gold-rimmed, rose-tinted style. The streets were perfectly clean and orderly. There wasn't any rubbish floating about, not even a single sweet wrapper. There was no chewing gum stuck to the black benches that lined the footpaths and not the tiniest bit of graffiti on the walls. The people were all skinny and though they weren't really alike there was something similar about each person they passed. It was like a gloss or shine – somehow everyone glowed.

"They're healthy, Violet," her father said when she brought it up. "The Archers told me this is rated the healthiest town in the world."

It was definitely true. There wasn't a chippers anywhere and she loved fish and chips on a Sunday evening – it was a Brown family tradition. She noted that down as another black mark against the town.

While her parents were busy chatting to another local who knew them by name, Violet quietly slipped away.

She passed by the Town Hall, an old building with four stone columns decorating its facade. Violet stopped and craned her neck back to get a better look at the huge clock tower that sat on the top of the hall's slated roof. She imagined it was possible to see the whole town and the mountains from up there.

Next to the Town Hall was the Archers' Tea Shop, painted in the same navy and gold colours as the tea packet which lay empty on their kitchen table from the night before.

A little further down Edward Street, Violet noticed a lane off to her left. High up on the wall was another black iron plaque which read "Archers' Avenue".

She turned off the main street onto the spotless cobbles. The right-hand side of the avenue was lined with two-storey stone houses while on the left was a tiny, almost hidden passageway which appeared to run down by the back of the shops that faced onto Edward Street.

The passageway, called Rag Lane, was dark, shadowed by the back of the shops on the left and a high stone wall on the right. It was uninviting too, unlike everything else she'd seen in Perfect so far.

Something about it drew her in.

A little nervous, she walked down the narrow passage, stopping at regular intervals to see if anyone was watching from the shadows. Her heart was racing, but she kept going. This was the only thing in the town that wasn't so perfect. It felt as if she was starting to walk downhill when the lane sloped a little to the right and she came to a dead end.

She turned around to go back and noticed she was behind the Town Hall. The glass windows of the clock tower loomed high above her.

She returned to the start of the passageway and instead of turning right towards Edward Street, she kept the wall on her left and decided to explore further along Archers' Avenue.

One of the stone houses on the right-hand side of the Avenue had another black iron plaque and she crossed the cobble dash to read it.

The Original Homeplace of Messrs George and Edward Archer, first sons of Perfect.

There was something else scratched in above the lettering. It was very faint but she could just make out the words *"and William"* roughly scrawled into the sign.

It must be the same Archers, but she hadn't heard of William.

She peered through the window beside her, curious to get a look at where the Archers were born. As her nose brushed the glass a face zoomed forward from the darkness inside.

An old woman stared out at her. Her skin hung so close to her skull that her blue eyes seemed to jump from her face. Her white hair wasn't exactly messy but it wasn't tidy either, like she hated brushing hers too. Her grimace was gapped with missing teeth and there was something else about her, something Violet couldn't put her finger on.

Shocked, Violet turned and raced back up towards Edward Street. In her haste, she tripped over a loose shoelace, knocking off her glasses. As she fell onto her knees to search the cobblestones, laughter echoed round her. It was the same haunting laughter she'd heard in the driveway the night before.

Finding the frames she frantically shoved them onto her nose and sprinted back onto the main street. She spotted her parents outside the Archers' Tea Shop.

"Oh, there you are, Violet," her mother smiled, "will we have a pot?"

Violet nodded, catching her breath.

Her mother pushed open the door of the tea shop and a bell chimed in the corner of the store.

The wall behind the counter was lined with wooden shelves all filled with navy and gold packets of tea that bore the Archers' portrait. Navy and gold mugs, tea strainers and pots hung from hooks in the rafters and beautiful, upturned wooden tea chests served as tabletops around the shop.

"Take a seat by the window," her mother said, as she headed for the counter.

Violet and her dad sat down at a table looking out on the pretty streetscape. To cover the awkward silence between them Violet pretended to be engrossed in people watching.

Rose came over with a tray in one hand and an ornate tea chest in the other.

"What's that for, Mam?" Violet asked, eyeing the chest.

"It's for the Tea Man, Violet. The woman behind the counter told me everyone has them in Perfect. You leave them at your door and the Tea Man drops your daily supply in it each morning. Isn't it beautiful? The tea is delivered fresh everyday, you know, just as the Archers said. No wonder it's so tasty. They're so nice here and the prices aren't too bad either, Eugene." Rose smiled, patting her pocket.

Eugene hadn't heard a word and continued to look out the window as Rose began to pour the tea.

"Mam," Violet said.

"Yes, pet?"

"My glasses fell off in the avenue just down there," she pointed in the general direction, "and I heard someone laughing at me. I heard the same voice last night when we arrived. I think someone's following me."

"Violet." Rose smiled, wrapping her arm around her daughter.

"Yes, Mam?"

"You know your imagination runs away with itself, pet. You're just like your father," Rose said, nodding at Eugene, who was still daydreaming through the window.

"But, Mam, I really did hear someone. What if it was a ghost or a monster or something? I don't think I like this town."

Rose laughed. "You're always jumping to the craziest conclusions. You'll be fine, Violet. What could go wrong in a beautiful place like this?"

She kissed Violet's forehead and rubbed a hand through her hair.

"Now have some tea, pet."

Violet did as she was told, trying to shake the voice from her head. Why didn't her mam ever listen to her? What if it really was a ghost or something? She stared out of the window at the picture-perfect people walking by and took a sip from her cup. Vanilla heaven floated over her tongue and she forgot all her worries. Maybe tea was the answer to everything.

CHAPTER 5

DREAMS OF GHOSTLY BOYS

After only two weeks in the town, the summer holidays were over. Violet didn't like the idea of starting a new school or making new friends. She had already tried with some of the local children, but it hadn't worked out.

Her mam was starting to embrace life in Perfect. She had taken Violet to a book club meeting to introduce her to some of her friends' children, who were having a mini book club meeting.

Drinking tea and eating home-baked cakes, the children discussed Roald Dahl's *James and the Giant Peach*. Violet told them she hadn't read it but loved some of his other books, like *Fantastic Mr Fox* and *The BFG*.

"If you haven't read *James and the Giant Peach* then

I'm afraid you can't take part in the discussion, Violet," one of the children stated.

For the rest of the evening Violet sat silently listening to them discuss the characterization of Aunt Sponge. At the end she left red faced and angry.

"How did you get on, Violet dear?" her mother asked, as they walked the tree-lined road towards home.

"Terrible, Mam," Violet replied. "I wasn't allowed to talk."

"Of course not, Violet, you hadn't read the book!" Her mother sighed. "But did you enjoy the evening? Don't you think they're very nice?"

"Too nice!" Violet snapped, remembering how each child had smiled and done whatever the adults told them to.

Her mother wouldn't listen. "I'm sick of it, Violet. 'Too nice', what does that mean? You'll really have to start making an effort. You're embarrassing me in front of all the other mums!"

"Mums"? When did her mam ever use a word like "mum"? She'd normally say mam or mammy but never *mum*.

In her old life Rose Brown didn't bake and she burned every dinner she ever made. She didn't do housework and always told Violet that a woman's work wasn't in the home. She worked hard and was usually back even later than Eugene in the evenings.

In this town she was different.

It had started with sorting out odd socks. By the second week, she'd joined loads of committees and had begun calling everyone "dear".

Every day she got up early and made breakfast for the family. Once she'd said goodbye to Violet's dad and cleaned the house, she'd head out to meet her new friends – the ones whose children Violet had to pretend to like. Sometimes it was for book club, or cookery lessons or even golf. In her short time in Perfect, Violet's mam had even become head of the town's baking committee. Rose was delighted, she'd smiled from ear to ear when she got the phone call and spent the rest of the night baking. Her cakes tasted nice but that wasn't the point.

Her old mother hated golf and would laugh at the idea of a book club. Now she was a "perfectionist" who shone like everyone else.

Her dad had changed too, but he wasn't shiny at all. He'd become dull and lifeless. Lately, he was always tired and even his smile had faded. He looked older. In two weeks he'd aged five years.

Violet had never seen her dad so sad and maybe it was partly her fault.

She still wasn't speaking to him. They used to talk about everything, but for the last fourteen days and five hours she hadn't said a word to him. At first he'd tried to carry on talking to her as usual, but by day four he'd realized he wasn't going to get a squeak out of her and he'd given up too.

Her parents were even different with each other.

Before, whenever they were together, they were always hugging and kissing. Violet used to think it was really embarrassing but now she wished they'd embarrass her, even just for a second. Instead her mother tried to be the perfect housewife and her dad was hardly ever home.

Violet had no friends in Perfect and it was beginning to feel like she had no parents either. Since they'd arrived she'd spent most days in her room alone, only coming downstairs for dinner when her mother presented another one of her concoctions.

The night before she started her new school, Violet overheard her parents in the kitchen as she climbed the stairs to bed.

Her father's voice made her stop.

"Rose –" he sighed, sounding worried, "will you please put that away and sit down. I need to speak to you."

"I can hear you perfectly well from where I'm standing," her mother replied. "I want to finish these buns."

"Rose. Please. Now," her father almost shouted. Violet stiffened. She'd never heard him that angry before.

"Just a minute, darling, I'm almost finished."

"I thought you hated cooking?" he snapped.

"Really? Whatever made you think that? I love it. Since I've moved here a whole new world has opened up!"

"I'm worried about this place, Rose." His voice softened.

"What was that, darling?"

Violet heard her dad sigh, then a chair scraped the tiles and heavy footsteps thudded across the kitchen. Violet froze.

"Rose," her father said, stopping in the doorway.

"Yes, darling?"

"You know I love you, don't you?" He sounded lonely.

"Of course, dear. Now do you want sprinkles on your buns or will I make my special icing? The ladies loved the icing last time round."

Her father didn't reply. He left the kitchen and headed up the hall.

Violet climbed the rest of the stairs as quietly as she could, slipped into her bedroom and jumped under her duvet.

A few minutes later her dad's figure appeared in the doorway.

"Violet," he whispered, "are you awake?"

She pulled the covers tight, and pretended to be asleep.

Her father tiptoed across the floor and sat gently on the edge of her bed. Her heart beat faster. He rubbed her hair. She wanted to sit up and hug him, because she knew he was sad, but she couldn't let herself. He was the one who had gotten them into this mess.

"Violet," he whispered, his voice shaky, "I love you, pet."

He bent down and kissed her forehead, then gently tucked in the edges of the duvet and slipped quietly from the room. She opened her eyes.

What had gotten into her family?

She was sad to see her dad so upset, but at least it meant he wasn't enjoying their new home either, and the more he didn't like it, the sooner they would move back to their old town.

Violet lay awake for ages. She was nervous about starting her new school the next day and couldn't sleep.

Sometime later she heard her dad's heavy footsteps passing her door and heading downstairs. She was beginning to doze off as she listened for his return, when something hit the floor.

Quickly she reached for her glasses on the bedside table but found nothing. Throwing her arm over the side of the bed she felt along the floor.

"Can't sleep, can you?"

Startled, Violet ducked back under the duvet. Someone laughed. It was that same laugh – the one she'd heard before.

"Why are you hiding under your covers? Sure you can't see me anyway!"

Violet pulled the duvet down a little to peer out. The room was fuzzy, but there was a black shadow moving in the far corner. Terrified, she ducked back under the covers.

"What do you want?" she squealed, her voice muffled by the sheets.

"I want all your money and as many sweets as you can give me or the doll gets it!"

"I haven't got a doll and I don't know where to get sweets," she quivered.

The boy laughed again. It was definitely a boy.

"I'm only messing! Oh they're coming –" he sounded panicked – "I have to go!"

Footsteps ran to the side of the bed. The intruder seemed to bend down and pick something up from the floor.

"Here're your specs. Enjoy school tomorrow!"

An object landed lightly on the covers and she reached out and felt her glasses. Quickly she pushed them on and switched on the bedside lamp.

The room was empty. Her heart pounded. Was she going mad? Maybe the sun was affecting her more than the others? She lay back down and pulled the duvet over her head, managing to fall asleep a little later, her dreams full of ghostly boys.

CHAPTER 6

SCHOOL RULES

After a restless night hidden under her duvet, Violet got up early the next morning and went downstairs to have breakfast. In the kitchen her father was half asleep at the table, leaning over some papers. He sat up quickly, gathering his notes as she walked in.

"You're up early, pet," he said, almost knocking over a cold cup of tea.

"I couldn't sleep," she replied. The words were brief but it was a relief to speak to him after such a long silence.

"Me neither." Eugene smiled warmly.

"What ya doing?" Violet asked.

"Just research for work," he said, packing the pages away under his notepad.

"Is it for the Archers?"

He nodded and pushed his chair back from the table.

"Would you like some cereal, pet?"

"Dad," Violet said, "do you like the Archers?"

"Of course, pet. They're my bosses."

"It's just, well, there's something strange about them and this place. Don't you think Mam is acting a little weird?"

"Violet, don't say that about your mother. It's just the stress of the move. You've been hard on this place since we got here. Give it a chance," he snapped.

For the second time in not even a day there was anger in his voice. What was it with adults? Last night he'd sounded like he wasn't sure about the town either.

"I hate it here, Dad, I hate this place! I never wanted to move here. You made us!" she roared, storming from the room.

"Violet, get back here this minute!"

His tone was terrifying and even though she wanted to be brave and walk away, she turned around and edged back into the doorway.

"Don't you ever speak to me like that again. I am trying to make a life for us here. I know it's not easy to move at your age but you have to give this place a chance."

"At my age! I'm not a baby. I *have* given Perfect a chance but I hate it. I HATE it! I have no friends and you and Mam are acting weird. Then last night I couldn't sleep because there was someone in my room. I wasn't even going to tell you because I knew you wouldn't believe me."

"What do you mean 'someone in your room'?" He looked alarmed.

"I heard a voice, Dad. It was a boy; he talked to me."

"Violet, it's just your imagination again. It's a new house. Look, pet, we're all trying to find our feet here. You'll make lots of new friends at school today and soon you'll forget we ever had this fight."

"No I won't, Dad. You never listen to me. I wish I'd never started talking to you again!" Violet screamed and ran from the kitchen.

This time she didn't turn back, though her dad called her name. She sprinted up the stairs, slammed her door and flung herself onto the bed.

For a while her dad clattered around in the kitchen below, then the front door banged, the car roared to life and he was gone.

Violet cried into her sheets loud enough so her mother would hear. She wanted her mam to give her a hug and whisper that everything was okay, like she would have before Perfect. But her mam never came and Violet got ready for her first day of school by herself.

A grey skirt, shirt and jumper rested on a hanger that

swung off the end of her bed: the local school uniform. She got dressed, sat on the duvet and pulled up her grey socks before sticking her feet into her polished black shoes. She walked over to the mirror and sighed. She was colourless.

Her mother had warned her to brush her hair so, in an effort to brighten up her look, she took a purple, a pink and a yellow scrunchie from the drawer, brushed her hair as neatly as she could and tied it up, then went back downstairs.

"Were you fighting with your father this morning, Violet?" her mother asked, joining her in the kitchen.

"No," Violet answered, her voice teary.

"Are you okay, dear?"

She raised her red-rimmed eyes to meet her mother's.

"I'm fine."

"Oh good." Her mother smiled, oblivious. "I've made you some ham sandwiches and a bun for lunch. Now brush your hair, Violet, I don't want you looking a mess in front of all the other mothers."

"I did brush it!"

Her mother tutted, then grabbed a brush from the windowsill and proceeded to yank at Violet's head. Her tears welled again as her mother took the coloured bands out replacing them with a single grey scrunchie.

They walked in silence down Splendid Road, past the

Archer Brothers' Spectacle Makers' Emporium onto Edward Street, and then turned right towards the school. The street went uphill a little and Violet panted as she followed her mother's march.

Soon they came to a halt outside a large, grey stone building set back a little from the road. The school roof was pointy at both ends, like two witches' hats. The entrance door was high and pointed too making the place look more like a church than a school. Violet shivered.

The playground was full of children waiting in neat rows for the bell to ring. Every child was dressed perfectly in the same grey uniform. None of the children were talking but some smiled politely at Violet as she passed.

"See," her mother whispered as they walked under the imposing entrance and into a hallway, "you're going to make great friends here. Friends for life!"

They were directed to the principal's office and, after a quick and formal introduction, Violet said goodbye to her mother and followed the principal to her classroom.

She stood nervously at the front of the class as the smart-suited principal whispered something to her new teacher. In her old school, the minute the teacher was distracted, Violet and her classmates would talk, pass notes and sometimes even switch seats. Here it was different; the students sat in silence. They didn't even smile.

The teacher, Mrs Moody, was short, round and granny

old. She wore the usual gold-rimmed glasses, a blue skirt, red cardigan and a white shirt. She had the Perfect shine.

"Violet dear," she said as the principal left the room, "take a seat. There is one at the back."

Violet walked to the end of the room and took a seat between a girl with pigtails and a curly-haired boy. They both smiled as she sat down.

"Now, class, say hello to Violet."

"Hello, Violet," the class responded on cue.

Violet blushed. Then Mrs Moody asked her to stand up and tell the class about her life before Perfect. Every student listened. No one chewed a pencil, chatted or fidgeted. When she'd finished, the teacher gave the class some work and came over to talk to Violet.

"Dear," she whispered, "we have a few tests here that each new student has to take so we can tell where you fit."

"What do you mean?" Violet asked. She didn't fit in anywhere.

"It's nothing to worry about. We just like to assess all our students. To tell what standard you have reached and if you have any defects – I mean problems – we should be aware of."

"Oh no, Mrs Moody, I don't have any problems." Violet smiled as nicely as she could.

"I don't mean problems as such, dear. It's just in this school we like to nurture the perfect student. Not all our pupils are perfect when they come to us. Take Michael over there," the teacher said, pointing to a blond-haired boy busy doing his maths, "he was quite excitable when he first arrived, couldn't sit still for a minute, but we soon worked that out of him and now he's picture perfect."

"Oh, I can sit still," Violet insisted, disliking her new teacher's tone.

"I'm sure you can, Violet dear, but there are all sorts of afflictions students are burdened with. We've had some here who made up stories, some who doodled all day, others like Michael who couldn't sit still. The list goes on. You may have no problems at all, dear, but we do need to know. Now it won't take long."

Swiftly, Mrs Moody put a piece of paper onto Violet's desk and held a pencil out in front of her. Violet looked at the pencil then back at her teacher, who smiled and nodded.

"Take it, dear."

Violet reached up and took the pencil.

"Ah, left-handed. Thought as much." The teacher tutted as she walked away.

Confused, Violet looked down at the paper on her desk.

Question one: What is your name?

She tried not to laugh as she filled in the empty box; this was easy.

The questions got sillier:

What was your first pet's name?

Do you visit your grandmother a lot?

Why would the school need to know those things?

Then they got stranger:

Have you ever felt the urge to run away from home?

Do you question adults?

She didn't know what to write and had only filled in a few answers by the time tea break was called.

An old woman with white hair curled tight to her head and wearing the usual glasses rolled a trolley into the classroom. A large silver canister with a huge Archers' Tea logo stuck to the side, rested on top of the trolley.

Everyone set down their pencils and took a mug from their desk. They queued up in an orderly fashion and pulled a lever on the side of the canister, filling their mugs with tea.

"Did you not bring a mug, Violet?" Mrs Moody asked, standing above her. "Take this one." She thrust a mug into Violet's grip before she'd even had time to respond. "We love our tea in Perfect!"

Violet looked down at the navy mug in her hand. Portraits of the Archer brothers smiled out at her sitting over the words *Archers' Tea is Perfect Tea*. She wanted to throw the mug out the window but thought better of the idea, seeing as tea was about the only thing she actually liked in Perfect.

She finished her mug and resumed her work. The questions got even stranger.

Have you ever had a secret? If so, give details.

Do you like art (this includes drawing, painting, singing, writing or any other form of expressing oneself)?

Violet's head was a muddle by the time lunch was called and she couldn't wait to get outside and play.

She followed a line of pupils from the classroom out into the playground. A grey, stone wall marked the edges of the playground and screwed to it, the whole way round, was a long wooden bench.

All the pupils walked uniformly over to the bench, took a spot, opened their lunch boxes and began to eat.

The sun was shining but everything was grey. There was no life in the yard, no screaming, shouting or laughing, which was normal in Violet's old school. Nobody ran, there was no football, no tig, nothing. She tried not to think about her old friends and what they were doing right now as she took a free spot on the bench.

Once they'd finished eating, kids began to close their lunch boxes and stand up. One group appeared to be marking out a hopscotch course on the ground while another group took out a long skipping rope. Maybe they did play games after all!

"Hello, Violet."

She was just closing her lunch box and looked up to see a red-haired girl from her class.

"I'm Beatrice," the girl said. "Would you like to join us for a game of skip?"

"Oh, erm…yeah, I'd love to!"

Beatrice smiled and Violet and her new friend walked over to the group of girls that had formed around the long skipping rope.

"Has everyone met Violet?" Beatrice asked. "She's new here; started today."

"Hello, Violet," the group said in unison, polite smiles resting on all their faces.

"Who'd like to hold the rope first?" Beatrice asked.

Violet stepped forward but the red-haired girl held up her hand.

"Not straight away, Violet. You have to learn how to swing the rope first."

Violet blushed and stepped back into the comfort of the crowd. She knew how to hold a skipping rope. When the game started, each girl stepped into the rope and jumped exactly three times. There was no laughing or joking and the rules seemed very strict.

When it came to Violet's turn she jumped nervously

in, the first two skips were great and she relaxed. To liven things up she decided to try a trick she used to do in her old school for her third skip. The rope came round and she crossed her legs as it passed beneath her.

Immediately the girls stopped swinging and everybody looked at Violet.

"That's not in the rules," Beatrice barked.

"I'm sorry," Violet stuttered.

"It's not in the rules, Violet," Beatrice repeated. "If it is not in the rules then you can't do it. What do you think rules are for?"

Violet didn't know what to say as she looked around at the angry faces. Suddenly Beatrice swung the rope again.

"It's okay, Violet." She smiled as though nothing had happened. "Maybe you should sit this round out to watch."

Violet did as she was told, finding a spot a little way back from the game. The girls jumped like robots until the bell rang, then everything stopped immediately and the pupils filed back silently into their classrooms.

School seemed really strange here; this town definitely wasn't perfect for children.

Back inside, Violet continued with the questionnaire. Why would the school need to know if she'd ever had an imaginary friend or if she daydreamed a lot? She was just writing that daydreaming was one of her favourite things when the pencil slipped from her hand onto the wooden floor. It was out of reach so she slid off her seat and under the desk. As she stretched for the pencil something etched into the bottom of her desk caught her eye.

William Archer was here, full of life and nothing to fear.

She turned awkwardly in the small space and ran her fingers over the roughly scrawled words.

It was that name again, William Archer.

It was weird that the Archers or her parents had never mentioned William. He had to be cool. Edward or George would never scratch their names into a plaque or a desk; no one in Perfect would.

She crawled back out and took her seat.

Just as she was about to start writing again, the silence hit her. Slowly she looked up. For the second time that day, all eyes were on her.

"You've decided to rejoin us, I see." Mrs Moody grimaced.

"Oh, I...I dropped my pencil," Violet said, holding it up.

"And you didn't think to ask permission?"

"Oh, I...erm..." Permission to pick up a pencil? That sounded stupid.

"Rules, Violet," the teacher snapped. "Beatrice told me about the skipping incident and now this. I'm afraid I will have to call your parents."

Call her parents because of a silly skipping trick and a lost pencil?

"But...I just..."

"No buts, Violet. You are on thin ice as it is, my dear. Now, class, back to work." Mrs Moody smiled.

Violet sat in shock for a while before returning to the questions.

What's the first thing that comes to mind when you think of Perfect?

Angrily she drew a dog poo. She had to get out of this town.

CHAPTER 7

IDDCS

The following afternoon, Violet sat at the kitchen table trying to do her homework. It was an essay titled "Why the World Needs Rules".

She didn't feel the world needed that many rules and had tried to debate the subject with the class earlier that day, almost causing Mrs Moody to have a heart attack. Nobody else agreed and for some strange reason she felt the whole exercise had been aimed at her.

"I've been speaking to your teacher, Violet," her mother sighed, walking into the kitchen. "She said you've been acting up in class and are not integrating with the other students…"

She let the sentence hang for a moment. Violet tried

to speak, but her mother held up a hand.

"They analyzed your test results. I can't believe I never saw it before. It's my fault. I take full responsibility."

"What do you mean, Mam? What test?"

"Violet, please, I know it's just your condition talking, but don't answer your mother back."

"Mam," Violet pleaded, "if you are talking about that test I did yesterday it was the stupidest thing I have ever seen. They even asked me the colour of my favourite pair of socks. You would have laughed. It's so strange here, Mam, this place gives me the creeps—"

"Stop it, Violet, I won't hear another word. You know, colour can tell a lot about a person, especially the colour of their socks! Now, Violet dear –" her mother continued; she was starting to love the word "dear" she sounded like Mrs Moody – "you have a condition called IDDCS. It's Irritable Dysfunctional Disobedient Child Syndrome. I can't believe I never picked up on it before. It has probably afflicted you all your life, dear," she said, reaching into her pocket, "that's why we're putting you on these."

Rose pulled out a small brown bottle and placed it on the table in front of Violet.

"You'll take one in the morning –" she said, shaking a yellow pill out onto her hand. Then she got up, filled a glass with water and put it and the pill down in front of her daughter – "and two in the evening. The doctor said to give you the morning one straight away as yours is a serious condition. I'll give you the evening ones when I get back. Don't worry about remembering, dear, Mrs Moody kindly gave me this alarm so I can set a reminder." She placed a small clock in the centre of the table. "They really do look out for your well-being at that school."

"But, Mam, I've only been there two days! Mrs Moody doesn't even know me. The test was stupid and I wasn't disobedient. I dropped my pencil and crossed my legs in skipping. Mam, please, I don't want to take pills. There is nothing wrong with me!"

"Violet, stop it now! I know it's your condition talking, but I do find it trying sometimes."

"But, Mam—"

"Enough, dear! Swallow that now. I have to meet my book club soon and I don't want to worry that you haven't taken your pill."

Violet glanced down at the yellow pill then back at her mother who looked like she was going to explode. She picked it up angrily, placed it on her tongue, took a gulp of water and swallowed.

Her mother smiled, patted her daughter's head and rose from the table.

"I bet you feel better already. I'm going out now, but I will be back in time to get you and your father dinner. Risotto tonight, I think."

Her mother floated from the room leaving Violet fuming at the kitchen table.

The woman she just talked to, though she looked like her mother, was definitely not her mother. She had to be an imposter.

Violet got up from the table and paced the room. Something was very wrong. She had to try and get through to her dad again.

He was at work so she grabbed her coat and ran as fast as she could all the way to the Archers' optician's.

CHAPTER 8

A CHANGE OF HEART

Violet stopped for a moment under the gleaming gold sign, *Archer Brothers' Spectacle Makers' Emporium*, to catch her breath. She was about to push open the painted navy door when a sudden thought hit her like a brick to the head.

Her mother was right.

She had IDDCS. She'd never heard of it before, but in that moment, she was 100 per cent sure she had it. Of course she was a disobedient child; Mrs Moody was right too. How could she have broken the skipping rules like that in the middle of the schoolyard? How embarrassing! And the pencil – she blushed as she thought about the pencil. Bending down under the desk without even thinking of asking teacher – what must the class have thought? Mrs Moody really had tried to help her by setting that essay about rules. How did she not see it before? She really was a bold child, but all that was going to change.

She turned around and walked back down Splendid Road towards home, but with each stride her reasoning weakened and by the time she'd reached her house she'd changed her mind again. Violet was totally confused.

She wasn't bold, she'd only been trying to liven up the game and at her old school nobody ever asked permission to pick up a pencil!

Violet sat down on the stone steps at the front door of her home. Her change of mind had been so quick it was scary. What had happened to make her think that way? She retraced her steps in her head like her mother always told her to do. What had she done that was different?

"THE PILLS!" she exclaimed, jumping up so fast she knocked off her glasses.

Her world went black and fuzzy. Quickly she sat back down and felt around for the frames. Something stirred on the gravel close by. Footsteps.

"It's me," the familiar voice spoke hurriedly. "I know your parents are changing."

It was that boy again.

Just as she turned towards his voice, heavy footsteps raced across the gravel.

"You," a man growled. "I'll make sure you never set foot outside them walls again!"

There was a rush of feet. Violet panicked and tried to stand up to get into her house but missed her footing and fell onto the gravel below, scraping her hands and knees.

"These are yours," the boy said, pushing the glasses into her hand.

She shoved them on, her heart pounding. There was no one about. The yard was empty. She turned over her hands, her palms and knees were bloody and her grey skirt was covered in pebble dust.

Was she going mad?

She'd felt the boy's hand this time – surely she hadn't imagined that? But why couldn't she see him? Who was he and why was he following her? Was he in trouble? Who was chasing him?

All these questions floated around her mind and she knew she had to find her dad. There was something going on in Perfect, something weird and she needed to convince him to leave. She had proof now, bloody knees and palms should be enough to get his attention.

She headed off on her third trip of the afternoon and marched back towards the Archers' emporium.

This time she didn't stop outside, she turned the polished brass knob and pushed open the door. A bell tingled above to announce her arrival.

"Mr Archer," she called.

There was no reply. The shop was empty. She walked past the gleaming glass cabinets on her left to the panelled wall on the far side of the room and traced her fingers along it until they felt a familiar bump in the polished cherry wood.

She pushed on the panel and the secret door opened inwards to the library beyond. Quickly she slipped inside.

There were voices coming from behind a door at the opposite end of the room. She tiptoed towards them.

"What are you talking about?"

"We're paying you well, aren't we?"

"But it's not right, Edward; morally, I just can't do it!"

"You'll do as you're told, that's what you'll do!"

It was the Archers – and they were talking to her father.

They were arguing. She hated it when adults fought, as sometimes they said horrible things to each other. It was kind of a good thing though as it sounded like her dad wasn't happy. Maybe he was thinking of leaving.

Not daring to disturb the men she tiptoed back towards the secret panel door.

"Violet Brown!"

She turned around quickly and stood almost nose to nose with Edward Archer.

"I'm sorry, Mr Archer, I heard voices. I was looking for my dad," she stuttered.

"You're not allowed in here, young lady," Edward Archer said, nodding behind her. "It's not mannerly to snoop."

"Oh, I wasn't snooping. It was an accident. I was just looking for Dad. I thought he might be in here."

"He's just stepped out, Violet. I'm afraid you've missed him."

"But I'm sure I heard him, he was talking to you in there." She pointed to the door behind him.

"Mrs Moody was right, you really are quite the handful," Edward Archer sighed.

"I...erm...I'm sorry, Mr Archer," Violet stuttered, stepping slowly backwards towards the shop, "I must have imagined it."

"What happened to you, Violet?" Edward Archer asked, taking in her untidy appearance. "Are you hurt, dear?"

"Oh, I fell. It's nothing,"

"Have you taken your pills, dear?"

She stepped further back. How did he know?

"Your mother told me." He smiled, as if reading her mind, "IDDCS, it's a serious condition, Violet, it mustn't go untreated."

Her heart was beating rapidly now.

"What's going on here?" snapped George Archer, stepping into the library behind his brother.

"Nothing." Edward smiled. "Violet here was looking for her father. She's just leaving."

"He's not here," George said, glaring down at Violet.

"I know, Edward told me," Violet stammered, then she turned and ran. There was something about George, something that made her nervous whenever she was near him.

Once outside and a safe distance from the shop, she stopped to breathe.

Why did Edward Archer know all that stuff about Mrs Moody and the pills. Why was he sticking his nose in her life? And her dad, why had they lied about her dad? She was sure it was him behind that door and he'd sounded angry. Why wouldn't they tell her the truth?

Avoiding home, she walked up Edward Street. The past few hours played over in her mind. First it was her mother and the pills, then her strange change of heart, her glasses, the voice, the Archers, their odd behaviour and her dad. There was something up with her dad.

A group of woman chatting outside the Hatchet Family Butcher's fell silent as she walked by – she could have sworn she heard one of them whisper *IDDCS*.

She crossed the road at the Town Hall and passed the Archers' Tea Shop resting in its shadow. A new display of beautiful hand-painted china cups decorated the window. She stopped for a look and noticed everyone in the busy shop had turned to stare out at her.

Quickly she continued on and turned left down Archers' Avenue, avoiding the eyes of Edward Street. Spying a bench by the high stone wall, she sat down to think.

What was going on in Perfect?

Violet knew her mother wouldn't listen. Her mam didn't care what Violet thought any more. Her dad wouldn't listen either. He'd be angry with her for sneaking around the Archers – she was sure Edward would tell him about that. Her dad was strict when it came to manners and she hadn't been at all polite to Edward Archer.

She looked up from the bench. She'd been on this street before.

On the wall almost directly opposite was that sign: *The Original Homeplace of Messrs George and Edward Archer, first sons of Perfect*, the words *and William* etched in above the letters.

She wondered if William Archer had scratched his own name into the sign and under her desk in school. If he did, it seemed he was a troublemaker just like everyone thought she was. Why had she never heard about him before? Maybe he'd left Perfect; maybe he'd hated the town just as much as she did?

Goosepimples prickled her skin as she wondered what had happened to William Archer.

CHAPTER 9

IRIS ARCHER

Violet's heart skipped. The same old lady she'd seen here on her first day in Perfect was watching her from behind the window of the house opposite. Quickly Violet looked away. When she dared to look back the lady was gone.

A few minutes later the door of the house swung gently open and the old woman resumed her place by the window.

Was she inviting her in?

Violet stood up from the bench and walked towards the house.

"Hello?" she called, stopping just outside the opened door.

There was no response so she stepped into the hall.

The interior was almost perfect but just like the outside there was something slightly off. The floor was a little wonky and creaked underfoot. The only light in the house seeped through dirty lace curtains and dust gathered thickly on everything in sight – it was like the place had never been polished, which was odd as dusting was almost an Olympic sport in Perfect.

A door off the hallway was partially open into a room on the left.

"Hello," Violet called as she peered round it.

The old lady was sitting in her spot by the window, a shadow cast across half her body.

"You opened the door," Violet said, edging further in.

"I did."

"Are you okay? Do you need some help?"

"No," the old lady croaked.

She had white hair that sat like a bird's nest on top of her head. Her dress was black and plain. She wore no shoes or socks and her thin bony feet poked out from under a black-laced hem. Her face was kind though her eyes were sad.

"Are you sure you're okay?" Violet asked.

The old woman didn't answer and turned once more to stare out the window. Then it hit Violet.

"You're not wearing glasses," she gasped.

"Eyes don't need glasses to see," the woman replied.

"They are the window to my soul, why would I curtain them?"

"But…" Violet stuttered, "how aren't you blinded by the sun?"

"It's the sons that robbed me."

Violet stepped closer into the room.

"Eyes mad." The old woman snapped a warning. "Eyes mad. Them sons makes eyes mad. Iris Archer, they all say, that son's no good. I protected him from Arnold, my William, my apple. Then jealous Ed and Georgie ate him."

"William Archer?" Violet asked. "Is he your son? What happened to him?"

"My son, my moon and my stars," Iris replied, her eyes welling with tears.

"I'm sorry," Violet said. "I didn't mean to upset you."

"He's not here," Iris continued. "They said he was bold as brass, a divided soul, but I knew he had spirit. A child without spirit is the sky without stars. He had stars, my William. A world full of stars. Are you in school with him?"

Violet shook her head.

"No. No, I don't think so. I'm new in school, my dad works for George and Edward though; they must be your sons too?"

"George and Edward, Edward and George? They took the light from my eyes. They've a streak like their father.

Everything in order, there must be order."

Violet stepped back towards the hallway. The old lady was clearly crazy and she didn't want to upset her any more than she already had.

"Erm…my mam has tea on and I have to go, it's risotto," she rambled.

"Don't drink the tea," Iris snapped, bolting up from the chair and moving quickly towards her. "Don't drink it, I tell ya!"

"Erm…okay, I won't, I promise," Violet stuttered stumbling backwards.

She was just about to step back into the hallway when the old lady spoke again. This time she didn't sound so mad.

"You remind me of him, Violet. You remind me of my William. There's spirit inside you too. Keep it close."

"Y-you know my name?"

"The boy told me. He's watching out for your spirit. You've connected with his soul."

"Which boy?" Violet hadn't met any boys in Perfect except for the ones in her class and they definitely weren't looking out for her.

Iris didn't answer, she had slipped back into her own world. Violet asked once more and when she got no reply, walked from the house into the sunshine and headed reluctantly back towards home.

CHAPTER 10

AN URGENT MEETING

Her mother was back by the time Violet returned home that evening. Rose was full of the joys of Perfect. She just couldn't stop describing Mrs Bickory's apple pie.

"The best I have ever tasted, Violet. I'll make it for dessert. June gave me the recipe. It's a family secret but she said she would share it with me. Everybody is so nice in this town."

Violet nodded as she took out her schoolbooks. "Oh good." Her mother smiled. "The pills are working already. I've never seen you so eager to study, dear."

Violet didn't answer. She wasn't any more or less eager to study than she had been before, but she hoped that by keeping her mother happy she might not have to take any more pills.

"Here, dear," her mother said, dropping two yellow capsules onto the table, "time for your medication."

"But, Mam, please I'm fine on the one you gave me earlier. I love Perfect." Violet forced a polite smile.

"That's great, Violet, I'm delighted, but it won't help your IDDCS. You do want to be cured, don't you, dear?"

"Can we wait for Dad to come home? Please?"

"Okay, but you'll take them then, your dad agrees with me. We both want you to be rid of this syndrome. It's holding you back. Think of how much you could achieve without it."

Violet smiled again and turned to her books pretending to study while Rose whistled as she prepared the risotto and apple pie. Violet had never even heard of risotto before Perfect, now it was her mother's speciality.

It was after six and her dad had not returned from work. He never missed dinner. In all the years he'd been her father, and that was all her life, he'd never spent an evening away without telling them.

She glanced up at the clock as her mother set the table.

"We can't wait any longer, Violet dear." Her mother sighed. "My apple pie will go soggy."

"But what about Dad?"

"Don't worry about your father, I'll save him some dessert."

"I'm not worried about your pie, Mam! Where *is* Dad? It's not like him to come home late. What if something's happened?"

"In Perfect, Violet?" Her mother laughed. "Of course nothing has happened to him. He's just caught up in his work, I imagine. He has the best job in the world working with the Archer brothers."

"But, Mam," Violet pleaded, "I thought you didn't like the Archers. The first night we came here you said they gave you the—"

"Violet!" Rose snapped. "Stop being so disruptive. I know it's the syndrome, dear, but it is getting out of hand. I have never, nor will I ever, speak badly of the Archers."

Rose picked up the two yellow capsules and handed them to Violet. She looked at the pills then back at her mother.

"Now!" her mother ordered.

Slowly she placed the yellow capsules under her tongue. Her mother filled a glass with water and handed it to Violet.

"Swallow!" she barked.

Violet did as she was told. Rose smiled and carried on dishing out the dinner. When her back was turned Violet quickly spat out the pills and shoved them in her pocket.

"Now," her mother said a little later as they were tucking into the risotto, "I bet you feel better already."

Violet nodded and didn't look up from her plate.

If she spoke she wouldn't be able to hide the teary tremble in her voice. Oblivious, her mam chatted about her day right through dinner and dessert. The meal was rounded off with the obligatory cup of tea but Violet remembered the old woman's warning earlier that day, and couldn't quite bring herself to drink it.

Later that night her father still hadn't returned and Violet's stomach churned. She felt sick thinking about her visit to the Archers' emporium. She'd definitely heard her father's voice. Why hadn't she questioned the Archers more? Why had she walked away? Something was wrong, she knew it. Her dad was in some sort of trouble.

Guilt hung over her as she climbed the stairs to bed. Just as she reached the top step, the phone rang. She paused. Moving closer to the banister, she sat down and listened.

"Hello, the Brown household," her mother said, in her new posh phone voice.

"Oh, Mr Archer. How may I help you?"

"Yes, I thought as much. Violet was worried."

"She was? Oh, really. She didn't tell me that."

"I'm so sorry if she upset you, Mr Archer. I'm afraid it must be the IDDCS."

"Yes, she's taking the pills. I watched her myself this evening."

"Oh, of course, Mr Archer, I know how children can be. I'll stand over her next time."

"Thank you for letting me know about Eugene, Mr Archer. I hope he's helping your research?"

"That's great to hear. How long will he be away?"

"Oh, perfect."

"Yes, I'll tell her. Goodnight, Mr Archer."

Why had the Archers rung to tell them her dad was away? Surely her dad could pick up the phone? Why couldn't he ring them himself?

"Violet!" her mother snapped, spying her on the stairs. "Were you eavesdropping?"

"Oh no, I was...I just wanted to hear if it was Dad."

"It was Edward Archer." Her mother smiled. "Your father's going to be away for a few days. He's gone to an opticians' conference. Very important apparently."

"Why couldn't he tell us himself?" Violet said, her voice louder than she'd intended. "He didn't even pack a bag!"

"Violet, please, you're giving me a headache. It was very kind of Edward Archer to ring and let us know. Your father had to leave quickly. It was urgent."

"An urgent opticians' conference?"

"Violet! Your condition is really getting the better of you.

It's exhausting, dear. Edward Archer was kind enough to enquire after your health. Everyone in this town is being so helpful and you repay them by being ungrateful. What were you doing in the Archers' emporium today?"

"I was looking for Dad," Violet snapped.

"You were snooping around in places you shouldn't be. It's lucky Edward Archer has promised not to take it any further."

"Any further?" Violet protested. "But I didn't—"

"Violet." Her mother sighed. "Enough is enough. Just be glad the Archers are so understanding. I'm sure your dad won't be when he comes home."

Violet didn't respond. There was no point. No matter what she said it was bound to get twisted.

She stood up, turned and walked down the carpeted hallway to her room, closed the door and collapsed on her bed.

Her world was crashing down around her. Her mother wouldn't listen and her father had disappeared. She'd been more than mean to him over the last few weeks and now she might never see him again. The Archers were behind all the weirdness she was sure, but even if she could prove it no one would listen. It was as if everyone in Perfect was under a spell. Her eyes welled up – she couldn't hold back the tears – and she cried until she had nothing left.

Exhausted, she crawled beneath her duvet and hoped that sleep would find her.

It didn't. That night, no matter what she did, Violet just couldn't get comfortable. There was a strange lump in her bed. After hours of tossing and turning she put on her glasses and got up to investigate.

She patted down the sheets but the lump was still there. Then she pulled them back a little and checked underneath in case something had got trapped when her mother was making the bed. There was nothing. It was as if the lump was actually inside the mattress. Maybe a spring had come loose or something.

In her frustration, Violet pulled the sheets right off the bed and inspected closer.

Bits of fluff poked out from a thin tear that ran along the top of the mattress. It was about the length of her arm from her elbow to her wrist. She wriggled her fingers through until they brushed against something solid. Squeezing her hand further inside she clasped the mysterious object and pulled it from its hiding place.

CHAPTER 11

INTRODUCTIONS

The small, flat box fitted neatly in her hand. It was dark blue and covered in a bendy ladder-like pattern. As she turned it over the ladders caught the light giving off a silvery sheen. There was a stamp on the cover with the words "Optical Prescriptions" in faded gold lettering. The box was closed on one side by a small magnet and rusted hinges held firm the other.

Slowly she prised it open. A pair of glasses sat proud on a dark blue velvet lining.

The frames were plain not gold-rimmed like the ones she got from the Archers and seemed to be made of rough-cut wood. The lenses were round and clear, not rose-tinted, and the arms of the glasses were cut in tiny segments making them flexible enough to bend round the ears.

A label, browned by time, sat centred inside the lid. It read *Optical Prescription Spectacle Makers, 135 Wickham Terrace*. Where was Wickham Terrace? She didn't recognize it as a street in Perfect.

She took off her gold-rimmed specs and fitted the wooden pair.

Strangely, she could see through them; the lenses suited her perfectly. She was just scanning the curtains when a figure caught her eye.

"Argh!" she screamed, throwing the wooden glasses from her face.

The room turned blurry and she scrambled for her gold-rimmed specs.

"You saw me?"

Violet grabbed her duvet and pulled it quickly up over her head. It flew from her grasp and fell to the floor.

"You saw me?" the voice said again.

"I didn't, I didn't!" Violet shivered. "I didn't see anything. I'm not talking to anyone, it's just my imagination."

"You did! You saw me." The voice sounded ecstatic. "You saw me standing by the curtains!"

Footsteps ran for the bed and suddenly Violet was bouncing from side to side as if someone was jumping on her mattress.

"The glasses, it has to be the glasses!" the voice said again.

The bed stopped bouncing and there was a thud. The footsteps started on the floor again, racing across the room.

"Here, put them back on."

Her hand was pulled open and the wooden glasses were shoved into her grasp.

"I promise I won't hurt you."

She'd heard this boy's voice before. He sounded sincere.

Slowly she moved the glasses towards her face and pulled the arms round her ears once more. She kept her eyes shut.

"Please," the voice said again.

A breeze swished past her nose as if a hand was waving back and forth in front of her face. Slowly she opened her eyes.

There at the edge of the bed stood a boy and he was waving madly in the air.

He was looking straight at her and was twelve, maybe thirteen, and dressed head to toe in black. He had jet-black hair that flopped round his ears and his white face was dappled in tiny freckles that mostly gathered round his nose. His eyes were deep navy, almost black, like the night sky. Something about them unsettled her.

"You do, you see me!" he said, jumping into the air.

A smile filled the boy's face and Violet couldn't help but return it. His teeth sparkled too like he'd never eaten sweets in his life. He had the most contagious smile she'd ever seen.

They stared silently at each other and a little awkwardness flooded the room. Violet tried hard not to blush as she racked her bedbrain for something to say.

"I'm Boy," the stranger said at last, breaking the silence.

"I'm Violet," she replied, shaking his extended hand. "Is your name really Boy?"

"Yes." Boy nodded.

"But that's not even a name."

"Yes it is. I've always been called Boy, just like you're called Violet."

"But what do your parents call you? You must have a name like Tom or Dara. I knew a few boys from home and they all had real names; none of them were called Boy."

"I don't have parents." He smiled.

"Oh!"

There was a little silence and, unsure of what to say next, she copied what adults said at funerals.

"I'm sorry for your loss."

"I didn't lose them." Boy laughed. "I just never had any!"

"You can't never have had parents," Violet replied. "Everybody has parents!"

"Well I don't and as far as I'm concerned I'm better off. Look how yours treat you!"

"Hey!" Violet exclaimed. "Don't say that about my parents, they're the best anyone could ever have!"

"Then why have you been crying for the last few hours? Don't deny it, I saw you."

She fell silent and looked away.

"I didn't mean to upset you, Violet," Boy said. "It's just I've been watching you for a while and I know your parents are changing."

"What do you mean?"

"They're changing. It's this place, it does that to people. After a while everyone changes."

"But what do you mean by 'changes'?" Violet asked, though she sort of knew what he meant already.

"Well I can only remember a few new people arriving in Perfect but they were all normal when they got here," Boy replied. "At first they can see me – I even spoke to one man – but after a day or two they go blind, then they get their glasses and start to change. First they ignore me, then they begin to change their clothes, their hair, the way they talk, even the way they walk, and all of a sudden they become just like everyone else in this town."

"I know," Violet whispered. "My mam has changed so much since we moved here. I can't talk to her any more."

"It's the rose-tinted glasses," Boy said bluntly.

"They do something to change reality."

"What do you mean? Without them I can't see."

"But without them you *can* see. You can see reality, it's just really fuzzy. Take these ones off," Boy said. Violet was still wearing the wooden pair.

She looked at him but didn't move.

"Trust me," he said.

Slowly she took the glasses off and held them firm in her grip. Everything was dark and blurry.

"Now," he said. "Can you see that?"

Something thick and solid moved across her vision. It was really fuzzy but she could see it.

"Yes." She nodded. "Are you moving your hand or something across my face?"

"Yeah!" Boy said. "Without any glasses you can still see me. You can see reality, it's just really fuzzy. Now put your gold-rimmed ones on."

He put them back in her hand. She could feel the hook of the arms slot uncomfortably behind her ears as she pushed them on.

She looked around the room. Boy had disappeared. She leaned over the side of her bed to check underneath it and then got out of bed and checked inside the wardrobe, but he was nowhere to be seen. It was really weird, as if he'd vanished into thin air.

The wooden glasses still sat on her bed. She climbed

back onto the mattress, took off her gold-rimmed pair and put them back on.

"See," Boy said, suddenly appearing right where he'd stood moments before. "Bet I disappeared altogether?"

"But how can I see you now?" Violet stammered, confused.

"It's the wooden glasses," he said. "I don't know how they work but they work and that's all I care about. It's not easy being invisible."

"But why are you invisible? Why can't I see you without these?"

"Beats me!" Boy sighed. "I was hoping your dad would know that. I came here the night you arrived to ask him to help me and my friends – I'd heard he was here to fix people's blindness – so I thought he might be able to figure out why we're invisible, but the Archers were here and I didn't want them to think your family was mad."

"My family *is* mad," Violet half whispered, looking down at her sheets.

Boy smiled, like he really knew what she meant. Maybe this boy could be her friend.

"Imagine if your dad was talking to me and all the Archers could see was thin air, your dad would lose his job straight away," he continued. "So I waited and waited for them to leave that night but it was getting so late I thought I'd be caught. I came back early the next morning but your dad was already blind, all of you were."

"But you kept following me," Violet said. "I heard you and at the emporium there was someone chasing you?"

"It was a Watcher." Boy sighed. "They don't allow us in to Perfect."

"What's a Watcher?"

"The Watchers guard Perfect and stop people like me getting over the wall into the town," Boy replied.

"The wall?"

"Yes, Violet, there's a huge wall separating my home from yours."

"But you got out?" Violet replied, puzzled.

"I wanted to give you those," he said, pointing to the glasses.

"Why me?"

"Because you were different." Boy smiled. "You weren't changing."

"But what can I do? I'm not a scientist. I don't know anything about glasses or why you're invisible or where you're from or anything. I don't even know much about Perfect," Violet said, her head frazzled.

"No, but you could tell your dad, you could show him the wooden glasses and tell him my story. He might be able to help," Boy pleaded.

"But I don't know your story. I don't know anything

about you," she snapped, thumping the mattress with her fist.

Boy looked down at his feet. Silence wrapped the room.

"I'm sorry." Violet's face was a little flushed. "I wish I could help you but Dad's gone to an opticians' conference, at least that's what the Archers told Mam."

"You don't sound too sure?"

"I'm not. I mean I don't know. I think he would have told me if he was going."

"That's parents for you!" Boy huffed.

"It's not *my* parents," Violet said. "I told you already, my parents are good. Or at least, they were before we came here."

Silence filled the air again.

Then Boy sighed. "Well, we've been invisible for so long I'm sure we can wait a little longer."

"Who's we?" Violet asked, unsure she wanted to know the answer.

"Come on, I'll show you," Boy said, grabbing her hand and pulling her off the mattress. "I'll show you my home!"

"Can't it wait until the morning?"

"No it can't. It has to be at night. The Watchers patrol in the day."

"Patrol where?"

"You'll see." Boy smiled.

CHAPTER 12

NO-MAN'S-LAND

"You took your time getting ready," Boy said when Violet finally joined him downstairs. "Girls are so slow."

"No I didn't," Violet snapped, following him through the hallway.

"Come on, we have to hurry! The Watchers'll be on duty in Perfect soon and if they catch me here I'll be in trouble."

"You make them sound really scary. I'm not going anywhere with you until you tell me what's going on."

"Ssh! Keep your voice down, Violet," Boy whispered, gently closing the front door behind them. "I told you, they're the Watchers. They make sure people like me and my friends don't turn up in Perfect. They don't want you to know we exist."

"So there's more like you?" she asked.

"Lots." Boy winked as they raced along the tree-lined avenue towards town.

They moved quickly up Splendid Road towards the Archer brothers' emporium. Then Violet followed Boy up Edward Street, stopping outside the butcher's where he pulled her into the darkness of the doorway.

"You have to be really careful from now on," he whispered. "I can't get caught on this side of the wall and you can't get caught going into the other. Just follow me and do as I say. Okay?"

Violet looked at him and nodded, her throat dry. She was scared but she wasn't going to let Boy know. She followed him silently as they slipped out of the darkness and headed towards the Town Hall.

With the wooden glasses on, Perfect didn't look quite so perfect any more. Even though it was dark, she could see that the paint was chipped and worn from buildings; the hanging baskets of flowers weren't as full or colourful as they'd seemed and even a little rubbish whistled past her feet down the empty street.

"It looks different," she said, sticking closely to Boy's side.

"It's not the same place really. Well, it is and it isn't," he replied.

They were approaching the Town Hall when Boy

95

stopped again and beckoned Violet into the darkness of another doorway.

"That's where the Watchers sit guarding over No-Man's-Land at night," he said, pointing up to the clock tower on the top of the Town Hall. "There should be some there now. Can you see them?"

Violet followed Boy's finger and looked up at the tower. She had to crane her neck to see the top. Glass windows glowed warmly against the night sky and she could see a shadow moving about in the light.

"There's one," she whispered.

"Well spotted," Boy said. "I always keep an eye on the tower and only move when no one's there. They don't normally look at the streets of Perfect as the curfew keeps everyone indoors at night. They mainly watch the walls but it's better to be safe than sorry."

They waited for a few minutes as the Watcher moved about inside the tower.

"Quick, he's gone," Boy said, pulling Violet out of hiding and past the Town Hall.

She didn't dare look back up and shivered imagining the phantom figure watching them from above as they snuck along the street.

Boy ducked left into Archers' Avenue and stopped. Violet almost walked into him in her haste. He raised his hand to signal silence and then stepped into Rag Lane and looked back up towards the tower.

"Coast's still clear," he whispered, moving quickly down the passage.

It was pitch black and goosepimples rose up on Violet's skin. She could barely see Boy moving just ahead of her.

"Where are we going, Boy?" she whispered. "This doesn't lead anywhere, I was here before!"

Boy didn't utter a word as they headed straight for the dead end. Violet stopped suddenly. A large arched wooden door stood in the middle of the stone wall ahead.

"There definitely wasn't a door here last time I came," she stuttered. "I'm sure of it!"

"That's because the Archers' glasses hid it," Boy said. "My home is behind that gateway, it's where my people live."

"And who are 'your people' exactly?" Violet asked.

"The outcasts. The unwanted – we've lots of names." Boy smiled. "But we're mainly called the No-Man's-Landers and we're definitely not perfect! You'll see."

Boy tapped out a gentle rhythm on the large iron knocker on the door in the middle of the gateway. It seemed to be some sort of code. Someone grunted and snorted as if in disgust, then there was movement on the other side of the wood. They waited for what seemed ages, when a hatch by the knocker slid across and a bloodshot eyeball stared out, searching the street.

"What are you doing standing out there, Boy? Have you lost your marbles, young man? And who's that with ya, I can't be letting no strangers in here."

"She's my friend, she got lost! She's new to No-Man's-Land and ended up outside the wall by mistake. I had to get her back!"

There was a short click and suddenly the door swung inwards. A round, red-faced woman dressed entirely in purple ushered them through.

"You'll get me in trouble wandering in and out like that, Boy. And who's this friend of yours." She turned to Violet before Boy had a chance to speak. "When did you get here young lady? Who's forgotten you?"

Violet looked at Boy, her face completely blank.

"She's a…she's a Harper," he said as he pulled Violet through the door.

"Oh." The woman smirked. "I thought your lot were perfect! Suppose there's an odd'un in every family. Well young Harper, make this your home, you ain't getting out of here now 'cept in a box!"

The woman's laugh echoed around the high stone walls that loomed over both sides of the narrow road, making Violet shiver. They were still in Rag Lane only on the other side of the gateway now. Violet could hardly believe she hadn't been able to see the door before. Her wooden glasses were revealing all kinds of surprises.

"Who is that woman?" she whispered as they walked further on.

"She's the gatekeeper," Boy said.

"Won't she tell on us? Tell the Watchers?"

"No, I don't think so," Boy replied. "She'll just think you're new. She won't be suspicious 'cause I never use the gate normally."

"Why did you use it this time?"

"You wouldn't be able to follow if I went the other way." He smiled.

"Yes I would!" Violet said, a little offended.

"Oh, really?" Boy laughed, pointing to the top of the wall that towered above them. "Could you climb up there?"

Violet didn't respond as her stomach did a dance. *Of course she could climb the wall*, she told herself, if she really wanted to.

She followed Boy as the lane sloped downhill and they came to a narrow set of steps that passed through a stone archway.

"Welcome to No-Man's-Land!" Boy announced proudly. Violet walked through the arch and into another world.

❊　　❊　　❊

The street they were standing on looked like it could have been in Perfect. It was the same width and had the same style of stone buildings and street furniture. In fact everything looked the same; it was just that nothing was *perfect*. There was broken glass in the street lamps, and in a lot of the windows of the buildings. Some of the homes were even missing doors, flower baskets hung empty and crooked on their perches, paint was chipped and flaking, weeds grew round the base of the buildings and potholes dotted the cobbled road. Everything was tattered and broken.

"Where are we, Boy?" Violet asked, looking around. "It feels like I'm in Perfect but not, if you know what I mean."

"Well you are and you aren't." Boy laughed at her confusion. He looked up at the wall again. "Perfect is on the other side of that," he explained. "No-Man's-Land is in the middle of your town surrounded by the wall and nobody knows we're even here."

"It's not my town," Violet said quickly.

"But you do live there!"

Violet ignored Boy and looked around. There were people rushing everywhere, as if it were the middle of the day instead of the middle of night.

"What are they doing?" she whispered.

"Working of course."

"At night?"

"Yes. Your night is our day. It's the only time we can work in No-Man's-Land. Once daylight arrives the

Watchers are on patrol and the No-Man's-Landers have to stay in their homes."

"Why?" Violet asked.

"Because the people of Perfect are out and about during the day," Boy said. "What if someone's glasses fell off and they heard strange noises floating over the walls? The Perfectionists would think they were going mad, just like when your glasses fell off and you heard my voice!"

Violet remembered the sensation clearly, but standing here now, in No-Man's-Land, a place she hadn't known existed, she still couldn't be sure her overactive imagination wasn't playing tricks on her.

"But why do the Watchers let you out of your homes in No-Man's-Land at all, if they want to keep you secret?" Violet asked.

"I'm not sure, but I've heard stories. I'm too young to remember but in the beginning when No-Man's-Land was first created, the Watchers locked up anyone caught trying to escape. No-Man's-Landers rebelled for a while until eventually both sides came to an agreement: the punishments would stop and the No-Man's-Landers would be given their freedom at night if they agreed to stop trying to escape and stay within these walls."

"Oh, that's why there's a curfew in Perfect. It's so we don't hear you lot at night," Violet blurted as though a light had gone on inside her head.

Boy nodded.

"But why did the No-Man's-Landers agree to that?" Violet asked. "It's still a prison, they're still locked inside these walls."

"People are proud of the deal, Violet," Boy said, a little annoyed. "There are no punishments now, well hardly any, and people can work. We live normalish lives except our day is reversed; we work at night and sleep in the day."

"Oh, erm that's good…" Violet said, trying not to offend.

Boy was quiet for a moment, and when he spoke again, he kept his head down.

"A friend told me once that it's easy to break a person's spirit." He blushed a little. "I think that's what happened to the No-Man's-Landers, the Watchers broke their spirit. Maybe it's why they don't rebel and try to escape any more, but any kind of freedom is still freedom, isn't it?"

"I suppose," Violet said, unconvinced, "but you're all locked up here, isn't that a kind of punishment? Why does No-Man's-Land exist? Is everyone in here a criminal?" A chill danced up her spine at the thought.

"No," Boy snapped, "we're not criminals, we're just… I don't know…we're just different. That's all. We're different from the people in Perfect."

"So they locked you up for being different?"

Boy shrugged.

"I can't really answer that, Violet. You'll have to ask the Watchers. People here are not like the Perfectionists though. You'll see…"

Violet looked around trying to ease her confusion.

The house opposite her was in disrepair. Planks of weather-worn wood were nailed to the windows, holding the place together. Daisies, dandelions and weeds sprouted round its base like decorations. A handwritten chalk sign was nailed to the door in lovely swirly letters that said "Angel Readings". Wafts of light purple and pink material blew through the glassless windows like ghosts in the night.

Each broken street lamp held a burning candle warming the darkness, allowing Violet to see that none of the other buildings around her looked quite solid. Painted wooden planks patterned their facades like colourful sticking plasters.

A man suddenly raced past her. He held a broken cane in one hand and an enormous tree branch in the other. Just behind him, a lady wearing a faded and torn pink ball gown puffed and panted as she pedalled a child's tricycle through the crowd. "Excuse me, late for the theatre!" she bellowed.

Boy tugged on Violet's sleeve pulling her away from the scene.

"Let's have some fun." He smiled. "Come on, there's lots to do here and not very much time to do it in.

"This is Forgotten Road," Boy told her as he ran ahead.

It was the main street in No-Man's-Land, and ran parallel to Edward Street on the other side of the wall. Three small cobbled lanes branched off it.

They ducked into the first lane, Violet wanting to explore. It was lined with shops selling everything from art classes and second-hand canvasses – "only used three times" the window sign read – to sewing twine and broken knitting needles.

Halfway down they turned left onto a narrow passage that linked to the second lane.

It was full of odds and ends, things that normal people would call rubbish. One shopfront proudly passed off a moth-eaten lampshade as a hat alongside a flat basketball.

They went into a bookshop, but some of the books were missing covers and others even missing pages. People sat reading in the cobbled lane outside on old suitcases and rubber tyres, while a woman stood by the shop doorway reciting poetry at the top of her voice.

The bottom of this lane opened onto a square overcrowded with greasy-haired men and women who had set up stalls to sell just about anything.

"This is the Market Yard," Boy said, as they pushed past. "We're in the heart of No-Man's-Land now. This is where most people do their business."

Winks and nods passed between the stall owners like a silent language. Children, their clothes and faces caked in dirt, ran barefoot through the crowds. Some of the kids were in gangs while others hung round on their own. They all seemed to know Boy.

Violet was standing by a fruit cart when a tiny, barefoot girl raced by and stole an apple right in front of her. The owner, a sweaty, fat man, spotted her and gave chase, knocking aside everything in his path.

"What will happen to her?" Violet gasped, pulling on Boy's shirtsleeve.

"There are street rules here. They're not written down or anything but everybody knows them. If he catches her, she'll get what she deserves."

"He won't hurt her, will he?"

"You've some imagination, Violet!" Boy smirked.

He took off again and skimmed his hand over the stalls as he raced by. When they rounded the corner he planted his back against the wall and picked two iced buns from his pocket.

"Let's hope they don't kill thieves," he joked, scoffing down one as he handed the other to Violet.

"But that's stealing. You can't steal from people!" Violet fumed.

"You sound like a Perfect girl," Boy mumbled.

"I am not!"

"Well eat it then," he teased.

She looked at the bun then back at her new friend. Desperate to wipe the smile from his face, she bit deep into its spongy core.

"No one's gonna take care of you here, Violet," Boy said. "You have to look out for yourself in No-Man's-Land."

Violet shivered at the thought and silently ate her bun while she watched the buzz around her. A shimmer of light caught her eye from across the market.

"What's that?" she asked, spotting an odd tree resting in the middle of the Market Yard. The tree was bent and shrivelled as if it was almost dead; there were no leaves on its branches but it seemed to be glistening in the darkness.

She moved towards it, negotiating the bustle. Boy followed her.

As she got closer she saw what was causing the shimmers of light. Gold and silver coins, pieces of glass, paper, dried flowers, ribbons and all sorts of other bits and pieces were tied to its branches. Most of the items were worn and faded like they'd hung there for ever while a few were vibrant and new.

A faded red ribbon caught her eye fluttering on the gentle night breeze. A woven message had been delicately hand-sewn into the material.

For the memories I lost to Perfect. I will never forget you, Mam. Your loving daughter, Pip.

"Pippa Moody," Boy whispered.

"Moody?" Violet started. "Could she be related to Mrs Moody my teacher in school?"

"Yeah," he nodded, "Pip was her daughter. We call this the Rag Tree. The people of No-Man's-Land used to leave messages here for the loved ones they'd lost. I think they hoped that someday their families might come looking for them, but that's hardly going to happen if they don't even know we exist. People don't really do this any more; they've stopped hanging stuff on the tree."

"So the No-Man's-Landers still have families in Perfect?"

Boy nodded.

"Nearly everyone here used to live in Perfect."

"But...but what age is Pippa?" Violet asked, confused.

"I think she was twelve when she was taken from Perfect. She's a lot older now, like twenty or something. There are lots more like Pippa."

"But why do they take children?" Violet asked. "What about their parents? Don't they notice they're gone?"

"No. Like you said, it's almost as if their parents are not their parents any more. Something happens to people in Perfect. I don't know what it is exactly, but I'm pretty sure it has something to do with the glasses. With the glasses on, No-Man's-Land doesn't exist and we –" he drew a circle with his finger around the people in the market –, "are all like living ghosts."

Violet gulped and tried not to think about how strangely her parents had been behaving lately.

"What happened to Pippa?" she asked.

"She was disobeying the rules. Nothing serious, but you know small things are big in Perfect. One night the Watchers came to her house, they snatched her from her bed and brought her here. She snuck out loads of times to try and get help from her family, but she was invisible to them. It didn't take long for them to forget all about her."

"But what if that happens to me?" Violet stammered. "Is it only children they take? Maybe they took my dad!"

"It won't happen to you," said Boy reassuringly. "Well, not yet anyway."

"But what about Dad? Do you think he's here?" she said, eyeing the crowd.

"I don't think so. Some adults have been here from the beginning when the Watchers first started locking people up inside the walls but that's unusual. Most of the adults in No-Man's-Land were taken when they were children, they've grown up here. Adults, you see, seem to fall under Perfect's spell more easily than children. They seem to like the rules."

"Why?" Violet shivered.

"Beats me!" he said, moving out of the market back onto one of the lanes. "Come on, we're late."

"What for?"

"Getting you home. The sun'll be up soon, the Watchers will be back patrolling No-Man's-Land making sure we're all inside. If they catch you in here there'll be trouble."

CHAPTER 13

THE WATCHERS

Boy grabbed Violet's hand and raced down the narrow cobbled lane back onto Forgotten Road towards the stone arch. Darkness was leaking from the sky as they climbed the steps through the arch and up towards the door.

The gatekeeper in her tight purple dress looked like an overgrown grape as she bent over packing up her bag. The large iron key hung in the lock. Boy whispered to Violet to hide in the shadow of the wall.

"I'll distract her while you get out, then wait for me at the top of Rag Lane."

Violet was about to protest when Boy left her side and approached the woman.

"Did you hear about the trouble in the market,

Mrs Snout?" Boy said, walking towards the door.

The woman looked up at him.

"Oh, Boy, I was wondering who it was talkin'. Shouldn't you be going back to the orphanage soon?"

"I was just passing and thought I'd call up. I know you get lonely on the door sometimes."

"Aren't you one in a million, Boy!" A gap-toothed smile stretched across Mrs Snout's rosy cheeks. "I'm always saying it, you're the best o' the orphans, poor creatures the lot o' ye! Now, what did you say about trouble?"

Boy stood facing Violet, so that Mrs Snout had her back to the door and began to tell a tale of trouble that Violet hadn't witnessed at all that night. The woman was engrossed, and her oohs and aahs of astonishment and delight echoed down the lane as the story unfolded.

Boy glanced over Mrs Snout's shoulder at Violet and gestured for her to move to the door.

Violet hesitated for a minute. Boy's eyes were now moving wildly from side to side, ushering her towards the large wooden door.

"Are you okay, Boy, is there something wrong with your eyes?" Mrs Snout asked.

"Oh, I just think, erm...I think something flew into one," Boy said, trying to cover over his strange expressions.

"Let me take a look."

Mrs Snout moved closer to Boy and grabbed both sides of his head with her large lumps of hands.

Violet pushed fear to the back of her mind and tiptoed to the lock. Slowly she turned the key until it clicked. Then she pulled on the huge iron handle. At first the door didn't move and Violet began to panic.

She looked over at Boy and Mrs Snout; the woman was now bent over her friend ogling his eyeballs.

Violet leaned all her weight back on the handle and pulled again. This time the solid door moved just enough for her to squeeze through.

Once on the other side, she pulled it shut and ran along the shadows of Rag Lane until she reached the top where it met Archers' Avenue. There she stopped and waited. And waited. It seemed like an eternity before Boy appeared from the bottom of the Avenue, his eyes bloodshot.

"Where've you been?" Violet said, her voice squeaking a little in panic.

"She almost pulled my eye out," he panted, bending over to catch his breath. "She said she couldn't find anything. She gave it a good look though!"

Violet tried not to laugh.

"How did you get past her anyway?" she asked, hiding her smile. "You're not coming from the direction of the gate." She indicated behind him along Archers' Avenue.

"I told you I don't usually go that way." He winked.

Boy didn't offer any further explanation as she waited for him to catch his breath. Once ready, he signalled for Violet to stay put and peered round the corner of Archers' Avenue up at the tower. Putting his finger to his lips, he beckoned her forward.

"You have to be quiet," he whispered, "some Watchers patrol Perfect at night. There's not many of them, but they're around the streets. I've even caught them going into people's houses, though I've never gotten close enough to see what they were doing."

The thought of the Watchers in her house gave Violet the creeps. She tiptoed after her new friend, her heart thumping.

As quietly as they could, they slipped through the early dawn shadows of Edward Street. All was still and she relaxed a little. They were just approaching the Archers' emporium when Boy pulled her into a doorway.

"Blasted early mornings," a gruff voice said. "He's always late. Expects me to be waiting around for 'im!"

Violet peered round the corner.

"That's Fists, he's the head Watcher," Boy whispered.

A large man paced back and forth outside the front door of the brothers' shop. He blew air into his giant, cupped hands to warm them against the morning chill. He was about the same height as Violet's dad but square like a cement block. His muscles were so big they almost burst through his clothes. He wore dark navy, from the tip of his toes to the top of his head, and scowled behind a red beard and thick caterpillar eyebrows. Tufts of fiery hair poked out from under his woollen hat.

"What took you so long, Bungalow?" he snarled. "You're late!"

Another man walked hesitantly down Splendid Road towards the emporium. He was a little smaller than Fists, but just as square. Dressed in navy again, but without a hat, his bald head reflected the rising sun. Bungalow's face was softer and a little more vacant. He seemed weighed down by a strange machine that was strapped tightly to his back. He carried a leather notebook under his arm and shook his head from side to side as he handed it over.

"What do you mean 'no show'?" Fists roared, staring at an opened page.

"I'm sorry, Fists, she just wasn't there. I waited for hours!"

"Of course she was there. SHE LIVES THERE! You know what the brothers will say when they hear about this. She's top of the list; get your thick head around that. She needs hollowing!"

Hollowing, what was hollowing? Violet looked at Boy wide-eyed.

"I know, but I swear she wasn't there. I couldn't do anything about it. I got her mother though. Please don't tell on me," Bungalow pleaded.

"Give me the Hollower. If you want a job done right you have to do it yourself!" Fists said, grabbing the weighty backpack.

"But it's almost daylight…"

"Shut up and go log in at the tower. I don't give a damn what time it is. I'll get her, and then we'll see what the brothers have to say about this!" Fists growled as he strode away from the emporium along Splendid Road.

They waited for a few minutes as Bungalow headed off towards the centre of town. Then Boy turned to Violet.

"Come on quickly," he whispered. "Just stay back a little out of his way."

They slipped down Edward Street onto Splendid Road a short distance behind Fists. Violet crossed her fingers and hoped that the Watcher would go into some other house along the way. He didn't and her suspicions were confirmed when he turned the corner at the bottom of the road and continued along the tree-lined avenue.

"I think he's going to your house, Violet," Boy said, looking straight at her. "I'll cause a diversion. You have to get back inside and act as normal as you can. Don't forget to put on your old glasses, the Perfect ones, then if Fists does pay a visit you won't notice a thing."

"But what if I see him by accident?"

"You won't," Boy said urgently. "The Perfect glasses do the same to the Watchers as they do to me, he'll be invisible. Trust me!"

"But why is he going to my house? I don't like any of this," Violet panicked. "What does he want?"

"I don't know, Violet. We don't have time, just do it!" Boy replied sharply, sprinting ahead.

They were just around the corner from Violet's house when they spotted Fists walking up the driveway. The two of them jumped over the low wall that surrounded the house and followed him as quietly as they could, hiding under the cover of the trees that edged the gravel yard.

"Right. Go. Now!" Boy whispered, pushing Violet towards the house.

As she sprinted for the steps, Boy raced towards Fists.

A painful cry echoed behind her but she didn't dare look back. Her legs were on fire and her chest heaved as she sucked in the early morning air. She cut across the gravel, up to the door and scrambled for the key her mother left under the potted plant. She was shaking so much she couldn't fit it in the lock.

There was another cry behind her.

She let out an accidental squeal as the key slid into the lock and turned. The door opened and she flew into the hallway, closing it gently behind her. Resting her back against the wood she stopped to catch her breath.

Suddenly she heard the lock in the door click once more.

She raced into the kitchen and opened the fridge, pretending to search for something. There were footsteps behind her. She froze. All the air flew from her lungs.

Act normal.

She picked up the milk as calmly as possible, closed the fridge and turned to walk back towards the table.

Fists stood right there, his black eyes boring into hers. Her heart thumped loudly. The glasses. She'd forgotten to swap the glasses.

Looking straight ahead she walked towards the table. He was in her way but she couldn't veer around him. Keeping course she prayed he would move. A step away from a crash, Fists slipped aside, his eyes still firmly fixed on Violet.

She breathed a silent sigh of relief as she sat down and poured a bowl of cereal. Then she picked up the cereal box and pretended to study the back. It shivered in her grasp and she quickly placed it back down. Her eyes continued to scan the words, not taking in a single one as Fists moved his face so close she could smell his stinking breath.

He blew in her ear. She didn't flinch.

He growled and stepped back, as if remembering something, then left the room and headed upstairs. Violet released a breath as she listened for footsteps. Fists was light on his feet and it was difficult to tell which room he was in.

A few moments later he was back in the kitchen. He took a seat near the door and watched her. She acted normal or at least as normal as she could with her insides knotted. She cleared up her place, got out some schoolbooks and stared blindly at the pages.

After a while, Fists grew impatient, and then, clearly frustrated, left the house.

Violet waited a few minutes to make sure he was gone, before running as fast as she could up the stairs and into her mother's room.

"Mam, Mam, are you all right?" she cried, shaking Rose awake.

"Violet, for goodness' sake. What time is it?" her mother slurred sleepily.

"You're all right!" Violet gasped, hugging her mam as tears slid down her cheeks.

"Of course I'm all right, dear, whatever has gotten into you?"

"Nothing, Mam, I just erm…I just had a bad dream."

"You and your imagination." Her mother smiled, rubbing her hair. "Are those new glasses, pet?"

"Oh yeah. I erm...I got them from school. I'll...I'll make you breakfast," Violet said, suddenly remembering her specs.

Back in her bedroom she found her gold-rimmed glasses and put them on. Everything looked shiny again. Placing the wooden pair in their box, she shoved them into their hiding place in the mattress, put on her school uniform and headed back downstairs to make her mam's breakfast. She yawned deeply as she poured the milk and imagined Mrs Moody's breakdown if she fell asleep in class.

She took off her glasses and listened for Boy. Nothing.

Violet remembered all the things Boy had told her about the Watchers and No-Man's-Land. What was going on in Perfect? Why did the Watchers keep Boy and his friends locked up, and what were they looking for in her house? She shivered as she remembered Fists' stare.

She listened for Boy again and still there was nothing. Where was he? Crossing her fingers she hoped her new friend was okay.

CHAPTER 14

A NIGHT VISITOR

Violet couldn't concentrate on her schoolwork that morning. She kept going over the previous night's events in her head. Why did the rose-tinted glasses make the people in Perfect act weird and those in No-Man's-Land disappear altogether? Why had the Watchers mentioned the brothers? Surely it was the Archer brothers they were talking about – they were standing outside their shop? What was *hollowing* and what had the Watchers been doing in her house? There was something up in Perfect and the more she thought about it, the more she worried about her dad. Where was he?

She was so distracted that Mrs Moody tried to make her swallow more pills but she spat them out as soon as her teacher's back was turned. She'd done the same that morning, when her mother had fed her a canary yellow capsule. Thankfully it was Friday and she wouldn't have to see the school or Mrs Moody for the next two days.

As the hours wore on she became convinced her dad was in trouble. He worked for the Archers and everything seemed to point to them; those two were definitely up to something. Her dad wasn't on a business trip. It was his voice she'd heard that day in the shop. She needed to talk to Boy.

Earlier than normal that evening, Violet told her mam she was tired and headed up the stairs to her room. Then she slipped the box holding the wooden glasses into her pocket and tiptoed back downstairs. She slid silently past the kitchen, where Rose was baking for a morning cake sale, and out the front door to the steps. The cold evening air made her shiver as she took up a spot to wait.

Making sure no one was watching, she carefully swapped glasses, putting her Perfect pair in the box.

Darkness fell on the yard as she waited. Where was Boy? She was sure he would come tonight.

It was getting late and he still hadn't turned up. What if Fists had done something terrible to him? What if he needed her help? She couldn't go back to No-Man's-Land and find him; she'd never get in on her own. Her only friend could be dead or in prison. What if she never saw him again?

Weary from lack of sleep, Violet dozed off on the doorstep, only to be woken later by the bitter night air. Shivering, she slipped back inside.

Her mother was long in bed and the lights were off all over the house. She picked her way along the hall and tiptoed up the stairs. She was just at the top when the front door clicked. Her heart jumped. Quietly she placed her hands on the banister and peered over. Breath caught in her throat. A figure was moving slowly through the hallway. It was too large to be Boy. As they drew closer she gasped. It was Bungalow, the Watcher from the night before.

Her mind raced as she snuck into her room. She kept on her wooden specs, took the box that held the Perfect rose-tinted pair from her pocket and placed them on the bedside table. Then she climbed into bed pulling the thin sheet right up over her head.

She lay still, her heart pounding so hard he'd surely hear. Her door creaked open. She could see Bungalow's shadow through the white sheet. Wearing the glasses was risky but it was the only way she'd be able to see him and find out what he was up to. Maybe in some way it'd help her find her dad.

Bungalow moved around quietly. How could someone so big make so little noise? He stopped by the edge of her bed, his eyes burning a hole in the sheet. She prayed he couldn't smell fear. He reached for her glasses' case. There was a faint creak when it opened. He moved his arm up and pulled something from over his shoulder. A short wet noise like someone was sucking snots up their nose filled the room. Then he put the glasses back in the box, snapped it closed and left, heading for her mother's bedroom.

Violet waited, listening. She heard the same sucking noise coming from her mother's room, before Bungalow headed silently back downstairs.

Violet reached for her gold-rimmed glasses to check them. They seemed exactly the same – she looked through the lenses and nothing was different. Quickly she slipped from the bed, forced on her runners and quietly opened the bedroom door. Waiting until the Watcher was in the hallway below, she tiptoed after him out of the house, across the yard, and down the avenue towards town.

She'd followed Bungalow all the way to the Archers' emporium when a hand grabbed her.

"What do you think you're doing?" Boy whispered.

"Oh, Boy!" Violet gasped. "You scared the life out of me. Thank goodness you're okay!"

"You *should* be scared," Boy insisted. "Have you any idea how dangerous it is to be out on the streets at this time of night?"

"I'm following Bungalow," she snapped. "He's been in our house again. He came into my room and did something with my glasses. I need to know what it is."

"What do you mean, he 'did something'?"

"He put my glasses in that machine he carries on his back. It made a weird noise, then he put them back and left. He did the same in Mam's room. I don't know what he was up to but I'm betting the Archers are behind it. They're the ones who make the glasses... And...and I think my dad is in trouble. I heard him arguing with the Archers and then he disappeared!"

"I thought you said he'd gone to a conference."

"Yeah, that's what Edward told Mam but I don't believe him."

"So that's why you thought he might be in No-Man's-Land?" Boy looked anxious. "It's not safe, Violet. You have to stay away from the Watchers."

Her friend fell silent and Violet noticed for the first time the blue bruise round his eye and a little blue mark just visible under the sleeve of his T-shirt. It looked as if someone had hit him.

"I'm so sorry, Boy," she said, reaching towards his eye. He pulled back.

"It's not safe, Violet. Don't mess with the Watchers. You don't know what you're doing."

"But somebody has to stand up to them, Boy. Why

were you at my house when we arrived if that's not what you wanted?"

"It is what I want, but you shouldn't get mixed up in it!" he snapped.

"Well it's too late now. Maybe you should have thought about that before you broke into my room!" Violet replied sharply.

They fell into silence. Ignoring Boy, Violet watched Bungalow.

"Look!" she said, triumphantly pointing over Boy's shoulder. "I knew it. I knew it. Bungalow has a key. He's going into the Archers' optician's. I know they're involved. We have to go in. It's the only way we'll find out what's going on."

"How do you know the Archers are involved, Violet? Bungalow has the key to your house too!"

"I just know, Boy, I can't explain it. I just feel it! Fists mentioned the brothers last night and he was standing outside the Archers' place and now Bungalow is going inside. They give me the creeps, Edward and George. I know they're behind all of this, they have to be!"

"Violet, have you not heard anything I've said? Whatever the Watchers are doing in the Archers' place you don't want to know. This is not a game."

"Did I say it was? All I know is that the Archers have my dad, and I have to get him back before Mam forgets he ever existed," she said, her voice quivering, "like Mrs Moody did with Pip!"

Boy's face softened a little. Violet held firm.

"I know what you mean about the Archers," Boy whispered, "they give me the creeps too but everyone in Perfect loves them. If they are involved nobody here is ever going to listen."

"But we have to find out, Boy," Violet insisted. "Remember what you said about the people in No-Man's-Land? They don't try any more, they've given up. But *you* haven't, that's why you were looking for my dad in the first place! If we find him, he can help. You and your friends won't be invisible any more. People in No-Man's-Land can go back to their families. Think about it, Boy, think about the Rag Tree."

Boy looked doubtful, his black eye suddenly shining on his face. "It's dangerous, Violet, I'm warning you."

"I know," she said, her tone softer now, "but it'll be safer if we do it together."

Boy looked at Violet for a moment then drew in his breath. "Okay. But you have to do as I say."

Violet nodded.

As the clock in the tower struck twelve, Boy grabbed her hand, and the pair snuck up the dark street towards the Archers' emporium, intent on breaking in.

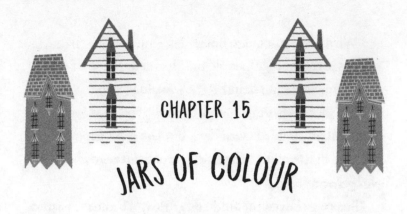

CHAPTER 15

JARS OF COLOUR

Violet followed silently behind Boy. They covered the distance to the Archers' emporium quickly. He signalled for her to stay back as he approached the door, but she ignored his orders and was by his side when Boy discovered it was locked.

"What will we do?" she whispered, making him jump.

"I told you to stay back!"

"It's *my* dad we're looking for!"

"Do you have a hair clip?" he asked ignoring her tone.

She pulled a pin from her ponytail. Boy fiddled with the lock, and after a few minutes there was a faint click, he turned the handle and the door opened.

"Have you been to jail?" she whispered, amazed.

"What? No, of course not!"

"It's just I thought people only learned that stuff in jail."

"Or in No-Man's-Land." He winked.

The shop was empty and they slipped in, closing the door behind them. It was dark but the glass cabinets still gleamed in the night. The thick carpet softened the sound of their steps.

"There's no one about," Boy breathed, after a quick investigation. "Bungalow isn't here, Violet."

"Then where is he?" she whispered. "We saw him go in, how could he get out without us seeing?" Then a thought struck her. "I want to check something. I have an idea then I promise I'll leave."

Quickly, Violet walked across the shop to the mahogany wall on the opposite side, and ran her fingers along the wood until they met a familiar bump. As she pushed gently, the wall gave way to the library beyond. She smiled back at Boy and entered.

It was darker than in the shop as there were no windows in the library. But a thin strip of light warmed the carpet from under the door at the far side of the room. A shadow passed through the light. Violet inched across the space and placed her ear against the cherry wood.

A familiar sound greeted her – a sucking noise. She pulled Boy alongside to listen. After a few minutes it stopped and the light went out.

They found a hiding spot behind an old leather armchair to the right of the door and waited for someone to come out.

"Any idea what that noise was?" Violet whispered.

Boy shook his head.

"It's the same one I heard tonight in my house – from the machine Bungalow carries on his back. We have to go in there and find out what it is."

"Not yet, Violet, let's wait a minute," Boy protested. "You don't know what you're saying. I've already told you to be afraid of the Watchers. They're seriously dangerous."

"Please, Boy," she begged, "you don't understand because you have no parents! My dad is one of my two favourite people in the world. I can't let anything happen to him. I need to find out what's going on."

Suddenly Boy's face changed. He was angry. Violet bit her lip. Maybe she shouldn't have said that. Maybe he wished he did have parents even though he said he didn't want any. Her dad always told her to think before she spoke in case she hurt someone's feelings. Maybe she'd just hurt Boy's.

"I'm sorry. I didn't mean it," she whispered. "I'd hate to not have parents."

Boy looked down at his feet, away from Violet. They fell into an awkward silence.

"I'm not afraid of the Watchers, you know," he said

after a while. "I can handle whatever they do to me."
Unconsciously, he cupped the bruise on his arm.

"I know."

"It's just we have to be careful, Violet. You have to promise you'll listen to me. I mean it this time."

"I will, I swear," she said, nodding her head earnestly.

They waited in the darkness a bit longer and, when nobody emerged from the room, Boy crept back to where they'd stood and listened. Violet followed. There was no sound behind the door. He turned the handle, leaned his weight against it and pushed gently. It opened just enough for the pair to slip through. Then Boy shut it quietly behind them.

Violet stood just inside the entrance. The room was long and narrow. Three rows of shelving about two metres high ran the length of both walls. These shelves were made of steel, a contrast to the rich wood that covered the rest of the emporium, and they were filled with glass jars – loads of them. Each jar held a strange-coloured gas that glowed in the dark, filling the room with a ghostly light.

"What are they?" Violet whispered, picking up one of the jars.

The gas was dull, a dark blue-green colour, and it moved sluggishly behind the glass. Boy picked up a second jar with slightly brighter colours, dark blue-greens mixed with hints of yellow and a single stream of bright red.

"Look," Boy whispered, pointing to a worn sticker on top of his jar. It read: *Mr John Bumsbury. Completed 9th Dec '05. Last top up 9th Dec '16.*

Violet looked up at her friend.

"I haven't a clue what it means." He shrugged.

She moved her jar towards Boy's for a little more light, then noticed it also had a label on the lid: *Mrs Charlotte Cotts. Completed 24th March '06. Last top up 24th March '17.*

Violet gasped. "I know that name," she whispered. "Charlotte Cotts lives in Perfect. She's in Mam's book club!"

"Come on," Boy said, putting down his jar.

He walked towards the far end of the room, not stopping until he reached a separate section of shelving where the jars were different. These were only partially full; the gas inside was brightly coloured, almost luminous and moved about rapidly behind the glass. The mixtures of colour were beautiful. Boy picked one up and read the label: *Mr Jim Joiners. Incomplete. Last session 14th June '06. NML.*

"I know him," Boy said, his voice shaky. "He lives in No-Man's-Land."

Quickly he put down the jar and picked up another: *Mr Raymond Splinters. Incomplete. Last session 1st Aug '06. NML.*

"I know him too."

Violet was reaching for another jar when a noise startled them both. Footsteps were approaching from the library. Someone was coming.

The pair scrambled for cover. The bottom shelf by her feet didn't have as many jars, so Violet ducked down and crawled into the space, pressing her back to the wall. She nearly knocked one of the jars over and just managed to steady it as the door opened and the lights flickered on. She held her breath and balanced precariously on a shaking arm.

The footsteps advanced down the room towards her hiding place. A pair of large, polished, brown leather shoes stopped millimetres from where she kneeled.

"Ah, Violet Brown," George Archer suddenly said. "I hope you've been a good girl."

Her heart stopped. She waited, terrified, but George Archer seemed to be distracted by something on a shelf above.

"That blasted Watcher!" he spat. "Still not enough. Do I have to do everything myself?"

There was a clatter of glass, and then George turned on his heel and marched down to the opposite end of the room from where he'd entered. The lights switched off, a door slammed and the place was plunged back into darkness.

"He was looking at that jar," Boy said, jumping out from his hiding place.

He ran to the spot where the tall twin had stood moments before. Violet crawled out shakily and stood by his side as Boy reached for the jar. It was about a quarter full of brightly coloured gas, which raced around inside at lightning speed. He passed it silently to Violet. She stared at the shiny new label stuck to the top: *Miss Violet Brown. Processing.*

Her legs weak, she handed the jar back to Boy, and felt her way onto the floor.

"What is it?" She trembled. "Why does it have my name on it?"

"I don't know, Violet," Boy whispered, crouching by her side. "But I promise we'll find out."

CHAPTER 16

THE WARNING

"What's going on, Boy?" Violet said, her voice barely a whisper.

They'd been sitting side by side in the darkness, too shaken to talk. Boy didn't answer.

"I mean what is that stuff in the jars?" she mumbled, mainly to herself.

"I don't know, Violet," Boy said, shaking his head. "But what was it you said about Bungalow taking your glasses?"

"He put them in a machine and it made a noise." She nodded weakly. "Just like the noise we heard a few minutes ago."

"So there's some sort of link between the Watchers,

the glasses and these jars...and the Archers," he almost whispered.

Violet didn't reply, lost in thought. The glow of the jars added a sinister air to their gloomy mood.

"But everyone trusts them, Violet," Boy piped up angrily. "They love the Archers here, they even have streets named after them – I never really suspected them, I mean I thought they were creepy but I still blamed everything on the Watchers. Maybe they're in this together?"

"I'm sure the Archers have my dad," Violet quivered.

"Come on," Boy said, after a while. "We won't solve anything sitting around here."

"Maybe you're right, this snooping is too dangerous." Violet hesitated. Seeing her name on the jar had unsettled her.

"But we can't let this go now," Boy insisted. "We have to follow George. It might lead us to your dad. At least then you'll be back together and your family can escape from Perfect."

"But what about you? Where will you go?"

"I'll be fine." Boy smiled, though it didn't quite reach his eyes.

Violet nodded. She trusted him. Boy was almost her best friend already and she needed his encouragement now she wasn't feeling as brave.

✳   ✳   ✳

George had disappeared through a door at the bottom of the room, but now the pair stood in front of a brick wall, feeling confused.

"It's a dead end," Boy stated, puzzled.

"I definitely heard a door bang when he went," Violet said.

"Me too," Boy agreed, staring at the wall in front of them. He thought for a moment, then straightened up and ran at it. He had to bite his tongue to stop from crying out in pain as he slammed into solid brick.

"Well that was a great idea!" Violet mocked.

"Can you think of a better one?" Boy snapped, cradling his shoulder.

"Actually, yes I can," Violet answered, running her hands along the wall. "I bet it's hidden somehow like the door from the Archers' optician's into their library…"

Her fingers slipped across a loose brick. She pushed it and the brick sprung out from the wall like a handle. Violet glanced at Boy and smiled. She turned the handle and the wall gave way to a landing behind. They entered quickly and gently closed the door behind them.

They were standing in what looked like an ancient passageway – a circular tunnel, made from solid squares of rock. A spiral stone staircase, lit by the flickering flame of a wall-mounted torch, led off to the left. Quickly Boy grabbed the torch from its perch and began to descend the stairs.

"The only way is down," he whispered.

Violet nodded, and followed close behind. Her earlier bravery was now being tested. "It's like we're inside a computer game," she said, trying to disguise her anxiety.

"A what?"

"You know, a computer game! You must have played some when you lived in Perfect?"

Boy fell silent. What had she said this time? How could talking about computer games upset anyone?

"Did I say something wrong?" she asked, confused. "Don't you like computer games?"

"I don't know what a computer game is."

"Oh, is that all." Violet smiled. "Are they not allowed in Perfect?"

"I never lived in Perfect," Boy whispered, so faintly that Violet barely heard.

"But how did you get into No-Man's-Land then?"

"I don't know. I was born there, I think. I don't ever remember anywhere else."

"Oh, I thought..." Violet didn't know what to say.

"Everyone my age in No-Man's-Land has family in Perfect. They all come from here," he said solemnly. "But I don't, and I don't know why."

"So you were born in the orphanage?" Violet asked.

"No." Boy shook his head. "I was left there. I don't know by who."

"That's good though kind of, isn't it?" she said trying to lighten his mood. "You said yourself you don't want parents. Look at mine, they're a mess."

"Yeah I suppose." He sighed. "Who wants to be told what to do all the time?"

Suddenly Boy froze and pushed Violet against the cold stone. He brought the flame round to his face, and put a finger to his lips, then pointed down the stairwell.

A chilling cry echoed up from below.

"I promise, I'll get her next time, sir," a voice whimpered.

"You'd better or you know where I'll be sending you."

Violet recognized George's voice.

"I don't want any newbies in No-Man's-Land, there's too many people in there already. Brown's daughter has to stay in Perfect. He's slow enough as it is. I don't want anything to stop him working!"

Violet gasped. She was right. They had her father.

"I understand, sir," the whimpering voice continued. "It's just this Violet, she's a hard'n' to crack, I think she's got too much. I'm doin' the same that I do t'all the rest but we've been at it nearly a month now, even with the pills, sir, she's just not coming round."

"I don't care how much she has, no excuses. Just figure it out!"

"I understand, Mr Archer, sir," The voice trembled. "I'll do me best."

"YOU'LL DO YOUR JOB!"

Footsteps pounded across the floor below. Then, after a few moments of silence, laughter erupted.

"I'll do me best, Mr Archer, sir!" a third voice snorted.

"Well what was I meant to say? If I don't get this one right I'll be off the hollowin' team an' workin' in the field growing them ugly plants."

"I love you, Mr Archer, sir," another voice sniggered.

Boy whispered to Violet to stay put. Then he quashed the torch flame with his foot and followed the stairwell to the bottom. Violet stood in the darkness listening to the squabbling voices below.

Moments later, Boy was by her side again. "There are three Watchers down there," he whispered. "Bungalow and two others. They're in a kind of dormitory. I think they're getting ready to sleep off their night shift. Won't be long before they're out for the count. Then we can move on."

"What about George Archer? Where did he go?"

"There's a passage leading off the other side of the room. He must have gone down there. We'll sneak through when the Watchers are asleep and follow him."

Violet shivered as she waited on the step, her head swimming in terrifying thoughts. What was the Watcher talking about? What did she have too much of? And what did the Archers want her dad to fix? Sometimes her imagination was her worst enemy but other times it was her best asset, at least that's what her mam told her.

She couldn't think about her parents now though, she needed to be strong if she was going to rescue them; her mother who was being lost to Perfect and her dad who was…who was just lost…

Boy shifted next to her and she sought out his hand on the cold stone. Slipping hers on top of his, she felt safe.

"You know," she whispered, "my parents can be yours too, when they're back to normal that is."

For a while Boy didn't reply and in the darkness Violet couldn't tell if she'd upset him again. Then he squeezed her hand.

"Come on," he whispered. "I think they've gone to sleep."

CHAPTER 17

DEADLY COLD

Violet got up and, keeping her left hand against the wall, tiptoed after her friend. As they neared the bottom of the stairwell, light trickled up from a doorway below. She held her breath; any sound could wake the sleeping Watchers.

Boy entered the freezing room first. Violet followed, though her legs wanted to run the other way.

The space was huge, lit only by a battery torch dangling from the end of a rope that was tied to a nail in the ceiling. The torch cast a circular glow round the centre of the room. About twenty rope hammocks hung from rusted hooks bolted to the stone above. All were empty except for three occupied by the sleeping Watchers.

Violet tiptoed round the hammocks, past an upturned wooden crate that sat directly under the torch, where a card game was laid out ready to play. Carefully she stepped over dirty uniforms and stinking giant leather boots that littered the middle of the floor. She held her nose to block out the sweaty stench.

"Down here," Boy whispered, ducking into a passageway at the far side of the room.

It was dark, but Boy didn't dare light the torch he still held in his grasp as they moved quickly on, keeping close to the wall for comfort. A little further down the tunnel Violet's fingers brushed over a cold slime. The walls were wet. Trickles of water ran down the stone forming small pools on the flagstone floor. It was freezing cold and Violet wrapped her arms around herself in a vain attempt to combat the falling temperature.

"Listen," Boy said, stopping suddenly in front of her. "Do you hear that?"

"What?" Violet asked.

"That noise, like running water. We must be under the river," he whispered.

"What river?"

"The river that marks the furthest edges of No-Man's-Land. There are walls on three sides and the river on the fourth. We must be underneath it now."

"Underneath it! So it's *above* us? What if the stones

can't hold it in? What if the walls burst and we drown?" Violet said, panic filling her throat.

"Violet!" Boy raised his voice to a loud whisper. "You don't half exaggerate! Does this tunnel look new to you?"

She shook her head and tried to calm the racing thoughts swirling round her mind.

"Exactly," he said. "It's centuries old. If the walls have kept the river out this long, I'm pretty sure they're not going to fall in on us now."

Boy's words made sense and Violet told herself to relax as they continued on their journey. Where had her bravery gone? She'd been determined to find out what Bungalow was up to earlier but now she was worried they'd gotten in a bit too deep. She wished they could just find her dad and leave.

"Have you ever crossed the river out of No-Man's-Land?" Violet asked, trying to distract her thoughts.

"No," Boy said. "It's almost impossible. There's only one footbridge and it's falling down. The Watchers patrol the other side too. I've heard rumours of people trying to escape across it."

"What happened to them?"

"They were caught by the Watchers. Nobody ever saw them again."

Violet didn't ask any more questions and they walked in silence as the ground beneath them began to slope gradually upwards like they were heading for the surface.

A slight breeze tickled her ankles and a mist seeped into the tunnel filling the stone space, its icy tongue licking Violet's skin. She searched out Boy's hand in the darkness. He was shivering.

"Are you okay?" she whispered.

He didn't reply.

"Boy, please, you're frightening me. Where are we?"

"Do you hear them?" His voice was weak.

"Who?"

Violet moved closer, wrapping her arm around his. It felt as if someone was watching them. She looked behind her but could see nothing in the thick black.

"Do you hear the voices, Violet?"

Boy sounded desperate.

"What voices? It's just the wind. Please, Boy, you're scaring me."

"They're crying. I think they're crying, Violet."

"Who's crying? Please, Boy, stop it!"

There was a rustle behind her. Violet panicked. Letting go of Boy's arm, she sprinted for the light that trickled down into the tunnel ahead outlining some stone steps in the darkness.

She rushed up the steps until her head broke through an opening above her into the night air. She squeezed her arms through the gap and wriggled out onto soggy grass using her elbows. A few moments later Boy struggled through onto the grass beside her.

"Where are we?" she whispered.

He didn't answer. His face was as white as her mother's starched sheets and it scared Violet. To steady her beating heart she ignored him and looked around. When she turned back, Boy was gone.

"No, please stop! Boy! Don't – i-it's a graveyard," she stuttered climbing onto her feet.

High crosses and half tombstones appeared to float in the fog either side of a stone path a little way away from her. The path cut straight through the graveyard. She could just make out Boy's grey shadow in the fog, and she followed him. She had no choice. Gingerly, she stepped round the graves to reach the path that was cracked and patterned in weeds. To steady herself, she counted them as she walked.

"One dandelion, two daisies, two dandelions… Ouch!"

Something sharp sliced the skin on her forearm. A rusted nail protruded from an old wooden stake. She looked up and screamed. A human skull was impaled on top of the stake and a roughly scrawled sign was nailed to the wood below.

KEEP OUT
IF YOU KNOW WHAT'S GOOD FOR YOU!

"Please, Boy! Please can we get out of here!" she cried.

The panic in her voice must have raised Boy from his trance and within seconds he appeared back through the mist.

"Violet, are you okay? What's wrong?" he panted.

As she pointed to the sign, something clattered up ahead. Boy grabbed her arm and yanked her down behind a broken stone cross.

"Stay here," he whispered.

She nodded, her voice stolen. Boy began to move away and she grabbed his sleeve.

"I have to check the voices out," he said, gently shaking her off. "One of them could be George! I'll be back in a minute. I promise."

He was gone. She was alone.

"Everything will be okay. Everything will be okay," Violet repeated.

There was a rustle behind her.

She closed her eyes, every muscle tensed. She couldn't move. Suddenly something scuttled over her foot, and she squealed and darted backwards.

A large rat rested at the base of the cross gnawing on a bone.

She panicked and ran blindly.

A wall surrounding the graveyard emerged out of the mist ahead and she scrambled across the graves towards it. Clambering over the top, she fell down the other side onto a bed of mossy grass.

As she sat with her back to the stone wall her fears engulfed her. Maybe Boy was right, she should never have got involved. More than ever she wished they hadn't come to Perfect. She wished none of this had happened. What if her mam just didn't love her any more? What if her dad had disappeared on purpose; maybe he had another family or maybe he didn't love her either and that's why he left? Maybe it had nothing to do with Perfect. She'd blamed the Archers for everything when really it was all her own fault. Her heart sank, pulling heavily on her chest. Every terrible thought she could imagine ate away at her until life seemed so bleak she couldn't see an escape.

She looked around for Boy. The mist had thickened. He'd left her too. Everyone who meant anything had gone. They'd all abandoned her. Pulling her knees towards her chest, she wrapped her arms around them, shielding herself from the outside. Soon the mist cocooned her from the world. She cried. For her mam and dad, for the friends she'd lost, for Boy and his lack of parents. She cried for all the bad things she had ever heard about in school, like homeless people or the starving children in Africa, and she cried for herself. This was how Boy found her.

"Violet," he panted, sitting down. "I was looking everywhere for you."

She didn't look at him. She was angry and didn't want him to see her cry.

"Where were you?" she stammered. "You left me."

"I'm sorry," he pleaded. "I didn't leave you. I went to see where the voices were coming from. I thought George Archer was there."

"But you left me in the graveyard."

"I'm sorry," said Boy, shamefaced. "I didn't think."

"Did you find them? The voices?"

"No." Boy sighed, his face still white. "I'm not sure they were real."

Violet shivered as the pair sat shoulder to shoulder in silence. The air grew thicker and a distant clap of thunder rumbled across the sky.

"Violet," Boy whispered a while later, "please look at me," he said, wiping the tears from his red eyes. "I know how you feel. It's this place. It brings out every bad thought you've ever had. I've heard about it before but I never believed the stories until now."

"What do you mean?"

"I'll show you," he said, getting to his feet and pulling Violet up from the soggy grass. "We have to be quiet, really quiet."

A blinking street lamp rested on the crest of the hill

ahead, yellowing the mists. They stumbled up the grassy rise towards it along a narrow path that had been worn into the hillside.

"It looks like we're not the only people who've come this way," Violet whispered.

Boy nodded but stayed silent. Nearing the top he pulled on her arm and signalled her to copy him. Quietly he got onto his knees and crawled up what remained of the hill, stopping by the street lamp.

Violet followed suit and was soon by his side, her elbows and knees sopping wet. From the top of the hill they could see down into a small valley.

A row of rusty, steel street lamps dotted along a cracked cement footpath dimly lit the scene below. Just off the footpath on one side were a group of unfinished cement block homes; some had just cavities for windows or doors, while two were shells without even a roof. Bits of steel fencing and old machinery decorated the weed-filled gardens at the front of the half-finished homes.

The place was nothing like the old world of Perfect or No-Man's-Land, it was modern and reminded Violet of the housing estate she lived in before she came to Perfect – except this one had never been finished.

Off the other side of the footpath was a black tarmac road that circled around a green common area in the middle of the houses.

Strange plants were growing in the green – about fifty rows of them. Their flower heads had white petals and were bent over as if sheltering from a driving rain, while their thick stems were coloured a deep blood red. They were about as tall as sunflowers.

"Where are we?" Violet whispered.

Boy pointed across the park. "Look over there."

Violet followed his finger and noticed two crumbling cement-block pillars marking what must have been an entrance. Beside the pillars was a faded billboard picture of a happy family. Each smiling parent carried a child on their shoulders towards a house that looked the exact same as the houses below them except for one thing – it was finished. Giant faded letters across the top of the billboard read: *Set your family up for life.*

Violet nodded.

"If you go through the pillars and follow the road it leads back to the footbridge I was telling you about, the broken one into No-Man's-Land. So we did cross under the river."

"But where are we, Boy, what is this place?"

"It's whispered about in No-Man's-Land."

"What do they say?" Violet quivered.

"That it's full of bad luck. Some say it's where the Watchers punished people during the rebellions, others tell darker stories about the graveyard and its bloody history. Most say it's…it's…"

"It's what?" Violet asked, her fear rising.

"It's haunted," Boy whispered. "People call it the Ghost Estate!"

CHAPTER 18

THE GHOST ESTATE

"Ghosts?"

Boy nodded. "I heard that the man who developed the estate was murdered before he could finish it because he tried to build on the land. It's right next to the graveyard and there's lots of dark stories about that place. Some people whisper that he built on old, forgotten graves and the spirits rose up to punish him. That's why it's supposed to be bad luck to come here."

Violet quivered. "Is that why I felt so sad in the graveyard and why you heard those voices, Boy? Was it the ghosts?"

Boy shrugged. "I'm just telling you what I know, Violet. Maybe it was ghosts, if you believe in that sort of thing."

"Dad says there's no such thing whenever I get scared. He believes in science and says that things need proof and there's no proof for ghosts," Violet stammered as confidently as she could.

"Well then I'm sure it's not true. It's probably just stories," Boy said reassuringly. "Anyway, look," he pointed to the path that was worn down to the estate, "people obviously walk this way."

The wind picked up and thunder boomed overhead. Violet jumped.

"It's okay, Violet. Like you said, there's no such thing as ghosts and George must have come this way. Don't you want to find your dad?" Boy looked straight at her. "Come on."

Without a word, Violet and Boy crept down the other side of the hill. They'd just stepped onto the cement footpath when a huge clatter echoed through the empty estate.

Boy grabbed her arm and they ran for cover behind a garden wall attached to the house beside them.

"It's just one of the fences. The steel makes a lot of noise. The wind must have blown it over," Boy panted, gathering his breath.

They were about to move when Violet suddenly ducked back down, pulling Boy with her.

"There's something inside the house," she whispered.

"Something moved, I swear."

She crawled quickly across the garden and ducked under the sill of the main window.

"What are you doing?" Boy whispered, ducking down beside her.

"I'm going to have a look," she said. "I got a strange feeling…"

Holding onto the edge of the sill, she inched herself up to peer through the window.

A red bulb hung in the centre of a room turning the walls blood coloured. Rows and rows of small potted plants covered the cement floor. They were just like the plants she'd seen growing on the green, except they were smaller.

Boy tugged on her leg.

"What?"

"Do you see anything?"

"I'm not sure…" she whispered, unable to look away.

The potted plants all had their heads turned towards the red light bulb, as though they were soaking in its warmth. The translucent-petalled flower heads were supported by pulsing red stems that looked like veins rooted into pots of dark clotted clay. The pots bubbled over with a gruesome red liquid that seeped across the floor. It looked as if a million people had been murdered in the room. Small plastic tubes in the side of each pot connected to a large barrel of thick liquid in the corner of the space. It seemed to be feeding the masses.

She stared into the room trying to make sense of the scene, when very slowly all the plants turned their heads towards the window and stared back at her.

She ducked down, her heart thumping.

"What is it, Violet? You're white as a sheet!"

"It's...it's..."

"It's what?"

"It's eyes. Lots of eyes, staring at me! Pots and pots of eyes. They're growing eyes, Boy!" Violet shuddered.

She wasn't making any sense. Boy pulled himself up for a look.

"It's eyes!" he gasped, darting back down to her side. "I don't understand, I thought they were plants. Eyes? Why would anyone be growing eyes?"

They sat under the window ledge in silence thinking frantically. An idea was forming in Violet's mind but she couldn't quite grasp it: the Archers, Perfect, the glasses, her dad...

"My dad –" she said, suddenly sitting upright, her bravery returning – "my dad is here, Boy. He's in this estate, I know he is."

"Shh," Boy whispered looking around to make sure no one was about. "What makes you think that?"

"It's the eyes. The Archers asked him to come and

work here because he'd won an award. I remember reading about it in *Eye Spy* magazine. I thought his whole idea was disgusting, but it had something to do with growing eyes for transplants."

"But why would the Archers want eye transplants... and so many?"

"All I know is that Dad is here. He has to be. And we have to rescue him. Please, Boy, will you help me check the estate? You take that side and I'll take this one."

"Really? On your own?"

"Yes, I'm not a girly girl, you know!"

"Well, you are actually." Boy smiled, then turned and crawled back across the garden.

Violet shivered as he dashed for the other side of the estate. She was on her own. She shook off her fear; her dad was here and she had to help him.

Quickly she crawled across the garden and over the low dividing wall to the house next door. Inside looked just the same as the last house: there were rows and rows of eye plants.

Ugh, it was disgusting. For a moment she thought she was going to vomit. Bile raced up her throat stopping short of her mouth. She steadied herself against the window sill. She was here to find her dad. She had to concentrate.

At the third house, a strange noise met her ears and, as she peeked through the window, her skin rose in goosepimples sending a shiver right through her shoulders.

Watchers lay all over the floor, snoring their night away. The house was packed with them. They were all fully dressed as if they'd collapsed exhausted where they stood. Some of their boots were caked in mud and dark clumps of clay were dotted over the concrete floor. Sets of muddy footprints traced from the door of the house, across the tarmac road to the green full of plants. The Watchers must be working there. She had to tell Boy.

She was about to move when suddenly the front door of the house opened. Violet pushed her body against the wall under the window sill and stayed deadly still, her pulse racing.

George Archer strode out across the green. She could see Boy on his knees peering through a window in one of the houses opposite. He was completely oblivious as the taller brother marched towards him.

All the air escaped Violet's lungs and she couldn't breathe. Her friend was caught. There was no way out. Clambering to her feet as quietly as possible, she followed after the taller twin at a safe distance, all the while searching her brain for a way to save Boy. If she screamed or threw something they'd both get caught and that wouldn't help anyone.

George was heading straight for Boy now. Her friend turned and the huge man was upon him. He pulled something from his pocket and sprayed Boy in the face. Within seconds he'd collapsed, unconscious.

George Archer threw Boy's limp body over his shoulder and turned. Violet watched as he walked to the house next door and pushed open the door.

The two disappeared inside and Violet quickly sprinted towards the house. Her legs were shaking, but she had to be strong.

She couldn't see anything in the front room so she raced around the back of the house just in time to see George carry Boy up the stairs, his legs dangling loosely down the giant's back. A few moments later George returned downstairs alone and disappeared out the front door.

She raced round after him, but the willowy twin was already striding across to the house with the sleeping Watchers on the other side of the green.

Violet wasn't sure what George Archer had done to Boy but she knew her friend was in trouble, deep trouble, and she was the only one who could save him.

CHAPTER 19

THE LOCKED ROOM

First things first, Violet had to get inside the house. She tried the doors, but they were locked. The windows! The upstairs ones at the back had no glass. Only white plastic sheeting covered the cavities.

She crept around the estate as quietly as she could, looking for something that would help her to reach the windows. In the back garden of one of the derelict houses was a battered workbench. Behind the bench a pile of tools and broken steel piping were gathering rust in the dirt. Hidden amongst them was a rickety old ladder. It looked just long enough to reach the upstairs windows.

The garden, like the rest of the estate, was eerie and a sudden chill danced up her spine. She remembered Boy's story about it being haunted, but she shook away the thought. This was no time to worry about ghosts.

The ladder was lightweight and she could carry it easily. She struggled to prop it up against the wall of the house where Boy was captive, tiredness taking hold of her limbs. It fell just short of the ledge.

With a deep breath she took her first step.

The metal clattered a little and she stopped for a moment, hoping no one had heard. It wobbled as she climbed up to the top, her legs shaking. Pressing her body firmly against the wall, she stretched until her fingers gripped the corner of the ledge.

The ladder slipped, scraping a little against the wall and she gasped, her heart thumping.

With all her strength she pulled and wiggled her way onto the window ledge. She tumbled through the opening, landing with a thud on the cold cement floor. She lay still for a moment, every muscle shaking.

Thunder boomed overhead, this time followed by a flash of white lightning that illuminated the empty landing. It was concrete, grey and barren. Shadows haunted every corner.

The house was silent. Deadly still.

There were four doors, two on either side of the landing. She crawled quickly to the first. The room was empty. She continued through the darkness to the second door. This room was bigger than the last and pitch black. The windows were blocked up with plastic sheeting that rattled in the wind. Violet felt her way across the floor as another bolt of lightning lit up the space, revealing a body in the corner – Boy!

She scurried towards him on all fours, a sudden lump in her throat. He had a leather collar round his neck that was secured to the floor by a steel chain. The chain was strong, too strong to break and the collar was locked shut at the catch. She searched frantically for something that might cut through it.

Suddenly a door slammed downstairs. Violet froze as voices filled the hallway below. Heavy footsteps walked past the stairs and into a room at the back of the house.

"Just like George to wake us. As if we're not working hard enough for him growing those things!"

"I know," the other yawned, "but the longer we're here minding that fella upstairs the longer we're away from weedin'!"

"What d'ya suppose he'll do with 'im?" the first snorted.

"Haven't a clue," the other laughed. "Experiments, probably."

"Ya reckon? He deserves it anyway. That boy was always a troublemaker. Could never get me hands on 'im. Slippery little customer. Blasted No-Man's-Lander!"

"Go up and check on him, will ya? Make sure he hasn't wriggled out of this one."

Feet pounded towards the stairs. The room was bare; there was nowhere to hide. Violet scrambled for the door on the opposite side of the landing and rattled the handle. It was locked. She yelped in fear.

"Crying like a girl, eh, Boy!" the Watcher laughed. He was nearing the top of the stairs.

Suddenly the door in front of Violet opened. A hand dragged her inside just as the Watcher stepped onto the landing.

Heavy steps stopped outside the door as Violet took in her rescuer, a dark-haired lady. The woman signalled for Violet to climb into an old wardrobe in the corner of the room. She did as instructed without question or sound.

"I definitely heard something but he's still out cold up here," the Watcher shouted downstairs.

"How stupid are you, ya twit!" The roar came from below. "Go'n check on your one. Make sure she's not up to no good."

Violet's heart pounded in the darkness as the door of the room she'd just entered creaked open.

"What are you playing at?" she heard the Watcher growl.

"Cards," the woman replied coolly.

"Mind if I join? I'd like to give you a good beatin'." He sniggered.

"Of course I mind!"

"Don't be so cheeky," the Watcher said, surging inside, "or I'll wipe the smile off that pretty little face…"

"Ah, ah, ah," the woman said calmly, "do you want me to report you to the Archers?"

"You…" the Watcher growled.

"What?" the woman replied. "You think I wouldn't do it?"

The door slammed as the Watcher thundered back downstairs.

"One of these days!" he roared up from below.

The dark-haired lady chuckled.

Violet remained in her hiding place. She was in awe of the woman's bravery, but for some reason she felt she had to stay in the wardrobe until asked to leave it.

"You can come out now."

She pushed the wooden door so it swung open, gradually revealing the room.

She hadn't had a chance to look at it properly before. It was a complete contrast to the rest of the house, lit with candles, which cast warm flickers of light and shadow across the ornate wallpaper. The room was full of rich reds and deep woody browns just like the Archers' optician's. As she stepped out her feet sank into the lavish carpet. Beautiful paintings, seascapes and country scenes, in gold gilded frames decorated the walls. They were wild and full of life like the artist was trying to paint freedom, but the room itself felt homely and safe.

"Have a seat, young lady," the woman said, gesturing to a chair by an antique wooden table.

Violet sat on the chair, her legs dangling over its edge.

"So what brings you here?" the woman asked.

What could Violet say? She stared blankly at her host.

She was maybe the most elegant lady Violet had ever seen. She was old though, probably as old as Violet's mother. Her hair was long, as long as Violet wished hers to be and, like a jet black veil, it fell down the back of the chair and pooled on the floor. Her face was pale and her large eyes were green, as green as the grass in spring. She wore a gold locket inset with green stones that caught the light in her eyes. Violet watched as she rubbed it between her thumb and forefinger. If ever the word beautiful fitted anyone, it fitted this woman. She was like a queen or a princess. Violet wished for a minute she could be just like her.

"Are you okay? Has the cat got your tongue?"

"Is there a cat?" Violet asked confused.

"Oh, it's only an expression." The woman smiled.

Violet shifted in the chair.

"Are you in trouble?"

Should she tell this lady? She wasn't afraid of her, but could she trust her? She was in need of a friend.

"Kind of," Violet answered. "Well, I'm kind of in

164

trouble but my friend, Boy, he's in big trouble."

"Boy?"

"Yes, I know." Violet smiled. "He's from No-Man's-Land. He says that's his name."

"Is he in No-Man's-Land now?"

"No, he's in the room next door chained up with a collar on his neck. I'm trying to free him so we can go and find my dad."

"Is your father in trouble too?"

"Yes. Well, I think so. I think the Archers have him and they're making him do some sort of experiments."

The woman's face changed. She turned and walked to the window that overlooked the estate, thumbing her locket again. She didn't speak for a while. Violet wasn't sure whether to break the silence, so she distracted herself with the writing desk and a half-written letter that lay on top of it. The handwriting was beautiful, swirly and delicate. Violet's teacher always told her off for her messy letters. She knew it wasn't right to read it but…

Dear Boys,
This is a day like all the others. I sit in my room and cry for all I have lost…

"What is your name, young lady?" the woman said turning sharply.

Violet blushed, tearing her eyes from the letter.

"I-it's Violet," she stuttered.

"That's beautiful." The woman smiled. "You must have wonderful parents to pick such a beautiful name."

"Erm…yes."

Images of her parents flooded Violet's mind. Her throat tightened.

"You know, your father is looking for you," the lady said mysteriously.

Violet sat forward. "Have you seen him?"

"No, I'm afraid not, Violet, but I know what it is like to lose your children and he will not rest until he finds you."

"He didn't lose me. I lost him."

"For a parent it's the same thing, Violet. He'll find you."

"Did you find your boys?" she asked; then quickly wished she hadn't.

"No," the lady replied looking away.

Silence flooded the room once more.

"I gave up my family a long time ago, Violet, but I will always love them. I know when it is my time I will see them again."

"Oh, I'm sorry. I didn't mean to be nosy."

"It's okay." The woman smiled. "Now, don't you want to free your friend?"

Violet nodded.

"Well then," the woman said, walking to the cabinet and pulling a knife from the depths of a drawer. "Take this. It should cut through the collar."

"Will you come with us?"

"No, Violet, but I wish you the best of luck."

"Are you a prisoner?"

"Of sorts."

"But you're not chained up?"

"Not physically, Violet, but the world has changed. There is nothing out there for me now."

"But this is just a room…"

"It's my room, Violet," the woman replied abruptly.

"I'm sorry, my dad would kill me for asking so many questions," Violet said, as she took the knife from the lady and walked to the door. "Thank you." She was about to turn the handle when the woman spoke again.

"Violet, I try not to spend too much time at my window but when I do I notice there is always a lot of activity over there." She pointed to a house two doors down from where the Watchers were sleeping. "I think perhaps your father is in there."

"Thank you," Violet said, feeling suddenly alive again. She slipped silently out the door and back across the hall to rescue Boy, aware that any moment the Watchers could mount the stairs once more and find her.

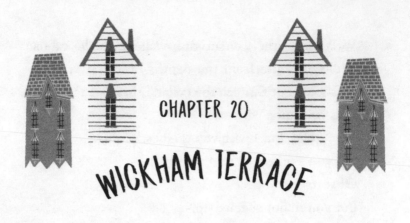

CHAPTER 20

WICKHAM TERRACE

Boy was still unconscious when Violet began to saw through the thick collar. Her progress was slow and he was gradually coming round as she cut.

"Ssh," she whispered when he started to groan. "It's me, Violet. I'm going to free you, but you have to be quiet. There are Watchers downstairs."

Boy slowly opened his eyes and grimaced.

"Shush, Boy," she hushed again. "We need to get out of here fast."

A chair scraped across the floor downstairs and Violet increased her speed until at last the leather snapped. Setting the knife down, she helped Boy up from the floor. He was a little groggy as he wobbled to his feet.

They shuffled to the door and peered round, checking the landing. All was clear.

"Thank you," Violet whispered as she passed the room across the landing.

"What for?" Boy mumbled, confused.

"I wasn't talking to you," she replied as they slipped quietly along the dark landing to the window ledge.

The plastic sheeting billowed in the wind, muffling the rattle of the ladder as they climbed back down. Boy was still a little wobbly and Violet crossed her fingers that he wouldn't fall. When they reached solid ground, she led him round the side of the house and they rested against the wall, catching their breath.

"What happened?" Boy slurred, his eyes still sleepy.

"George Archer caught you. I saw him spray something in your face but there was nothing I could do."

"Oh, I think I remember some—"

"I met a woman," Violet interrupted urgently. "She said she knows which house Dad is in!"

"He's here?" Boy said sitting upright.

Violet nodded and filled him in on all that had happened while he'd been unconscious. Once Boy was up to speed and steadier on his feet, they decided to sneak back across the estate to the house the woman had pointed at.

Taking care to stay low, they ran round the tarmac road

past the pillared entrance until they reached the house. Then, they crawled up the garden, and crouched underneath the windowsill.

"You have a look," Violet said, her voice shaking. "I'll keep an eye out for any Watchers."

"He's your dad, don't you want to…?"

"No, no, just in case he's not there."

"But I thought you said the woman saw him?"

"She didn't *see* him exactly, she just said there was a lot of stuff happening in there," Violet snapped, glaring at Boy. "Please, just do it."

Boy looked at his friend, his face a little red. Then he shrugged and peered up over the rim of the concrete sill.

"I'm not sure I can remember what your dad looks like," he said, bobbing back down to Violet's side. "There's a man in there and he kinda looks like him but he's a bit thinner than I remember. It could be him…"

"What do you mean *could be him*?" Violet said, quickly peering up over the ledge.

This room was different from any she'd seen on the estate so far. The floor was filled with shiny, wheeled, steel tables like the ones used in hospitals. Glass boxes sat on top of the tables. In each box a small red light shone down on a solitary eyeball plant. Another larger table dominated the centre of the room; it looked like an office desk and overflowed with papers that streamed onto the floor. A whiteboard crowded with calculations and red arrows filled the back wall.

A man in a white coat was standing by the board looking a little perplexed.

"Dad!" Violet gasped.

He'd lost weight; his eyes, underlined by half-moon shadows, bulged from slightly sunken cheeks. He looked worn and sad. What had the Archers done to him?

She was about to knock on the window when someone entered from the far corner of the room. It was Edward Archer. She ducked back down quickly.

"Edward is in there with my dad. We have to do something!" she hissed.

"I don't know, Violet," Boy said. "I can't think straight. It must be the stuff George used to knock me out. My head's all cloudy."

"But we have to get him out now," she pleaded.

"Can't we go somewhere? Just for a bit. If I get some rest it'll be easier to think straight and come up with a plan. If we rush in now we'll get caught. There's a room full of Watchers asleep just a few doors down, Violet. We can't be stupid about this."

"I'm not being stupid!" she snapped, a little too loudly.

"Just listen to me," Boy whispered through gritted teeth. "Right now it's too dangerous."

"No!" Violet insisted. "We have to do something *now*! Who knows what's going on in there – what they're doing to him?"

"Violet, please be quiet. Edward's in there, remember."

"You don't *want* me to get my dad. Just 'cause you have no parents, you want me to be an orphan and live in No-Man's-Land just like you!"

"What did you say?" Boy stared at her in disbelief.

Everything stopped, including Violet's beating heart.

She was too angry to speak. Boy stayed under the sill for a minute or two longer then, silently, he crept across the garden onto the tarmac road and out the estate entrance.

Violet didn't look around. She didn't need Boy, saving him had given her confidence. She was fine on her own. Her eyes watered but she wouldn't cry.

Shakily she crawled away from the window round the side of the house and rested her back against the wall. Her dad needed her now.

How was she going to break him out? She got onto her feet and snuck across the back garden. Unlike the other houses she'd seen on the estate this one was almost finished. It had all its windows and doors and the only means of getting in that Violet could see was through a frosted-glass window upstairs that was partially open. She needed a ladder, and she knew exactly where to get one.

She snuck back to the house where Boy had been captive and slipped round to the back garden. The ladder still rested against the wall. Dawn was creeping into the sky and she hoped the Watchers inside were asleep and wouldn't see her skulking about in the half-light.

She was just moving the ladder when someone cleared their throat. She froze. The hair on the back of her neck stood up. Then the foul smell of morning breath infected her nose.

"Well, well, look what I caught," Fists whispered into her ear.

Violet turned quickly, her muscles tensed. Her back was pressed against the rungs of the ladder and Fists' tree-trunk arms rested either side of the rusting metal, blocking her escape.

His fiery red beard dangled in front of her and she pulled it hard. He winced and grabbed his face as she dashed under his arm. She raced down the side of the house and was about to break out onto the tarmac road when he grabbed her top, yanking her back. She squirmed but couldn't loosen his grip.

"Well now, won't I be Mr Edward's favourite," he laughed, shining a torch directly into her eyes.

Blindly she kicked and wriggled but couldn't get free.

"DUCK!" somebody suddenly yelled.

Violet did as she was told, and a large rock whizzed

over her head, landing smack on the bridge of the Watcher's nose. Fists fell to the ground roaring in pain. Violet looked round. Boy stood silhouetted on the road. She was about to say something when he raced forward, grabbed her hand and took off.

As they reached the green, sleepy Watchers were emerging from the house across the way to give chase. Boy and Violet sprinted through the rows of plants, heading for the billboarded exit out of the estate.

Suddenly Violet tumbled – one of the plants had wrapped itself round her leg. She tried to kick it off, when she caught sight of an eyeball glaring out at her from beneath its translucent petals. These plants were eyes too, just like the ones in the houses, except bigger. Her stomach churned.

Boy tried to pull her free, but the plant wouldn't let go; it clung on like a crazed animal. The Watchers were almost upon them when he grabbed the pulsing stem and ripped it as hard as he could. Blood gushed in all directions from the severed vein and Boy sprayed it at the Watchers, slowing their advance. Then he shoved the plant in his pocket.

Suddenly a terrifying shriek cut through the night like a thousand wailing cats. The once-sleeping plants pulled back their petals to reveal masses of bloodshot eyeballs and screamed. The plants flung themselves at Boy and Violet in a frenzy as they hurtled past.

Barely escaping the green intact, the pair dashed by the faded billboard of the happy family. They were out of the estate and on a potholed road, barren fields stretching either side of them.

"Hurry," Boy said, sprinting ahead. "No-Man's-Land is just across the river."

A footbridge appeared in the early morning light. It was elaborate and looked like it might have been there for centuries. Two tall, thin metal spires stood on either side of the river. They were connected by thick wire ropes that stretched across the water, dipping low in the middle. Thousands of thinner wire threads, which must have once supported a wooden plank floor, were broken now and dangled in the water; hardly any of the planks were left. The bridge was just wide enough for one person.

"We can't cross that! There's hardly a floor!" Violet exclaimed, watching the river rushing past below.

"We have no choice. Come on, we don't weigh much," Boy said, clocking the advancing Watchers.

Quickly Boy jumped onto the first plank. It wobbled, but he held tight to the wire ropes and managed to balance himself.

"Come on, hurry!"

Violet looked at the waters speeding below.

"I can't," she said; the words were out before she meant them.

"You have to," Boy replied urgently.

She checked back. The Watchers weren't far behind. She looked at the plank ahead and tried to blot out the image of the water. She bent her legs to jump but nothing happened, her muscles were frozen. She tried again, but still she couldn't move. An image of her parents flashed across her mind. She had to do this for them. She had to save them and that was impossible to do if she was captured too.

She jumped; time slowed. It seemed like an eternity until her feet hit something solid. Time resumed, she wobbled and grabbed the wire rope to steady herself. Boy had already moved on. She followed him across the broken footbridge, her legs on fire.

Suddenly the bridge started to shake as the Watchers began to haul themselves across. A loud crack and a roar broke the morning stillness and she looked around. A Watcher dangled from one of the thick wires as his friends tried to pull him back up.

Boy was already on the other side shouting at her to hurry. She jumped from the last plank and rolled onto the grass bank, finally landing in No-Man's-Land. He pulled her from the ground and raced ahead.

Boy ducked down a lane to their left, it was signed *Wickham Terrace* and flanked either side by rows of dilapidated houses. She recognized the name of the street, but couldn't remember why.

"Check the doors," her friend gasped. "There has to be one open."

Violet tried a few handles, but they were all locked. She could hear the Watchers grunting as they began to catch up. An old shop sign hung out on the street: *Prescription Optical Makers*. She pressed on the door handle and it opened easily.

"In here!" Violet said. The pair hurried inside and gently closed the door behind them. With their backs to the worn wood, they rested for a moment, as outside the Watchers darted past.

"Who goes there?" a man suddenly shouted from the shadows.

"W-we don't mean any harm," Violet insisted, looking at Boy. "We were being chased and—"

"Where did you get those?" the man croaked. His voice was dusty as if it hadn't been used in a while.

Violet looked at Boy, who shrugged.

"Answer me!" the man snapped.

"Where did I get what?" Violet replied shakily.

"Your glasses, where did you get them?"

"I, erm, I found them," she said.

"Don't lie to me, girl. Where did you get them?"

"I found them, I promise. They were under my mattress," she insisted.

"Give them here," the man ordered, stretching out his hand.

Violet looked at Boy again, and he nodded. She took the frames slowly from her face and held out her shaking hand. The man grabbed the glasses from her grasp.

"How did they get under your mattress?" he growled, stepping out from the shadows. "I think you're telling fibs, little girl. The last time I saw these they were in the hands of my brothers. You're working for the twins, aren't you? Trying to set me up again, are they?"

The man walked to the window and pulled back the dirty lace curtain, checking the street. The early morning light fell across his face. Violet recognized something in his features and his suspicion suddenly made sense.

She looked at Boy, her eyes wide, then addressed the man.

"I think...I think I know who you are," she stammered. "You're, you're...William Archer."

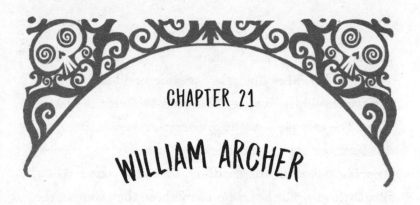

CHAPTER 21

WILLIAM ARCHER

Boy looked at Violet as if she had ten heads. He grabbed her sleeve and gestured towards the door.

"And you are?" the man continued.

"Violet – Violet Brown," she stuttered. "And this is my friend Boy."

William Archer was a tall man though not as tall as George. He was also a wide man though not as wide as Edward and this combination meant he was completely in proportion. He was unkempt, dirty and looked like he'd spent a thousand years in his clothes. His hair was long and streaked with tones of grey. His beard was long too and he wore both beard and hair wrapped like a scarf round his neck.

His face was kind but his eyes were unsettling; it was almost impossible not to stare at them. One was dark, almost black, while the other was a cold blue like an icy winter's morning. Violet's dad had told her that some people were born with different-coloured eyes, but William was the first one she'd met.

A cluttered table stood by the front window and William cleared it before gesturing for them both to sit down. Violet sat on one side and Boy on the other.

A net curtain hanging in the window was stiff with dirt and a murky brown light trickled through it across the beaten wooden table. Rusted springs, a cracked magnifying glass and lots of small parcels wrapped in browned newspaper were piled up under the chipped, white painted window sill. Dust from years of stillness danced in the light as William moved books from a seat to make space.

"Excuse the mess." He coughed. "I haven't had guests in a while."

"It's fine," Violet replied in her polite voice. "It's just like my room."

William smiled uncomfortably, maybe he wasn't used to the company of children – or any company at all.

"Have you lived here long?" Violet asked, breaking the awkward silence.

Boy stared at his friend and frantically gestured towards the door.

"It's okay, Boy. He's not like his brothers."

"And how do you know I'm not like my brothers?" William asked a hint of a smile in his voice.

"Because I saw your message under my desk at school and because I met your mam. She said you were a good son."

"She did?" William asked, his eyes glassing over. "How is Iris, is she well?"

"I think so. I only met her for a minute though."

"I've been here so long," William whispered almost to himself. "I'm not sure I remember what she looks like any more."

"Everyone remembers what their mam looks like, no matter how long they've been away," Violet replied without thinking. "She's your mam, isn't she?"

She glanced across at Boy then down at her hands. Maybe not everyone remembered their mam.

"You're a wise one for someone your age!" William Archer laughed.

The gentle sound filled the faded shop and Violet knew immediately, though she'd kind of known it already, that she liked William Archer. Boy seemed to know it too and he began to relax.

"So," William said, running his fingers over the frames in his hands, "how did you *really* find my glasses?"

"Oh!" Violet exclaimed, suddenly jumping up. "I'm not wearing any glasses. But I can see! I'm not blind."

William laughed again, a big, full laugh that almost shook the shop. It was infectious and suddenly Boy and Violet found themselves laughing too.

"So you're from Perfect." He smiled, regaining a little control.

"No I'm not," Violet snapped. "I've lived there for a bit, but I'm not *from* there."

"She is from there," Boy teased. "I'm not though, I'm from here."

Violet shot Boy a dirty look.

"You might not come from there originally, but you've lived there. You must have, why else would you be blind?" William continued.

"But I'm not blind now," Violet said. "That's what I'm trying to say."

"I know that, Violet, and I'll let you in on a secret – you never were blind. They just made you believe you were."

"The Watchers?" Violet asked.

"No. My brothers. The Watchers work for them, haven't you two figured that out yet?"

Violet looked at Boy and smiled.

"We kind of have," Boy said, "but we just weren't sure. Everybody loves the Archers in Perfect."

"I know," William sighed. "My brothers made everyone in Perfect blind and now they're all too blind to see how blind they are. It really is a conundrum."

"But why would they make people blind?"

"It's a long story, Violet," William said, "and you still haven't told me how you came across my glasses?"

"I didn't know they were yours. I just found them in my bed." She looked sheepishly at Boy.

"Well, how did they get there?" William asked, his voice still disbelieving.

"I put them there," Boy said.

"Ah," William smiled. "I thought it might have something to do with you. All the children in No-Man's-Land have nifty fingers."

"I didn't steal them," Boy replied angrily. "I just had them."

Violet stared down at her hands afraid she'd gotten Boy in trouble.

"You still haven't answered my question," William Archer said, staring at Boy.

"I swear I didn't steal them. I've just always had them, since I was born. In the orphanage they joked that I was born wearing them, then one of the nurses told me that the glasses were hidden in my blankets the day I arrived."

"Oh," William replied.

His brow furrowed and he fell into a deep silence. Boy and Violet glanced across the table, afraid to break the quiet.

"And the nurses, did they say anything else?" William suddenly asked.

"No. Nothing."

Boy was silent now too. His head dropped forward and his hand slipped down off the table. He began to fumble with something in his pocket.

"There is one thing," he mumbled. "This was left with them. I think it's from my mother or something..."

He pulled out a piece of paper from his pocket and unfolded it. Catching the look of surprise on Violet's face he blushed a rosy red as he passed the note to William.

The once-white paper was now grey and worn, like it was long since ripped from a notebook. Violet watched Boy as William Archer read. Then the older man carefully folded it and without a word, handed the note back to her friend.

"Can I have a read?" she asked. She was afraid he might not want her to, their fight in the estate still fresh in her mind.

Slowly Boy passed it over and Violet opened the note. She imagined Boy's mother scribbling the mysterious message. It read:

So you will never be invisible.

Something about it was oddly familiar. She stared at

the note for a moment then gently folded the precious paper and handed it back to her friend.

"It's beautiful, Boy."

He smiled, looked at it once more then carefully put it back in his pocket.

"Does it mean anything to you, Mr Archer?" Violet asked.

"Erm…no, no, Violet, it doesn't," William said, rising from the table. "Now I'm being a terrible host. Would you like some tea? I could do with a cup after all this excitement."

"Yes please!" Violet smiled. "Do you have any of the tea from Perfect? I went off it for a bit but I'd love a cup right now!"

"No, Violet, there's only normal tea here, I'm afraid."

William Archer left them at his table and walked back into the shadows of the room.

Violet's taste buds slumped. She'd been dying for a cup of Perfect tea; she hadn't had any in ages. Her mouth watered and she was lost in a world of longing when Boy interrupted.

"Where do you think he's gone?" he whispered.

"The kitchen, I suppose." Violet shrugged.

"Violet, after everything that's happened you're still a little stupid. Do you really trust him? He's an *Archer*. I think we should get out of here."

"No, Boy, he's a good man, I can tell. Just give him a chance. Anyway, if he was evil why would he own a pair of glasses that could make the people in Perfect see reality again? Surely if he was like his brothers he wouldn't do that – and what about the most obvious thing?" Violet whispered, leaning further across the table, "He lives here, in No-Man's-Land. Who'd choose that?"

"Oh, thanks," Boy huffed.

"Well, you didn't really choose it, your mother did and she must have had her reasons. I think she was a good person."

"What do you mean?"

"Well, I mean your mam must have known what was going on in Perfect. If I had a kid I wouldn't like it to grow up there. I'd choose No-Man's-Land too, but only if I knew what was happening in Perfect; most people are blind to it. And I think she left you the glasses because she wanted you to know what was happening too so you could do something about it. If she couldn't maybe she hoped her son could?"

"I never really thought about it. Anyway who even knows if it was my mam? It could have been anyone. Like I said, I have no parents, but you have some imagination, Violet. All that from one little note."

They both fell into an awkward silence.

"I'm sorry about what I said earlier," Violet whispered

as she fiddled with a rusted spring that was lying on the table. "I mean about you being an orphan."

"It's okay." Boy half smiled. "They wouldn't take you into the orphanage anyway," he teased, just as William Archer walked back into the room. He was carrying a tray laden with a teapot, chipped mugs and a handle-less jug of milk. Staring at the mugs, Violet slipped into memories of the tea in Perfect and all the delicious cups she'd missed the last few days. Her taste buds were watering when suddenly it hit her.

"THE TEA!" she shouted, jumping up and almost knocking the tray from William's hands. "It has to be the tea!"

"Yes, calm down, Violet," Boy smirked. "It is *only* a cup of tea!"

"No, Boy, you don't understand – it's the reason I can see again without glasses; I haven't had any tea in ages. I never drank tea before I got to Perfect. Then the first night we arrived the Archers were there and they had tea ready. They told us everyone drinks it in Perfect and when I tried it I knew why. It tasted like anything I wanted it to – an ice-cream sundae, fizzy cola bottles, apple drops, anything. I had two cups that night, so did mam and dad, and the next day we were all blind. I never thought... I mean everybody drinks it! Even in school we have tea breaks all the time. It was only after I met Iris the other day – she said something to me in her house about not drinking it so I didn't have any that night at home and I haven't had any since. Now I can see again. It can't be by accident."

"My brothers must have gotten better." William sighed setting down the tray. "In my time they were using drops. They prescribed them to everyone for all sorts of eye ailments, it didn't matter what. They even poured them in people's drinks when they weren't looking. It was a messy business. The drops – and now I imagine the tea – distort the retina at the back of the eye rendering a person almost blind, therefore in need of glasses. The glasses my brothers give you, when you come to them looking for help, counteract this distortion but that's not all they do. They're called BR glasses and they're very clever, they make you see whatever my brothers want you to see and anything they don't becomes invisible. They also have an earpiece that filters out any sounds that they don't want you to hear. Genius really!"

"What's BR stand for?" Boy asked.

"Oh, excuse me," William said, "it's the scientist in me. BR stands for *bended reality*. That's what the glasses do; they're programmed so that the wearer's reality is controlled by my brothers and they only experience the things my brothers want them to. Of course the hearing only works when a person is wearing their glasses – I presume that's still the case? It's a flaw Ed and George could never get around!"

"Yes." Violet nodded. "Whenever my glasses fell off I could hear Boy – I kinda thought I was going mad! We think that's why there's a curfew in Perfect, so the people don't hear the No-Man's-Landers at night."

"So nobody in Perfect can see or hear me, or any of us in No-Man's-Land," Boy added, now red-faced with anger, "because the Archers don't want them to?"

"Precisely," William said. "Now you're getting it!"

"Why didn't you stop them?" Violet asked.

"Well, at first I tried and I had some support," William began. "You see, in the beginning it took a while for people to change, the drops weren't efficient enough and so those who weren't changing noticed what was going on and tried to do something about it. Soon though, most people succumbed to the effects; the town appeared perfect to them and they stopped listening. Then the Watchers came on board. Edward hired them straight out of prison. They were paid to keep the remaining rebels in check. Later, my brothers decided they didn't want people who disagreed with their ideas of perfection living in Perfect at all! They walled in part of the town, now called No-Man's-Land, and threw all of us in here. They got the Watchers to make certain we stayed put by whatever means necessary," he finished angrily.

A silence filled the shop as William Archer gathered his emotions. The strain of the memories was written on his face.

"I didn't give up," he continued at last. "I set up my workshop so I could start work on my own glasses, ones that would show the people of Perfect the reality they were living in," he said, picking up the wooden frames from the table.

"You said the last time you saw those glasses your brothers had them?" Boy asked.

William looked at the box in his hands. "Yes." He nodded. "I believed that my mother and Macula had gone under the effects of Perfect – they hadn't turned up in No-Man's-Land, you see – so I snuck into town with the glasses; I was hoping that if they could just put them on they'd know I hadn't left, that I hadn't gone away. But I never reached them. One of the Watchers caught me and brought me to Edward and George who took the glasses. I was beaten alive that day."

An awkwardness settled over them and Violet rattled her brains for something to say to ease the tension of William's memories.

"Who's Macula?" she asked.

"Just someone I knew once." William moved his hands in front of his face to shield his tears and Violet wished she hadn't tried to change the subject. Quickly he wiped his cheeks, and began to pour the tea.

"But how did *I* get the glasses?" Boy asked quietly.

William and Violet looked at him and the group fell into silence.

"I think I know!" Violet said, sitting forward, her imagination on overtime. "I bet your mam worked for the Archers and she probably eavesdropped and knew what was happening. Then maybe she found the glasses in the shop and tried them on. Maybe she was scared and she loved you so much that she saved you and put the glasses in your blanket so one day you could save her too – when you were older, of course; a baby wouldn't be able to save anyone!"

Boy looked uncertainly at William.

"It's plausible. They did have different ladies cleaning the shop over the years, Boy. It is highly possible someone found out about their plot." William nodded, handing him a cup.

"I'm okay for tea, thanks," Boy said.

"It's safe." William smiled. "I'm not like them. I'll never be like them."

His tone was firm and Boy accepted the cup. Violet looked over at her friend then took the first sip.

CHAPTER 22

THE REIMAGINATOR

"I think I have an idea," Violet said, placing down her cup.

"Oh no! Not another one," Boy teased. "Your last idea ended with the Watchers trying to kill us in the Ghost Estate!"

"Ha ha, very funny, Boy!" She turned to William, who was now lost in thought. "If it's the tea that's making everyone blind then we need to get rid of it! If the people in Perfect stop drinking the tea then they'll be able to see again. Don't you think so, Mr Archer? ...Mr Archer?"

"Oh yes, sorry, Violet, what were you saying?"

"The tea...if we get rid of the tea then everyone will be able to see again."

"I'm not sure it's so simple, Violet. The glasses my

brothers invented don't just alter the wearer's perception of the world around them; they're much cleverer than that." William cleared his throat. "Have you ever noticed how the people of Perfect are very open to suggestion? Tell them the sky is falling and they'll believe you! That's because the glasses also suck out their imaginations. During the day tiny metal pads on the earpiece attract the imagination like a magnet, and store it. At least that's how they worked in my day. At night the Watchers sneak into people's homes, put the glasses into a special machine called the Hollower, and pull out the stored imagination. Then the Watchers bring it back to my brothers' shop for safekeeping."

"That's what we saw in the Archers' storeroom Violet. All those jars of colour – they must have been imaginations," Boy said, getting excited.

"But why?" Violet asked William, ignoring Boy's enthusiasm.

"Oh, it's simple really. People are much easier to control when they have no imagination. They don't ask questions and they believe anything you tell them. The simple fact is, a human isn't much at all when they lack imagination."

"Why do they store the imaginations then? Why not just destroy them?" Boy asked, a little confused.

"Fortunately you can't destroy the imagination, Boy!"

William smiled. "You can steal it and keep it hidden but once it's freed and given a helping hand, it will always find its rightful owner."

"But what about me? Why didn't the glasses work on me?" Violet asked. "Why do I still have my imagination?"

"Well I'm not sure, Violet," William said thoughtfully. "It happens sometimes – my brothers just can't control some people no matter how much they try."

Violet was silent for a few minutes before she spoke again. "Mam gave me yellow pills, they made me think strange for a while, not like myself. They said I had IDDCS, Irritable, Dysfunctional, Disobedient Child Syndrome."

William laughed, almost choking on his tea. "IDDCS? Well, that's original. They do crack me up my brothers sometimes. They're persistent, I'll give them that. I imagine those pills are accelerators used to loosen the imagination, making it easier to steal. If someone wasn't changing fast enough, my brothers would drop them a tablet to speed up the transition. It rarely worked though, if the glasses don't get you, not much else will."

"What happens if the glasses don't work and the pills don't work?" Violet asked nervously.

"Well, then you end up here, in No-Man's-Land. If my brothers can't steal your imagination then they can't control you and that doesn't make for a perfect society.

I imagine given a little more time, Violet, you would have been thrown in here too. Needless to say they'd tell your family some story or other and they'd simply accept it."

"Like Mam did with Dad," Violet said. "The Archers told her he'd gone away on business and she believed them. Dad would never have done that without telling us."

"Exactly, Violet. Your mother has become a *Perfect* citizen so to speak."

"But I still don't understand why it didn't work on me?" she said again.

"Well, I believe some people just have too much."

"Too much what?" Boy asked.

"Too much imagination. They either have vast stores or they can easily regenerate it if some is taken away. I'm not sure which. Most people just have a set amount that can be taken pretty quickly. They may produce tiny residual amounts every year thereafter but it's nothing a quick top up of the Hollower can't handle. The likes of you, Violet, are always producing more, no matter how much is stolen; you'll always be an independent thinker."

"Bet I have more than you, Boy." Violet smiled.

"Yeah, you're a bit of a freak." He laughed.

"My studies have shown it could be genetic," William continued. "You said your father was also taken to No-Man's-Land, Violet – which proves my point."

"No I didn't," Violet replied, her voice breaking. "The Archers have my dad. He's being kept in the Ghost Estate. We're trying to save him."

"Where?" William asked.

"The Ghost Estate," Boy said, pointing in the general direction. "The place across the river over the old footbridge."

"I know where it is," William continued, "I just wasn't sure I'd heard you right."

"It's haunted," Violet piped up.

"Oh, that nonsense." William laughed. "I don't know who started those rumours but I've heard them. I expect it saves the Watchers patrolling the riverbank too often. No one's going to escape from No-Man's-Land into a haunted estate. I knew the developer of that place, Mr Lashes. He was found dead out there – years ago, before Perfect. Nobody ever discovered what happened to him. The builders abandoned the job saying it was haunted and that building next to an ancient graveyard brought bad luck. It was a tragic affair." He shook his head as he remembered. "I don't believe in that rubbish. Anyway, isn't that place deserted?"

"No," Boy said. "It's full of Watchers."

"What are Watchers doing out there?" William asked, confused. "Are you sure they're not just guarding the riverbank so we don't escape?"

"I'm sure. It's full of them," Boy told him. "We were just there looking for Violet's dad."

"What is he doing there?" William asked Violet.

"I don't really know." She shrugged. "But I think it has something to do with his experiments. The Archers asked Dad to work for them after he won an award from *Eye Spy* magazine."

"He sounds like a clever man." William smiled.

"He is," Violet said proudly. "The Archers said they needed him to research why people were going blind and fix it."

"We know now that was a lie!" Boy snorted.

"When we arrived in Perfect," Violet continued, "Dad started to act strange, but not in a *Perfect* way, like Mam. He was distracted and tired and hardly ever home. He seemed to work all the time. Then one day he just disappeared. The Archers told Mam he'd gone to an opticians' conference but I didn't believe them. That's why myself and Boy broke into the Archers' Emporium and…"

"Aha." William smiled shaking his head. "Let me guess, you found the tunnel? I never thought of that, my brothers are clever. They could go in and out of that estate and nobody would ever know."

"How do you know about the tunnel?" Boy asked.

"Mam used to own the Archers' Emporium. She sold

all kinds of local crafts from there, but it always embarrassed my brothers, they never thought it was a real business. When the twins got older she gave it to them to set up their optician's. The tunnel comes out in the old graveyard. Perfect's a medieval town; people reckon there are lots of tunnels like this one underneath the place, but I never could find another. Anyway, what are they doing with your dad out there?"

"Growing eyes," Violet said.

"Growing *what*?" William coughed, spitting out some of his tea.

"Eyes," Boy replied, "they're growing eyes, just like this one."

Boy pulled the half-dead plant from his pocket, dropping it in front of William. The thing wriggled and squirmed for a moment, then a clump of congealed blood oozed out onto the table from its severed vein. The eye looked slowly from Violet to William finally resting on Boy before it shuddered and died. William's face lost all colour as he picked up a pencil and prodded the specimen.

"I can't believe…" He stopped mid-sentence and rose quickly to peer out the window. "You two, in the back now!" he commanded. "Down that way there's a door. Go through it and wait until I come and get you."

He was suddenly stiff and stern.

"What is it? What's wrong?" Violet asked.

"The Watchers, they're searching the street, probably looking for you two. I'll try to get rid of them."

Violet and Boy did as they were told and slipped into the shadows. The place was dark and they had to put their arms out in front of them so as not to bump into anything. Boy hit the door first and grunted.

"Not a sound!" William growled across the room.

Searching in the darkness, Violet found the handle and turned it as quietly as she could. The pair slipped through the door closing it gently behind them.

They were standing in an extremely messy office.

A single dirt-caked bulb clung to a wire in the middle of the ceiling casting a faint yellow glow around the space. A table by the far wall overflowed with piles of notebooks and loose papers; a few sheets had fallen onto an old swivel chair below. The floor was covered in coloured markers and pens that crunched under their feet. Violet tiptoed round the mess and had just picked a notebook from the pile when Boy beckoned her over.

"Come here," he said. "Listen."

He had his ear to the door. She crept over carefully and took a spot next to him.

"They ran past about half an hour ago," a voice barked.

"Well, as I said I haven't seen them. I've been shut up in my office all night and am about to go to bed."

"Working on your experiments, I suppose." One of the Watchers laughed.

"I gave that up years ago, boys, you know that. Happy to toe the line these days."

"That's what you say all right. So you don't mind if we come in for a look then?"

Violet's eyes widened. Quickly the pair scurried around the room looking for somewhere to hide.

In her haste, Violet tripped over a lump in the carpet. She bent down to inspect the threadbare rug. It was raised up as if something was underneath it. She pulled it back to reveal a trapdoor. A worn metal ring inset in the old wood was raised up slightly. She lifted it and pulled hard, her face turning red with the effort.

"Boy, quickly," she gasped.

Within seconds he was at her side and had yanked open the secret door. A rusted iron ladder reached up from the darkness below. Violet quickly descended. Boy followed, pushing down the metal ring and pulling the carpet back on top of the trapdoor before closing it silently above him. They held their breath as footsteps entered the room above.

"Do you think they heard us?" Violet whispered.

Boy shook his head.

Something brushed Violet's ear and she jumped almost losing her grip on the ladder. A piece of cord swung silently beside her. She reached for it in the darkness and pulled.

There was a faint click, a small sizzle and suddenly the room lit up. They were perched halfway up a ladder in the middle of a deep cellar.

The walls of the cellar were stone and thick beams of dark brown wood intersected them, as if they were holding the room together. Thinner wooden beams striped the ceiling and uneven stone slabs covered the ground. It was cold and Violet's breath formed foggy clouds in front of her.

They climbed down to the floor.

Hundreds of sheets of paper plastered the walls, covered in drawings of glasses with arrows running from one picture to another as if piecing together a puzzle. Hand-scribbled notes patterned the drawings. It was clear William Archer had been experimenting with different ways to make his own glasses. All the notes were dated and were at least ten years old.

There were also lots of theories on the imagination worked out across the yellowing pages. One drawing titled the ReImaginator stood out. It showed a strange contraption made up mainly of what looked like lots of bagpipes sticking out of the side of a central glass cabinet.

"Violet," Boy whispered.

Engrossed in the strange diagram, she ignored her friend.

"Violet," he said, this time a little louder.

Again she ignored him, busy with her reading.

"Violet, you have to see this!"

"What, Boy?" she snapped, turning around.

Violet gasped. Boy was standing in front of a worn wooden workbench. On top of the bench rested the actual ReImaginator. It seemed almost exactly the same as the drawing.

It was about Boy's height and looked like a strange musical instrument. Eight gold pipes of various lengths rose up from the back of the machine like a church organ. Each pipe was connected to a separate brown leather bag at the bottom. The bags hung off the machine like giant lungs, four either side of a gold-framed glass cabinet that was the centrepiece of the ReImaginator. It was empty now but the drawing showed it filled with coloured gas.

"What is it?" Boy whispered.

"The ReImaginator," Violet slowly replied.

"The what?"

"It gives people back their imaginations," Violet said.

There was a sudden shuffling noise above. Boy dived for the cord and with a sharp click the room plunged back into darkness.

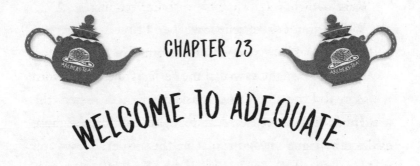

CHAPTER 23

WELCOME TO ADEQUATE

"I see you found my den." William Archer's silhouette peered down from the trapdoor above.

"Yes," Violet replied, relieved it was William and not the Watchers. "Your drawings, they're amazing!"

"Oh, that was all a long time ago," William said, brushing off the compliment. "Now come on, you better get out of here. It took a lot of persuading to get rid of those Watchers and I'm sure they'll be back."

"How did you get rid of them?" Violet asked as she climbed back into the room above.

"I told them I knew nothing. I haven't put a foot out of line in a long, long time so nowadays the Watchers believe me." William smiled half-heartedly. "Several years ago that would never have happened."

"Why not?"

"Well, I didn't exactly lie low when I first came here as you can see from my experiments. But I've been a good boy since. You might even call me *Perfect*," he joked.

"Why did you stop?" Violet asked.

"There was no reason left to fight." William sighed, closing the trapdoor and replacing the carpet. "Now you two better go. I don't want to get into trouble again after all these years."

"But please," Violet said, "you could help. We saw the ReImaginator. We could fix Perfect."

"Violet," Boy warned.

"Please," Violet said again, "please, Mr Archer, we could do it. Now that we know about the tea and we have your invention and all your research, I know we could save Perfect. We could save my family."

"Violet, let's go," Boy said, pulling her away.

"Please, Mr Archer?"

"Enough, Violet!" William snapped. "Perfect is fine as it is. I gave all that up long ago and I'm happier for it. I am sorry about your father but I'm afraid I can't help. You will have to suffer the same fate as the rest of us and get used to No-Man's-Land. The sooner you do that, the better for you."

"But you *can* help, I know you can. I can see you're not happy."

"Violet, you've gone too far now. You don't know me at all. Please, both of you leave. I've helped you enough."

He herded the pair across his shop and out the door leaving them alone in the road. Violet was devastated. She'd thought William Archer would be nice, she'd thought he would be different.

It was now mid morning and both were extremely tired as they found their way back through the Market Yard and along one of the lanes coming out halfway down Forgotten Road.

The streets were empty so the Watchers weren't hard to spot as they patrolled No-Man's-Land making sure everyone was inside. Boy knew all the hiding places and they avoided getting caught, sometimes by the narrowest of margins. Quickly they scuttled along in silence, stopping outside a large stone building near the end of Forgotten Road.

"We're here," Boy said. "Everyone will be going to bed now so you can stay today, and tonight we'll figure out what to do next."

"Where are we?" Violet asked sleepily, her eyes struggling to stay open.

"My home," Boy smiled. "The orphanage. I'll sneak you in and you can sleep in the playroom. It's better we don't tell anyone yet, just in case the Watchers are looking for you. After a few days, when it's all blown over, I'll tell the nurses. I'm sure they'll give you a bed."

"But I don't want to live here, Boy!" Violet panicked. "I live with my mam and dad. I want to go home!"

"Ssh, Violet, please," Boy soothed, hugging his friend. "We'll figure something out, but for today you'll stay here."

Boy tilted over a small marble birdbath that sat by the front door and pulled out a large rusted key. Quietly he unlocked the door.

Checking the coast was clear, they tiptoed down the enormous marble-tiled hallway and Boy disappeared into a doorway on the left.

"In here," he whispered, his voice echoing in the silence.

The room was sparse and cold – the ceiling seemed to stretch right to the sky. The walls were covered in plain white wallpaper, which was torn away in places revealing years of chipped paint. A rickety bookcase holding a tiny collection of ageing books and a small box of broken and tattered toys rested in one corner, the only decoration in the lonely space. The room was huge and empty and not anything like Violet's home, where she felt safe.

Large wooden shutters rested by the sides of the windows and Boy pulled them shut, blocking out as much daylight as was possible, until only slivers fell across the floor. Then he left to get some blankets.

Seeking out a small space, Violet crouched down and nestled into the far corner of the cavernous room.

Tiny footsteps sounded through the ceiling above as the orphans prepared for bed. Faint echoes of children's voices haunted the space and a shiver danced down her spine.

For comfort she thought of home again, but she was wrong. She wasn't even safe there any more. An image of her perfectly preened mother holding out two yellow pills flashed through her memory. Maybe she wasn't loved either. Tears watered her vision and Boy was a blur as he tiptoed back into the room.

"Violet," he whispered.

"Over here, Boy."

"What are you doing?" he laughed, finding her curled up in the corner.

"I don't know," she half smiled. "It felt safer."

"Don't worry, you are safe. They don't let us play in here much, so you won't be disturbed. I'll come down before night to wake you. Here, take these."

He handed her a worn blanket and pillow and left a cup of hot water and an apple on the floor beside her.

"Is this yours?" she asked, looking at the blanket.

"I'll be fine," he replied, "I never get cold anyway."

"No, I can't," Violet insisted, handing it back.

"I'm a boy," he laughed, running over to the door, "we can take the cold."

"Boy," she called, just as he was about to slip out.

He turned and looked at her.

"Do you think we'll save my dad? The Archers know we've been in the estate now. What if they do something to him?"

"He'll be fine, Violet," Boy whispered. "The Archers need your dad and they won't see us as a threat anyway, we're only kids! Don't worry, we'll figure something out, we'll save him."

Violet smiled as her friend snuck quietly from the room. Even though she pretended she didn't, she needed him sometimes.

Spreading the blanket out on the floor she lay on top, grabbed the corner and rolled, wrapping it tight around her narrow figure to make sure there were no air holes. It felt weird now not having to take off her glasses at bedtime.

Then she pulled the pillow in under her head and fell asleep, exhausted.

❋   ❋   ❋

A rising cold took Violet from her sleep, as the dim evening light filtered through the cracks in the shutters. There wasn't a sound in the huge house; everyone must still be in bed. She lay awake, her mind whirring with worries, as her breath formed circles in the space above her head.

Unable to fall back asleep, she sat up and scanned the room, spotting the small bookshelf in the corner. On the count of three she raced across the freezing tiles and surveyed the shelf. Most of the books were for young kids and she had just picked one up when she noticed another tucked in behind it.

This book was worn and tattered. It was called *A History of Adequate* and a picture of what looked like Edward Street in Perfect rested proudly on the cover. She cradled it and raced back into the warmth of her blanket. Biting the apple Boy had left her, Violet opened the book.

Welcome to Adequate, our perfect little town.

She flicked through the pages. Adequate was definitely Perfect. Violet recognized the streets, the shops, even some of the faces. Just one thing was different. Nothing was perfect in Adequate. The town wasn't glossy, it was nice, lovely even, but it was normal. The people looked normal too, good normal, not shiny at all.

She turned the page and her breath caught. There was a picture of a wedding scene. A beautiful young couple stood at the centre with their families either side; behind them was the Town Hall in Perfect. The caption read: "Macula Lashes and William Archer, son of Iris and the late Arnold Archer, residents of Adequate, surrounded by family on their wedding day."

"Boo!"

Violet leaped from her bed, dropping the book.

"Got you!" Boy laughed.

"Boy!" Violet snapped, catching her breath. "What if I'd screamed or something?"

"Sorry." Boy looked a little ashamed. "But your face was hilarious!"

Violet forced a smile, sat down on the blanket and picked up the book.

"I didn't know you could read," Boy teased.

"Stop messing about, Boy," Violet said, "you have to see this. I think I know how we'll get William to help us."

"No, Violet," Boy replied, suddenly serious. "He doesn't want to help us, I could see that yesterday. You can't force him. We'll find another way."

"But I'm telling you, he'll want to," Violet said, pushing the book under his nose. "Look."

"Is that William?" Boy said, running his finger over the picture. "On his wedding day? That's hilarious, look at the faces on George and Edward, they don't seem too happy."

"Oh yeah, I didn't see them. They look like they'd prefer to be anywhere else!" Violet smiled. "But what about *her*," she said, pointing to William's bride.

"What about her?"

"She's the woman I met."

"Which woman? When did you meet her?"

"When you were in that house in the Ghost Estate, the one I rescued you from…"

"I rescued you too you know!"

"It's not a competition, Boy," Violet mocked. "Anyway, she was the woman in the room across the hall. The one I told you about. She's a bit older now, but it's definitely her!"

"Really? You're sure? What would she be doing there if she's William's wife?"

"Well how do I know? Maybe the Archers kidnapped her, but she wasn't locked in. She didn't want to leave the room; she said that there was nothing to leave for. William said the same in his house, remember? He said they took everything from him and that's why he won't fight. Maybe she's the *everything* they took?"

"That still doesn't mean he'll help us."

"But when he finds out where she is, he'll want to rescue her," Violet said. "Then maybe he'll help us rescue Dad too. I think he just needs a little push to get brave again."

"Get brave again! That's a good way of putting it. What happened to the scared Violet? I think she's turned into a monster!" Boy joked.

She elbowed Boy in the ribs and smiled, climbing up from the floor.

"Come on. Let's get William brave again!"

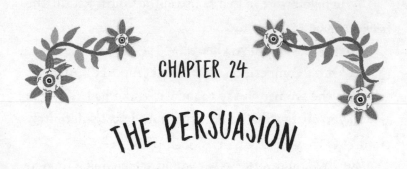

CHAPTER 24

THE PERSUASION

"Not you two again." William Archer sighed, as he opened his door a crack, spilling light onto the dark street.

"Please, Mr Archer, can we come in?" Violet asked. "I have something I need to tell you."

"Violet, I told you this morning I'm not interested in helping you. Now please leave me a—"

"It's about Macula."

William's face changed. He glanced down the street in both directions and quickly ushered them inside. Closing the door, he paused against the wood then turned to face them.

"What do you know about Macula?" he asked, his tone firm. "This better be good, children, because you have worn my patience thin."

Violet looked at Boy then pulled the book from under her jumper.

"I found this," she said, handing it over. "I've marked the page."

William took it from her hands, walked to the table and sat down. His body slackened as he looked at the picture. Unconsciously, he thumbed the paper.

"You looked beautiful that day," he whispered.

Violet walked over to the table and sat down too. Boy followed her lead.

"I found it in the orphanage," she said. "Was Perfect once called Adequate?"

William nodded.

"When did it change?" Boy asked.

"It'd been happening for a while but the big change was when my brothers created No-Man's-Land about twelve years ago." William sighed, lifting his head from the page for the first time. "You see, Adequate was a lovely town. It had its good and bad points but on the whole it was a happy place. Balanced."

"So what happened to it?" Violet asked.

"My brothers of course," William replied, his fist clenched over the opened page. "They were always too big for their boots. They were perfect in school and perfect at home but they didn't get the praise they thought they deserved from their peers and teachers, or from our mother. On the other hand, I wasn't perfect, I was a bit of a joker. I had loads of friends and I was our mother's pet. It wasn't that she didn't love the twins, she did, but for some reason she protected me fiercely. Maybe she was protecting me from them, I never really asked her. Either way it sparked a vicious jealousy in my brothers."

"Because you were her favourite?" Violet asked.

William nodded. "I wasn't perfect but I was popular. That killed the twins. They couldn't understand how I could constantly fail in school, break all the rules and still be popular. They got straight A's, never acted up and were the picture of perfection, yet people didn't really like them and no matter how hard they tried they couldn't turn Mam against me. It ate away at them. This was all bubbling under the surface and then one day Macula arrived in our town."

"She's beautiful," Violet said, looking at the picture.

"She turned up like an exotic bird. Her dad was building the estate, your Ghost Estate." He nodded at Boy. "She wasn't meant to stay long but he died tragically as I told you and she'd nowhere to go. Mam took her in and we fell for her immediately. All of us did. In fact, every young man in Adequate was in love with Macula Lashes. My brothers tried everything possible to win her heart. George sent her flowers, Edward wrote her poems, but nothing worked. I did nothing. I was too shy and never thought she'd like me. The strange thing was doing nothing seemed to work. That's women for you." William smiled at Boy, who blushed.

"We fell in love and, added to everything else, it broke my brothers, at least that's how it seemed at the time," he continued. "From that moment on they plotted to get rid of me and anything else that didn't fit with their vision of a perfect world."

"So they developed the tea!" Violet said.

"Well it was the drops in my time, *before* the tea."

"So they made people go blind and because they were blind they went to the Archers, who fitted them with glasses and stole their imaginations in order to control them. Just because they wanted things their way, wanted things perfect, they made everyone suffer? That's psycho!" Boy spat angrily.

"I couldn't have put it better myself." William sighed. "That's how Adequate came to be Perfect. Little by little, they changed our town. My brothers got what they wanted. They became powerful in Perfect, popular even, and those who didn't conform were imprisoned in No-Man's-Land under the threat of the Watchers. We're only a stone's throw from family and friends who go about their lives oblivious to the fact that we even exist. That's the cruellest bit. If they locked us up somewhere else, far away, it might be easier but I think my brothers like it this way. They always had a cruel streak."

"That's awful," Violet whispered. "How could anyone want people to suffer like that?"

William shook his head.

"When I was caught taking the glasses into Perfect, they locked me up alone for a few years. I wasn't allowed outside; even the limited freedoms of No-Man's-Land were denied to me. They took my life away." His voice trembled as he continued, "They let me out once they thought they'd broken me enough to make me toe the line. So that's what I do now. At least when I was locked up I could pretend that I would take some sort of action when I got out. But now, well, I just accept my lot like everyone else in here and I hide myself inside this workshop. It's strange, that life, in whatever form it takes, goes on outside these walls while everyone in No-Man's-Land just exists; I just exist." William stood up and walked over to a cabinet by the wall.

"This is her," he said, pulling a black-and-white portrait picture from the drawer and joining them back at the table.

"She really is beautiful," Violet added.

"Was beautiful," William sighed, his voice barely audible. "She left Perfect. Met another man George told me. They were both killed on honeymoon when their hot-air balloon crashed."

"Oh," Violet laughed.

William looked up from the picture. "Do you think that's funny?" he snapped.

"No, just George's story – I didn't know he had an imagination. I thought he only kept them in jars."

"Violet, are you sure?" Boy hissed across the table. "I really don't know about this!"

"About what?" William said, glaring at Violet.

"Well," Violet continued, "I don't think Macula was in a hot-air balloon or with another man."

"What do you mean?" William said pushing back from the table.

"I met Macula." Violet smiled. "I met her last night in the Ghost Estate."

William looked at Violet, his face turning deathly pale. Slowly he put down the portrait, then without a word he strode into the shadows and through the door to his office.

"I knew we shouldn't have come, Violet," Boy whispered, leaning across the table. "Let's go, please. I don't think he's too happy with us."

She was about to answer when a door banged and William Archer emerged back through the shadows. He stopped short of the table and flung something down onto the wood. A gold ring wobbled and rolled before falling over dead.

"Her wedding ring, taken from her finger after she

died," he snapped. "Now please leave this house. I have lost all but a morsel of my patience."

Violet picked up the delicate gold ring and stared at the inscription inside.

To my love, everything is clear when I'm with you William.

"But..." she said. Her hesitation hung in the air.

Boy got up from his seat and grabbed her hand.

"Come on. We have to go. I'm sorry, Mr Archer. We didn't mean—"

"Her eyes," Violet said suddenly, "her eyes are green. Really green, like grass."

William Archer walked to the door, grabbed the handle and wrenched it open.

"And she wore a locket," Violet stammered, as Boy pulled her through the doorway, "it was gold with green stones. She held it almost all the time I was there."

The door slammed behind them and Violet and Boy were left alone on Wickham Terrace.

"It was her, Boy, I swear it was!" Violet sobbed, as they reached the corner.

Suddenly another bang shook the street. The pair turned to see William Archer standing outside his house, his features hidden by the night.

"Tell me that again, Violet!" he shouted.

She looked at Boy, who pushed her forward towards William.

"Tell him," he whispered.

"Erm…she had green eyes."

"After that."

"Her locket! She wore a gold locket?"

"You'd better come back in," William said, disappearing through his front door.

Violet looked at Boy, who shrugged and together they walked back up the street.

William Archer was sitting in his chair by the window. The pair took their spots at the table and for a while there was silence. William swirled the gold wedding ring round his little finger.

"You said she held the locket all the time you were there?" He looked up at Violet.

"Yes." Violet nodded. "She rubbed it constantly. I noticed because it was beautiful."

William's eyes glassed over and he dropped his head into his hands.

Violet glanced at Boy, who looked as shocked as she felt. She was about to say something, but when her friend shook his head she stopped. After a few moments, William continued.

"I gave it to her. Emeralds for love and hope. We'd been

separated a lot you see and we were arguing a bit. The separations were my fault. I'd been trying to rally support against my brothers and was hardly ever home. It was a crazy crusade, Macula said, and one she disagreed with. None of us really knew what was going on then. We knew people were going blind and I had suspicions my brothers had something to do with it but that was all. Sometimes I think Macula thought I was going mad. In a way she was right, it did consume me. The locket was a peace offering. I gave it to her on our wedding anniversary, New Year's Eve twelve years ago. My brothers captured me early the following year and I never saw Macula again. Our anniversary was the last time we laughed together." William choked back his tears.

"I'm sorry," Boy said. "We shouldn't have come."

"No, Boy. I'm the one who is sorry. It's just I haven't spoken about Macula in a very long time, but I think of her every day. As soon as you mentioned the locket, Violet, I knew you really had met her," William looked up from his shaking hands. "How is she?" he asked.

"She's okay," Violet replied. "She helped me. She saved me from the Watchers. I asked her if she wanted to escape but she said she had nothing left. I think she was scared."

"And she held the locket all the time?"

Violet nodded.

"Maybe she thinks of me too." William smiled shyly. "Did she seem well? Healthy?"

"Yes, she seemed healthy," Violet said, "but I don't think she was happy."

William stood up from the table and paced the room. The sadness left his face. His mouth narrowed and his eyes darted from side to side. He was thinking hard.

"They told me she was dead!" he said angrily, colour rising in his cheeks.

He marched towards the table. His hand held firm in a white-knuckled fist, he slammed it ferociously into the solid wood. Everything jumped including Violet and Boy.

"My brothers!" William snarled. "They have made their last pair of spectacles."

He walked to the cabinet and pulled out a notepad and pencil.

"Now tell me everything you know. I need all the details," he said, rejoining the pair at the table.

Violet smiled at Boy then up at William.

"I told Boy all we had to do was make you brave again."

CHAPTER 25

TIME FOR TACTICS

Violet and Boy told their tale with enthusiasm, starting from the very beginning when Violet arrived in Perfect with her family and had her first cup of tea, to her mam's changes, her dad's disappearance, Boy, the wooden glasses, No-Man's-Land, the Watchers, the Hollower, the tunnel, the Ghost Estate, Macula, the eyes, finding her dad and right up to meeting William and spotting the ReImaginator.

William interrupted with questions. He pushed them to remember every detail and when they'd finished, they were both exhausted.

"I've never had to think this hard about anything." Boy yawned, rubbing his forehead.

"We have to get everything down on paper, Boy. My brothers are formidable opponents and we can't go into battle ill-prepared."

"We're going into battle?" Violet gasped, her eyes huge.

"Yes." William smiled. "We're going to cause mayhem and madness. My brothers won't know what's hit them. I've been feeling sorry for myself for a very long time and you two have made me see sense. I can't sit and wait for somebody else to stand up to those two; I have to make it happen. Waiting is a coward's game. I have to fight for what I want."

"Well *I* want my family back," Violet said, sitting upright.

"As do I, Violet," William replied.

Boy sat silently fidgeting and Violet blushed.

"Boy, imagine," she joked. "Once I get Mam and Dad back you'll be free of me."

Her friend smiled but it didn't feel real.

"My brothers must be using the Ghost Estate as their headquarters," William said, pushing up from the table. "Right from the beginning, I could never find where they based themselves. Perhaps all the stories of hauntings made me overlook the estate. I've only been there once and that was before Macula's father died. Do you two think you could draw an accurate map marking exactly where things are: the eye plants, Macula, the Watchers – everything?"

"And where my dad is," Violet added.

"Of course, Violet," William said, mumbling to himself as he walked back into the shadows of the room.

Violet and Boy were arguing over the number of houses in the estate when William rejoined them at the table. He was laden with bits and bobs of equipment, reams of paper and a jar of gooey water in which the dead eye plant was suspended.

"Eeeeugh!" Violet said, as the jar was placed in front of her. "That thing is disgusting. At least the smaller ones didn't look as bad!"

"Smaller ones?" William asked.

"Yes, they're growing in some of the houses under a red light. The larger ones are outside on the green!"

"Oh, I suspect the small ones are seedlings. I imagine they're put out on the green to flourish, then once they get to a certain size I'm sure they're harvested."

"That's a lot of eyes," Boy said.

"Well there's a lot of people in Perfect, and they each have two eyes!" William smiled grimly. "My brothers have a big plan up their sleeves. I confess I did a little investigation after you left last night. It reminded me of the old days." William smiled as he picked up the limp eyeball. "I think I may have discovered what my brothers are up to with these little beauties."

He handed the plant to Violet and then to Boy, pointing out an incision he'd made in the centre of the eye.

"See this," he said, gently lifting a thin layer of rose-coloured film from the pupil. "It's made from the same material as the lenses Ed and George put in their glasses. It's the advanced technology I told you about – BR or Bended Reality. I remember Edward's main frustration with Perfect was that it *wasn't* perfect, not when everyone in the town wore glasses. With these new eyes that problem is solved. Genius – in a twisted kind of way."

"You mean they're going to take out people's eyes and give them new ones?" Boy said, going pale.

"Exactly, Boy." William smiled. "I don't expect my brothers would explain it that way though. No doubt they'll make a big announcement and tell the town that Violet's father has solved the problem and they can now pinpoint why people have gone blind. They'll probably give some explanation, which of course nobody will question, and then a solution, such as laser surgery to fix the problem. I've heard it's all the rage in the world of optometry these days. I can see their tagline now: *Imagine a life without glasses*. The funny thing is no one would be able to imagine, as they have no imaginations left!" William laughed.

"Then how will they steal people's imaginations without the glasses?" Violet asked.

"Oh, Violet." William smiled. "No matter what I say about my brothers I have to give them one thing. They are extremely clever. I expect people will need a number of check-ups after laser surgery, don't you think? Three or four sessions should be sufficient to steal a whole imagination these days, and then a check-up or should I say a top-up once a year would work nicely for any residue!"

"Oh!" Violet gasped. "We have to stop them! If they swap people's actual eyes there'll be no hope of them ever seeing reality again."

"Exactly," William agreed. "And we have to act quickly."

"What are you planning?" Boy asked.

"I propose a full-on assault: storm the estate, rescue Macula, and Violet's dad of course, and destroy the eyes."

Violet was watching William frantically scribble notes when she noticed Boy signalling from the other side of the table.

"Erm...I'm not sure that's the best idea," Boy said, quietly.

William looked up from his papers.

"And why not?" he asked.

"Well, firstly, how do we get across the river—?"

"A minor detail," William interrupted.

"The Watchers aren't stupid," Boy continued. "I've spent twelve years finding that out. They know we know where Violet's dad is. They also know we know about the eye plants. They won't feel too threatened as we're only kids but they'll still be on high alert for anyone going in or out of the estate. And how do we get in there? The footbridge won't hold enough people for us to be able to attack, and sneaking through the Archers' tunnel again is too dangerous. I really don't think it's a good idea to go there first." He looked at William, then at Violet. "I know you want Macula and Violet wants her dad but the Watchers will be expecting us to go back there. We'll walk straight into their trap."

Silence filled the room as all three sat thinking.

"I kinda agree with Boy," Violet said eventually, shifting in her seat. "I mean I really want to save Dad but Boy's usually right about these things and if we mess this up, Dad will be in more trouble than ever."

William Archer stood up and began pacing the room.

"Boy, I'm impressed," he said. "I was going to run into this like a headless chicken. All thoughts of Macula have clearly clouded my vision and put my own needs ahead of the town. I've been selfish and that could have been a fatal mistake. This can't be about what I want. It has to be about Perfect. Perhaps we need some lateral thinking."

"Maybe if we list the problems first," Boy said, "it will help us to come up with a plan to solve them."

"Careful. You're sounding kind of intelligent," Violet joked.

"I like your approach, very mathematical." William smiled, ruffling Boy's hair. "There may be a scientist in you yet!"

"Well, the most obvious problem," Violet said, "is everyone in Perfect is blind."

"And controlled because they've no imagination," Boy added as William wrote vigorously in his notepad.

"So if we could get them to *see* again and then get the ReImaginator to give them back their imaginations everything would be fixed!" Violet jumped up excitedly.

"That's great, Violet, but can you rewind a little?" William said, looking up from the page. "Why is everyone blind?"

"Because of the tea." She smiled. "If we can stop people drinking it for a while then they'll be able to see reality again, like I did!"

"They'll never stop drinking it." Boy sighed, shaking his head. "They're addicted to the stuff. It's delivered to people's homes, given out in school at break and the most popular place in town is the tea shop."

"They may not have to stop," William said, chewing on his pencil.

"What do you mean?" Violet asked.

"I invented a reversing agent for the eye drops years ago, maybe it'll work on the tea. I'll see if I can find my notes."

"That's brilliant!" Violet said, eagerly. "So if we can get everyone to see again, then your machine can give them back their imaginations?"

"Does the ReImaginator actually work?" Boy asked.

"I'll get it working," William assured.

"But how do we change people? The Watchers are everywhere; we'll never get past them into Perfect!" Violet said, her excitement waning a little.

"Exactly how many Watchers do we think there are?" William asked. "Can we overpower them if we get other people to join us?"

The three spent a few minutes piecing together the number of Watchers they thought existed but they couldn't get a figure they all agreed on.

"Let's just say there's lots," Boy said, trying to put a stop to the argument.

"But who's going to take on the Watchers?" Violet asked. "There's only three of us!"

"The No-Man's-Landers might come out to help us," William half whispered. "But we'd need to win them over; tell them our plan and show them the ReImaginator. I think we could convince them."

"They're already defeated though," Boy said, looking straight at William. "I don't think the No-Man's-Landers have the spirit to fight any more."

"They'll get it back, Boy." William smiled warmly.

"They just need to be reminded it's still there!"

"Do you really think we can do this?" Violet asked.

William stopped writing. "I've been locked up too long now, Violet. It's that or die trying."

They set to work formulating a rough plan for "Project Perfect". Then William beckoned the pair into his office to begin Phase One – give the Perfectionists back their eyesight. Boy and Violet sat down on the ground and watched as he riffled through the reams of paper spread across his desk and floor.

"I had it here somewhere." He frowned, throwing a pile of notes over his shoulder. "I'd been working on reversing the effects of their drops, but abandoned the plan figuring myself mad for even trying. However, I'm not altogether sure this mixture will work on the tea. They didn't have that in my day."

"Maybe they use the same stuff in the tea as they did in the drops. They probably just use more of it," Violet smiled.

"Good point, Violet. Aha, here it is!" William exclaimed, zoning in on a particular page.

William Archer the scientist sprung to life. Keeping his notes aside, he shifted the rest of his papers from the desk onto the floor in front of the door, blocking the entrance.

Once the desk was clear, he folded down the front panel revealing a hidden workspace behind. Glass flasks and thermometers were piled high and he muttered to himself while he reached for them.

It was a long night and the children were exhausted. Boy fell asleep beside Violet and, as she watched William at work, her eyes gradually drooped to a close.

❋   ❋   ❋

The sun was just rising when William gently shook them both from their dreams and handed over a flask of greenish-pink liquid. He was beaming from ear to ear.

"This should reverse the effects of the tea if I've done it right." He smiled, wiping the sweat from his brow. "Now do you remember the plan?"

"Yes?" Boy said, sleepily taking the flask. We'll go to the tea factory…"

"Out on George's Road," William interrupted, his eyes red with tiredness.

"I know, I've been there before," Boy sighed. "We break in…"

"Sneak in, sneak in, Boy," William corrected, his face now a little anxious. "Find the tank with my brothers' blinding concoction. It'll probably be suspended above the factory floor and sprayed down onto the Chameleon plant. I can't imagine any other way to do it on such a large scale. Then pour this in…"

"I know, we've gone through the plan a million times.

Don't worry!" Boy replied taking the flask from William.

"Brilliant," the older man said, his face still a little stressed. "I'll expect you back this evening then. Hopefully at that stage I'll have rounded up some others to join our ranks."

"Great," Violet said, her heart hammering in her chest. "Now all we have to do is sneak out of No-Man's-Land without the Watchers finding us, through Perfect and sneak *into* the tea factory. Sounds easy!"

"Easy when you've grown up in No-Man's-Land." Boy smiled reassuringly.

His confidence was infectious and Violet didn't feel as worried as she gave William a hug and snuck out from the house into the early morning light. Armed with the flask, she clung desperately to the hope that they really could save Perfect and her family.

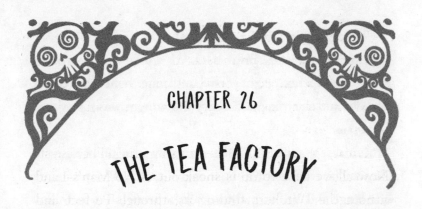

CHAPTER 26

THE TEA FACTORY

"Sometimes I really don't like adults," Violet whispered as they edged along Wickham Terrace, "but other times I love them – their hugs always make me feel safe."

"I've never had a hug before," Boy stated, carefully checking round the corner ahead.

Never had a hug! Violet tried to imagine what that must be like as she followed behind him in sombre silence. They passed through the emptying streets of No-Man's-Land onto Forgotten Road, then turned right towards the arch leading to Rag Lane.

The gatekeeper had already gone and the gate was locked.

"What are we going to do?" Violet asked, a little panicked.

"What I always do." Boy smiled.

Violet followed him back down onto Forgotten Road and turned right. The morning light made her nervous and she imagined every movement was a Watcher on patrol.

Boy disappeared into the doorway of a tall house up ahead. The front door hung loosely across the entrance on one hinge and Violet had to duck underneath it to follow him inside.

"Up here," he whispered.

He was halfway up a rickety flight of stairs. Violet stepped round an old stool blocking the way. A mouse skirted by her foot and she jumped. The stairs were covered in a moth-eaten brown carpet and creaked with every step. When she reached the landing, Boy was nowhere to be seen.

"Up here," he called again.

She looked around. The staircase turned back on itself as it led up to the floor above. Boy stood at a broken railing looking down at her.

Violet continued her climb and stepped onto the next landing. It was decorated in orange wallpaper that was ripped away in parts and covered in graffiti.

"Do people live here?" she asked.

"Sometimes." Boy shrugged. "No one really owns anything in No-Man's-Land, so if somebody needs a place to stay, they come here. We share things; it's different to Perfect."

"Oh." Violet tried to imagine what it would be like to share her house with strangers.

Boy pushed open a brown-painted door off the landing. Violet followed him into the large bathroom behind. Everything from the wall to the toilet and basin was a pale sickly green.

Boy climbed out an open window above the bath onto the roof.

"Come on," he said, "we have to hurry."

Violet pulled herself up to look. The roof slanted away from her and she shuddered.

"Violet, hurry –" by now Boy was perched on the apex of the next roof across – "we have to get over there. The other side of that wall is Perfect."

He pointed to the top of a stone wall just peeking out behind another rooftop a little away.

She felt dizzy.

"Violet!"

"I'm coming," she snapped.

She took a deep breath and climbed out onto the slates. Slowly she edged her way to the bottom of the roof. She didn't dare look down as she jumped across the gap between the houses and scrambled up to the apex of the next roof where Boy was waiting.

She was panting and held onto the edge for her life.

"See, you're fine." He smiled, moving swiftly on across the remaining rooftops.

She followed unsteadily until, finally, they reached their destination.

Boy picked up a rope, tied at one end to a chimney stack of one of the houses, and threw it over the wall into Perfect.

"Watch me," he said, disappearing.

They were up so high Violet wobbled as she looked over the edge to watch Boy descend. He held tight to the rope and leaned out over the street below planting his feet firmly against the wall. Slowly he inched his way to the ground.

"Your turn," he mouthed up on reaching the bottom.

Violet took the rope. She was shaking.

"Don't look down, face in towards the wall," Boy whispered, his voice barely audible.

She listened to his directions and began to descend. She wasn't nervous now, her mind focused on survival.

"Well done." He smiled as she found solid ground. "That was brilliant for a first time."

Violet steadied herself against the wall, as Boy threw the rope back up over the top.

"Where are we?" she whispered.

"In Perfect!"

"I know that, but where exactly? I've never been in this part before."

"We're at the bottom of Archers' Avenue; it's a blind spot in the wall. I've tried every section and this is the only place the Watchers can't see from the tower. It's how I sneak in and out."

"I think I prefer the gate."

"Don't be such a girl." Boy laughed.

Violet elbowed him in the ribs.

"Hey! What's that for?"

"A present from all the girls." She smiled, moving off the wall.

The pair reached Edward Street and stopped to check the coast was clear. With no one about they headed onto George's Road where a big pointed-finger sign read: "Archers' Tea Factory".

Elegant three-storey buildings lined one side of the street and Violet was aware of curtains moving in the windows as people began to wake.

"Morning, young Brown," a voice called.

Violet looked over at a man in a checked dressing gown and slippers, who was picking up his freshly delivered tea box from the doorstep.

"Morning," she said, trembling.

"Act normal," Boy whispered. "Remember they *can* see you."

"I'm trying," Violet said through gritted teeth. "It's easy for you to say, you're invisible!"

Violet kept in the morning shadows as they walked along George's Road. When they finally reached a high grey stone wall on their left, Boy smiled.

"We're here."

There was an entrance ahead marked with black iron gates. A trickle of people walked in under an arched sign spanning above the entrance which read: "Archers' Tea Factory".

Violet and Boy stopped outside, looking in.

"Are you okay, Violet?" a voice asked.

Violet turned around, her heart pounding. A woman wearing a navy cap and coverall that both sported the gold Archers' Tea logo, stood looking at her.

"Yes, I'm fine," Violet said politely, trying to think on her feet, "I'm just waiting for my class; we're going on a school tour to the factory."

"Oh wonderful," the woman smiled, "you'll love it. Maybe someday when you grow up you'll work here too and be the pride of Perfect! By the way you're not wearing your glasses, dear!"

"Oh, erm…" Violet tried not to panic. She'd forgotten to bring her glasses. "They're broken. Mam is getting them fixed today."

"That's nice, dear," the woman said patting Violet on

the head before continuing through the gates to work.

"We're lucky they don't question things in Perfect." Boy laughed.

"That was close." Violet sighed, looking around. "We need to get in before more people see me, Boy."

"Well come on then," he said.

Straight ahead through the gates was a huge corrugated warehouse.

Boy passed under the arched entrance and headed across the concrete yard towards it. Then he slipped into the warehouse through a large opening big enough for a truck. Violet followed making sure no one had seen her.

They were standing in a huge space filled at one end with wooden boxes marked with the Archers' Tea logo. Stacked at the other end of the warehouse were hundreds of weird-looking bales. Violet had seen straw and hay bales before on her cousins' farm but they didn't look anything like these.

She walked closer and pulled out some of the strange grass from one of the bales. It was a silvery colour and when she waved it in the air, it reflected everything around her including herself.

"It must be the Chameleon plant," she whispered. "It doesn't just taste like anything you want, it looks like it too!"

"They must harvest it out of town and bring it here," Boy said, pointing to a tractor and trailer.

"But where's the factory?" she asked. "This is just a warehouse."

They spotted another large doorway just in front of the stacked tea boxes, crept across to it and peered outside.

Straight across a yard was a long rectangular red-bricked building. It was much larger than the warehouse and looked more like a hotel than a factory. Steps in front of the main building led up to a white-pillared entrance flanked by two enormous bronze statues of the Archer brothers in their famous bowler hats. Violet almost choked.

The windows of the factory were fogged up inside and smoke billowed from six chimneys that spanned the length of the roof. Above the entrance, right across the middle of the building, shiny gold letters spelled out *Archers' Tea Factory*.

"Look, Boy," Violet whispered.

Walking out the entrance, laughing and joking, were two Watchers. They took up sentry positions at the main door either side of the statues.

"What are they doing?" she asked.

"They must be on guard duty," Boy replied. "I didn't think they'd have Watchers at the factory as well."

"How are we going to get past them?"

Suddenly a loud beeping noise filled the air and a yellow forklift rattled round the side of the factory, heading for the warehouse.

"Hide, Violet," Boy hissed.

They raced down towards the Chameleon bales and hid behind the tractor trailer. The forklift entered the warehouse just where they had been standing moments before. The driver lowered the forks and moved forward towards the tea boxes.

Violet watched as the forks slid under a stack of boxes and lifted the whole lot straight up into the air. The loud beeping started again and the forklift reversed outside with its cargo.

Boy and Violet ran back to the entrance and watched the forklift disappear into the factory.

"They're taking the boxes inside," Boy said. "They must be going to fill them up with tea leaves. If we hide in one each we'll get in without anyone seeing us!"

"I'm not sure, Boy, what if they feel our weight?"

"It's a forklift, Violet! It's easy, come on," he said, as he climbed the stack next in line for collection.

He opened the lid on one of the boxes.

"There's loads of room, if we curl up we'll fit in one each."

Cautiously, Violet climbed up the stack beside him and peered inside. The box seemed small and cramped and she imagined being locked in it for ever, like a coffin or something. She hesitated.

"Come on, Violet," Boy said, looking back out the door, "we have to hurry."

Reluctantly, she climbed inside and pulled her legs up so her knees met her chin. She looked out at Boy then watched as the world went dark. He banged the lid above her, shutting it tight.

"Wait for me to come get you," he said.

She lay still and listened while Boy fiddled with the lid of his own box.

After what seemed like an age, the beeping started again, growing louder as the forklift reached the warehouse. The machinery clinked as the fork was lowered and there was a short bang when it hit the ground.

Then the box shuddered. Violet's heart pounded in her chest and she braced herself against the sides of the wood.

All kinds of horrible thoughts raced through her mind as they began to move. She tried not to panic, but the sides of the box seemed to cave in around her and she suddenly felt extremely hot. Sweat rolled off her forehead and dripped down her back.

She felt faint, but knew she mustn't lose control. She focused on her dad. She wouldn't let him down. As her head spun in despair, the movement suddenly stopped and she felt herself descending. There was a short jerk as the fork hit the floor and then silence. She waited in the darkness for Boy, but he didn't come.

She was about to attempt an escape when the lid popped off above her.

"Come on," her friend whispered, his head appearing above the rim of the box, "they've gone."

His face looked decidedly green and, like her, he was covered in telltale droplets of sweat.

"Are you okay?" Violet asked, climbing out.

"I'm fine," Boy snapped.

"It's just—"

"I said I was fine, Violet!"

"Oh I get it! I'm not the only one afraid of small spaces, am I?" she said gleefully, all of a sudden feeling much better.

Boy ignored her, and Violet tried hard not to laugh as they climbed down onto the floor.

They were standing in a white room beside three stacks of Archers' Tea boxes.

In front of them was a conveyor belt like the ones in airports. Tea boxes were lined up single file on the belt, which wound out of the room through a hole in the wall to their left.

Yellow lines marked walkways on the concrete ground. Violet followed one of them to a white door. A sign above it read "Factory Floor" in big red letters.

"Here, put these on," Boy said, handing her a navy coverall and hat just like the ones the woman at the gate had worn.

"Where did you get those?"

"They're hanging on a hook over there." Boy pointed behind the boxes. "They're a bit big, but they'll help us to blend in."

"That might not be a problem," Violet said, watching steam ooze in around the edges of the door, "they'll never see us through all that!"

She was just rolling up the sleeves of her jacket when a deafening siren reverberated through the factory. Violet grabbed Boy's arm and pointed.

The conveyor belt started to move and the tea boxes on it were shunted one by one through the hole in the wall onto the factory floor. The place was full of noise: beeps, whooshes and swooshes flew around them and Violet couldn't hear a word Boy was saying.

He pointed at the door.

"WE SHOULD GO OUT THERE!" he roared, just as the noise stopped.

Suddenly the room was deathly quiet, but for the echo of his words. Petrified, Boy and Violet stood frozen stiff, waiting for someone to arrive.

CHAPTER 27

WILLIAM'S POTION

Violet shivered. *Someone's walking on your grave* her dad would have said. She shook off the thought. She eyed the door, then Boy, then the door again. Neither moved and after a few minutes, Violet sighed with relief.

"I don't think they heard you," she whispered.

Boy exhaled, washing some colour back into his face. He was about to speak when the siren went off a second time and the boxes began to move once more.

"The conveyor belt must be on a cycle," he whispered when the noise stopped again. "Next time it starts we'll open the door and get onto the factory floor; nobody will hear us in that racket. Then let's both search for the tank William told us about, get the antidote in it and get out of here!"

"It might be quicker if we split up," Violet said.

"Okay I'll go right, you go left. We'll meet back here in ten minutes."

Violet nodded and they both waited nervously for the horn to sound again. On cue Boy opened the door.

The room flooded with steam. It was blinding and Violet's eyes stung in the prickly hot air. Boy had already disappeared into the clouds on her right, so she made her way gingerly from the tea box room, turning left onto the foggy factory floor.

The workers were nothing more than hazy shadows through a veil of steam as they passed by her, busy with their duties. They all wore the same navy coveralls and hats. Violet pulled her cap further down to blend in with the crowd.

On her right, she could just make out another conveyor belt. Winding through the room suspended directly above it, was a long metal pipe, dotted with handles and dials. Every so often the pipe rattled until a gush of steam jetted out of it as if releasing pressure.

The belt overflowed with long, loose stalks of the Chameleon grass they'd seen baled in the warehouse earlier. The grass was moving towards a ceiling bed of knifes that rapidly chopped it into tiny particles resembling mirrored tea leaves. Violet followed the belt forward.

The temperature began to rise and she fanned her coverall as she watched the tea leaves, which now passed under a giant heater. On the other side they were a toasted brown colour and had lost their shimmer.

William had guessed that in some part of the process the leaves would be sprayed with his brothers' concoction but Violet hadn't seen any sign of it yet. She hoped Boy was having better luck.

The siren started again. She had to concentrate but it was so hot. Sweat dripped into her eyes. She rubbed it away with the sleeve of her navy coverall and tried to suck air into her lungs. A little dizzy, she stopped for a breather.

"Everything okay?" a voice said behind her.

"Urgh yes," she replied quickly scooping some tea leaves into her hand, "I'm just erm...checking the con... consistency!" she said, picking a word her mother used when she talked about cake mixes.

The man nodded and moved away. She waited for him to disappear into the steam then hurried onwards, following the belt as it snaked to the right.

Then she stopped.

Up ahead the leaves passed under a large showerhead that sprayed them with a liquid. It was connected to a huge conical tank suspended high in the ceiling above. This had to be what William was talking about.

Her thoughts raced; she needed to find Boy. Suddenly someone grabbed her and a hand flew over her mouth.

"Shush!" Boy whispered into her ear. "Follow me!"

Violet gave a silent gasp of relief and, steadying herself, followed her friend towards a door in front of them. Boy opened it and Violet stepped inside.

The room was dark and it took a moment for her eyes to adjust. To her right was a long glass window with a grandstand view of the factory floor; to her left lots of pictures of George and Edward sparkled from gold frames on the wall.

In one photo, the twins stood proudly in front of the factory, in another all the workers were lined up behind them, beaming, like an enormous soccer team. Above the pictures was a sign: *Comrades in Work and Life; an Archers' Worker is a Perfect Worker.*

A polished wooden table in the middle of the room was dotted with mugs and navy packets of Archers' Tea. On the opposite wall was a white board covered in daily details.

"Did you see the tank?" Boy asked.

She nodded.

"It has to be the potion. There's a metal staircase that goes up to it," he said. "Nobody seems to use it. I think we'd be noticed if we did."

"Well then we need a distraction," Violet said, feeling a little more confident.

"It's not that easy, Violet," Boy replied. "There are workers everywhere and I spotted a few more Watchers prowling around. They can't find out we've been here or our whole plan will be ruined!"

"What about the tea boxes?" Violet said, pointing out the window. "Look!"

After the tea was sprayed it went under a second heat lamp to be dried and then passed over a lower conveyor belt carrying the tea boxes. The loose tea leaves were tipped from the higher conveyor belt into the boxes below. Once each tea box was full, it moved off and was replaced by the next one. It was an exact system and any slight hiccup would upset the whole line.

"Maybe if we cause a blockage in the tea-box room the whole operation will stop working," Violet suggested. "It's all connected. The tea leaves will pour onto the floor and everyone will be in a panic. The Watchers will have to come to help. I bet the workers won't have a clue what to do, they can't think for themselves."

"That's brilliant, Violet, it might just work." Boy smiled. "You've been hanging around No-Man's-Land too long. They won't want you back in Perfect now!"

"Hopefully there won't be a Perfect when we're finished."

They planned their attack and waited to pick their moment. It had to be exactly right.

Boy would cause a diversion in the tea-box room by blocking the conveyor belt that held the boxes. When the tea boxes stopped moving, the loose tea leaves would spill all over the floor causing the workers to panic.

In the commotion, Violet would climb the stairs and drop William Archer's antidote into the tank. From then on, all tea leaves on the conveyor belt would be sprayed with it and in a day or so the people of Perfect would regain their sight. Easy.

"Remember to wait for my signal," Boy said as he left the room on the sounding of the siren.

Violet remained behind, pacing the boardroom. The Archers' portraits watched her from the wall. Everything appeared to be normal on the factory floor. The boxes hadn't stopped moving and the longer Violet waited, the more nervous she became.

A second siren had gone off since Boy left and still the boxes moved steadily along. A third came and went, but nothing changed. Her heart pounded as she played with William Archer's flask.

Suddenly a sharp screeching sound bounced off the walls. It cut right into her. She peered through the window and watched as chaos took hold outside. Securing the flask in the waistband of her trousers, she took a deep breath and slipped out onto the factory floor.

Workers sprinted through the steam towards the conveyor belt. Whatever Boy had done, had worked; tea leaves were spilling all over the floor. People ran in every direction bearing buckets. Realizing she looked out of place moving steadily through the madness, Violet sped up. The stairs to the conical tank were just ahead. She ran for them holding tightly to the flask and had just reached the first step when a hand grabbed her.

"We're losing the tea, we're losing the tea," a man shouted in a panic, thrusting a bucket into her hand.

She took it from him and the flask slipped and slid rapidly down the leg of her trousers. It was about to hit the floor, but in the nick of time, she dropped the bucket and managed to grab it.

"We're losing the tea, we're losing the tea! It's a disaster, a disaster," the man was still roaring. He pulled her towards the belt where everyone stood watching the tea leaves spill onto the floor.

Suddenly two Watchers appeared. Violet looked away, afraid they'd notice she'd seen them. She had to remind herself constantly that the Watchers were invisible to everyone in Perfect.

Her hand shook as she secured the flask once more in her waistband and pulled her cap further down in case they'd notice she wasn't wearing glasses.

"These people are so stupid sometimes," one of the Watchers snarled as he grabbed a bucket from the crowd to catch the falling tea leaves.

The worker he'd taken the bucket from looked blankly at his empty hands. "Did you see that?" he said to the man beside him. "My bucket's moving by itself."

"That's 'cause they're automatic," the second man replied. "The Archers invented them. If we stand here long enough the buckets will know what to do!"

Violet couldn't believe her ears. William was right – people really were nothing without imagination.

She needed to move away and get to the stairs, but the Watchers would notice. She looked around for Boy but couldn't see him.

"Give me that, you stupid fool," the Watcher said, grabbing a bucket from another unsuspecting worker.

"Are you going to help me fix the blockage or what?" he snarled at a fellow Watcher who was standing idly by. "Stop gawping. You're as bad as the rest of these idiot workers!"

"Fix it yourself," the other Watcher snarled back. "I'm sick of you ordering me about!"

"You're what?" the first Watcher snapped, dropping his bucket and clenching his fists.

The workers began to panic as tea leaves were once again spilling all over the floor.

"There's something wrong with the buckets, there's something wrong with the buckets," a woman screamed, running around in circles.

Violet took her chance. She raced up the stairwell to the tank just as a roar rose up behind her. She looked back, afraid someone had seen.

The two Watchers were rolling around the floor fighting as other Watchers ran in to break them apart. All around them the workers stood open-mouthed as, in their eyes, an invisible force hurled buckets and tea leaves in all directions.

Violet sped up the steps. Reaching the top she pulled out the flask. A steel landing hugged the circumference of the tank. She ran frantically around it but there was no opening to tip the contents of the flask into.

A ladder on the side ran over the top of the steel cylinder. If anyone looked up now they'd see her scaling the tank, but luckily the Watchers were still focused on the fight.

She took the flask in her teeth, grabbed the sides of the metal ladder and quickly climbed to the top. She couldn't help looking down. The ground seemed miles below, her arms shook and dizziness hit her. She steadied herself for a few seconds.

There was a small circular handle like a steering wheel on top of the tank. Her heart pounded as shrieks reached up from the factory floor. She crawled over to the handle and twisted it with all her strength. It was stiff at first but quickly loosened in her grip, opening up a small trapdoor into the tank.

Ripping the cork from the flask, she kissed the murky glass and emptied its contents into the liquid below. Then she closed up the door and climbed back down the ladder.

The fight was still in progress as she descended the stairs and snuck back to the boardroom where Boy was waiting for her.

With a quick nod, she followed her friend through the steam towards the exit. All the Watchers were now occupied inside so Boy and Violet slipped out unnoticed past the bronze statues of the Archer brothers.

The pair sprinted across the yard and hid their coats in the warehouse.

"You got the liquid into the tank?" Boy asked, bending over to catch his breath.

"Yes," Violet panted.

"No one saw?"

"No, I don't think so. They were all too busy with the fight."

"So we've done it? The people of Perfect will soon be able to see again!"

Violet nodded, lost for words; she couldn't quite believe it herself.

Full of energy from the morning's excitement they

followed George's Road back into the middle of Perfect. The town was busy when they hit Edward Street and while Boy was invisible to the townsfolk, Violet kept her head down, afraid she'd be noticed.

Her heart pounded as they entered Archers' Avenue and she was just turning onto Rag Lane when Boy pulled her back. "No. This way, Violet!"

She followed him down past Iris Archer's house to the bottom of the Avenue, stopping by the wall where they'd landed earlier that morning.

Boy, lizard-like, used little nooks and crannies in the stone to scale the height. He reached the top, smiled and disappeared. A few moments later the rope fell down the wall beside Violet.

"Come on," he said, "grab it."

Cautiously Violet did as she was told.

"Now put your legs against the wall and walk up. It's easy!"

"I'm not sure I'd use the word easy!" Violet grimaced as she grabbed hold of the rope.

Her arms strained as she moved her legs slowly up the wall. She got to the top, exhausted, and scowled at Boy before peering over the edge back down to the ground. She wobbled and he grabbed her arm.

"Thanks," she gasped.

They were up so high she could see across No-Man's-

Land and Perfect – one town hidden inside the other, separated only by a wall. She'd been so nervous earlier she hadn't noticed the view that morning. How beautiful the town would be if only it wasn't divided.

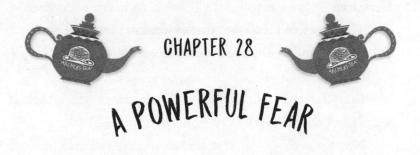

CHAPTER 28

A POWERFUL FEAR

Carefully, Violet and Boy ran back across the rooftops until they reached the bathroom window. They climbed inside and hurried down the three floors out onto Forgotten Road.

It was almost midday and all was quiet on the main street. They kept out of sight of the Watchers as they snuck back through the town. Nearing Wickham Terrace, the energy in the air changed. Something was amiss. Suddenly a woman rushed out the door of her lopsided house.

"That's her!" she snarled, pointing at Violet. "That's her!"

Another woman, about Violet's mam's age, ran from

the same door and grabbed her top, pulling her roughly back.

"The cheek of you!" the second woman roared. "Don't you think we have it hard enough without setting the Watchers on us?"

"Let go of me!" Violet yelled, struggling to break the woman's hold. "I haven't done anything wrong!"

"Not yet, young one, but you're trying, you and that boyfriend of yours. Just leave us alone! We don't need any trouble!"

"She hasn't done anything," Boy shouted, pulling Violet away to stand between the pair of them.

"They're talking revolution in Will Archer's place. No-Man's-Landers sneaking around in the daylight will be risin' suspicions from the Watchers. Your names are all around the place as the ones behind it. Know anything about that, do ya?" the woman hissed, almost nose to nose with Boy.

Quickly, Boy grabbed Violet's arm and they sprinted towards William Archer's. They raced through the tiny streets and, without knocking, pushed open the door of the ramshackle house.

The heat hit Violet first then the smell of sweat. The room was packed with people and they had to push their way through a sea of legs to get near the front of the crowd.

Violet recognized a few faces from the streets of No-Man's-Land but others she'd never seen before. Some seemed happy but most grunted and growled as William faced the room from the top of a rocky old footstool.

"What about the Watchers? There's not enough of us in No-Man's-Land to take them on," one man shouted.

"We'll have numbers when we change the Perfectionists back," William said. "Then we fight. I'm willing to give my fists an airing if you are, gents...and ladies, of course."

"We'll never beat them," another man called.

"We will with a bit of luck," William replied. "Once our friends and families in Perfect realize we're still alive, they'll join us, you'll see."

"And how do you propose they'll see us? Hasn't that been the problem all along, William? I thought you stopped talking this nonsense long ago. It's doing none of us any good. We're here to stay in No-Man's-Land and it's about time some of us accepted that!"

"A man of your imagination stands defeated, Frederick?" William replied, looking straight into his eyes. "They will see us again, I promise you."

"It's a promise you can't keep, William!"

"Yes he can." Violet stepped out in front of the crowd.

"Violet!" William exclaimed, jumping down from the stool. "Thank heavens you're all right. And Boy? Is he with you?"

"He's there," Violet said, pointing him out in the crowd.

"How did you get on?" William whispered anxiously.

Violet pulled the empty flask from her trouser belt and handed it to him. Cupping the glass in both hands, he held the bottle tightly to his chest, and inhaled long and deep.

"Our families *will* see us," he shouted, jumping back onto the stool.

He shoved the flask into the air for all to witness. "My two young friends made sure of that!"

The crowd began to whisper and William waited for them to settle again before he started to explain.

"Archers' Tea is blinding our families and I've developed an antidote that will reverse its effects. My two brave friends here administered it to the tea leaves in the factory right this very morning. It's my brothers' pride and joy, I've been told, that freshly brewed tea is delivered to every home and workplace in the town each day and because of this, by tomorrow, our families will see us again – if we were to walk down the streets of what once was our town! They won't however recognize us yet and that's the next part of our plan – to zap them with the ReImaginator. If we can do all that, Perfect will fall."

"The what?" Someone laughed, at the end of the room.

"The ReImaginator," William repeated seriously,

before explaining how his brothers' rose-tinted glasses robbed the imagination, how their BR technology made people see only what the Archers wanted them to, and how his machine, the ReImaginator could fix all that.

"And why do our families not fight back, why do they not question anything – our disappearances, the regime in Perfect? Because nothing seems out of the ordinary to them, they have lost their ability to imagine an alternative life. They've lost independent thought," William finished.

Someone laughed from across the room. "Well, I'm delighted I stayed to hear you answer our questions, William, because now I know for sure that you're crazy. I'm out of here," a red-bearded man shouted, pushing aside the crowd as he forced his way towards the door.

"They called you crazy too, Sam. There was a time nobody could stop you doing what you loved. Remember when people called you a dreamer? It's why you're here in No-Man's-Land! It's why we're all here. We were all dreamers once. Can we not dream together again?"

"I've grown up, William, and you should too. Accept where you are and move on. Build a life here. It's all you've got now!"

Others began to move too, passing out of the house in silence.

"Why now, William?" another man asked. "I mean, I was with you at the beginning but then you disappeared and we all gave up. What's happened to bring back your fight? What's brought you out of hiding?"

William turned to face him. "It's Macula, Merrill. My brothers have her. I gave up because I had nothing to fight for. I thought she was dead. Then with the help of Violet and Boy here I found out she's still alive. That's what's brought me back."

The crowd still trickled out the door.

"Look, we are in No-Man's-Land because we are different!" William shouted, addressing those slipping from the room. "What's happened to your imaginations? Where is the fight? You're all acting like Perfectionists! We have a responsibility to our families in Perfect. It's up to us, the outsiders, to show them the way, to wake them up. If we don't at least try then we're just as controlled as they are, except we've no excuse for our ignorance!"

"Grow up, Archer! No-Man's-Land is our lot, what's the point in fighting? I remember the rebellions, the beatings, the blood, I remember it all. I don't want to go back there. If you draw the Watchers down on us you'll have me to answer to," a woman roared as she left the house.

The crowd filtered steadily outside and William stepped down from the stool.

"It's no good," he said, his head in his hands, "they won't fight!"

Violet stepped forward. "It's okay," she said. "We can do it without them. I know it will be harder but we can still make it happen."

"Violet." William smiled, looking down at her. "You're a lovely child. Your enthusiasm knows no bounds, but in this case, three against so many just won't be enough."

"What about four?" A figure stepped forward from the shadows.

"Merrill! I thought you'd left with the others?"

"No, William, I thought about it, I must confess," Merrill said, "but I've missed the adventures we had taking on your brothers. Making toys serves me well here but it's no substitute for my family. It's time to get them back! So, where do I sign up?"

CHAPTER 29

LITTLE HELPERS

William wrapped his arms around his old friend.

"Who's that?" Violet whispered.

"Merrill Marx, the toymaker." Boy smiled. "He has the nicest shop in No-Man's-Land. Gives free stuff to the orphans."

Violet liked the sound of him already, but there were still only four of them. They needed an army large enough to overthrow the Archers and their Watchers if they were to save Perfect and her dad.

"If we could just prove to the No-Man's-Landers that they can be reunited with their families, then I know they'll join us and fight," William said.

"But how?" Merrill asked. "It sounds great but it's

just a dream, William."

"We use the ReImaginator. We give the Perfectionists back their imaginations and show the No-Man's-Landers. Then they'll revolt in here. I know it will work!"

"But that's still not enough people to overthrow the might of the Watchers, William," Merrill said quietly, "the rebellions in the past showed us that much."

"Yes, but it won't be just us. We need to stage an uprising here and while the Watchers are dealing with that we'll sneak into Perfect and change the Perfectionists. Then we'll have numbers large enough to take back our town!"

"But to use your machine we need people's imaginations so we can give them back," Violet said. "How do we get them from the Archers without being spotted?"

Boy, who'd been sitting quietly by the window, suddenly stood up. "I know where we can get an army. They might be a little small but they'll have lots of energy." He smiled. "They'll help us get the imaginations."

"Who are you talking about, Boy?" William asked.

"The orphans. My family!"

"No." William and Merrill both shook their heads.

"They're only children, Boy!" Merrill said, looking straight at him.

"It's too dangerous," William added.

"We're kids too, if you haven't noticed," Violet said, stepping forward, her hands on her hips.

"Don't underestimate them." Boy smiled. "These kids have grown up on the streets of No-Man's-Land. They're much braver than any adults I know."

"Okay, so what's your plan?" Violet asked, ignoring the two older men.

"Well, we need a lot of hands to get the imaginations. The orphans are light on their feet, quick and nimble. We could start with, say, twenty imaginations. Would that be enough to convince the No-Man's-Landers that our plan will work?" Boy asked.

William nodded slowly. "Yes I think so. If we could change twenty Perfectionists and bring them back here, nobody could dispute our plan."

"Brilliant. So we get twenty orphans. We cross the river – the bridge shouldn't be too risky as they're all small and light. Sneak through the Ghost Estate at night, when the Watchers who look after the eye plants are sleeping, into the graveyard, through the tunnel to the Archers' storeroom. Then we grab the imaginations and bring them back here."

"But what about the hollowing team?" Violet asked. "They might be in their den."

"If we time it right they should be out on patrol."

"It sounds very risky, Boy," William said.

"Yes, but if it works the orphans get to go home. I live in the orphanage, I hear them crying all the time. Most of them still dream of their old lives only to wake up here in No-Man's-Land. That's why I went looking for Violet's dad in the first place. I thought he might help get their families back. I think they'll be willing to take the risk."

"Okay, if you're sure, Boy; you put across a convincing case," William said, looking at Merrill and Violet. "What do you two think?"

"I think kids are way smarter than adults!" Violet smiled.

"Well that's a yes I take it, Violet," Merrill joked. "I'm in too. I understand what Boy's saying about the orphans, they come to my shop most days and play, just so they can be kids again. As long as they're happy to go then I won't stop them."

"The Archers can't have any idea we're after the imaginations, if they get a whiff that something's up, we're finished," William said, looking sternly at Boy.

"They won't," Boy said solidly. "Twenty missing imaginations won't be noticed among all the other jars on the shelf. And we'll go the back way, through the Ghost Estate. No one will have a clue we've been to the storeroom at all. Like I said, we orphans are used to sneaking around unseen!"

The foursome discussed their plans until Boy and

Violet couldn't hold their eyes open any longer. William insisted they should sleep while he and Merrill worked on the ReImaginator.

❋   ❋   ❋

It was almost dusk; the sun was setting behind the high stone walls of No-Man's-Land, when William gently prodded the two children from their slumber to reveal a humming machine.

"I knew it'd only take a tweak," he said, proudly polishing the brass. "Now all we need are a few imaginations!"

"We're going to sort that out now." Boy smiled. "The orphans should be getting up soon."

"Are you sure this plan will work?" Merrill asked.

"Of course," Violet replied. "Nothing's ever difficult for children. It's adults who complicate things—"

"You remember the meeting point, William?" Boy interrupted.

"Don't worry, Boy, we'll be waiting by the Rag Tree with this old girl."

Boy and Violet said goodbye to their friends and, for the second time in as many days, left William Archer's house on a mission. Violet followed Boy, predicting every turn they took; No-Man's-Land was no longer a mystery to her.

They snuck onto Forgotten Road and along to the orphanage. Boy took the key from under the birdbath and jiggled it in the lock. Moments later they were standing in the enormous hall.

"This way," he whispered, tiptoeing across the tiled floor.

The place was quiet and sounds echoed through the empty hall like ghosts. Fear crawled up Violet's spine. They reached a wooden stairwell and climbed two floors, the steps creaking under their weight, then walked down another corridor to a set of wooden double doors.

"Be really quiet," Boy mouthed, pushing one open.

He slipped through the narrow gap, Violet in tow.

"Stay here," he whispered, leaving her side.

Shards of late evening light came through the shuttered windows and she could see the rusted metal frame of a bunk bed beside her. A small thin figure moved beneath a threadbare blanket in the bottom bunk. There were at least twenty other bunks in the oversized room, all occupied by similar small figures.

The air was cold and wisps of foggy breath formed in front of her nose. Moans and groans followed Boy round the room like a chorus, as he quietly made his way from bed to bed pulling each child gently from their sleep. When he finally got back to Violet, the room was humming.

"Is it time to get up already?" a small voice complained.

"Shush, yes, it's almost night time," Boy whispered, "and I have a favour to ask. Please don't make a sound or the nurses will come rushing down here and we all know what'll happen then."

Shushes and giggles danced round the room.

"Right, I'm going to turn on the light now," Boy warned. "Not a sound."

There was a faint flicker from above. Then another, that lasted a little longer, and finally the light came to life. Twenty miniature, messy-haired heads peered out from under dirty sheets.

"What is it, Boy?" a little girl in one of the upper bunks asked, grabbing the rusted, white railing that ran round the edge of her bed. "Is it Santy?"

"No Anna." Boy smiled. "It's not Santa. I have a job that I want you to help me with. If it works you'll go back home to your family."

"Just me?" Anna asked.

"No, everybody," Boy replied.

"Really? We'll really go home?" a child a little younger than Boy said, jumping up on his mattress. "Like home, home, Boy? You're not joking, are ya?"

"No, no, I'm not joking. You'll go back to your real home and family, I promise."

"Well then I'm in, I don't care what I have to do!"

"You can come live in my house, Boy," Anna said, "'cause you don't have a family of your own."

"Thanks." Boy smiled, lifting the little girl into his arms. "Now listen. I want you all to think about this really hard 'cause it's going to be dangerous."

"Woohoo, danger!" Another little boy laughed and did a somersault on his bed.

"What sort of danger?" an older orphan asked.

"The Archer twins have stolen the imaginations of the people in Perfect, Jack, and we need to get them back so they'll remember us."

"I knew it, I knew the Archers were evil," a little boy said. "I wrote a story about it in school then the Watchers came and took me!"

"Yes, you're different, you see, just like the rest of us. That's why the Watchers put you here; they couldn't steal your imagination."

"But what can we do, Boy?" Anna asked.

"The Archers are keeping the jars of imaginations in a secret storeroom behind their shop. We can get to it through a tunnel in the Ghost Estate. We take a jar each and bring it back here. It sounds simple but I want you all to know it could be very dangerous."

"Does that mean we have to cross the river?" a little girl said, sitting upright. "But it's haunted over there, I've heard all the stories. If we go, we'll be killed!"

"I'm not sure about ghosts," Boy replied, "but there are Watchers in the Ghost Estate, that's why I want you all to think hard about this mission. Like I said, it is dangerous and if you don't want to come, you don't have to."

"But it's an adventure," another child piped up.

"Yeah," loads of voices joined in, "an adventure!"

Each child was as excited as the next and it took a lot of shushing to calm them down as Violet and Boy outlined the details of their plan. By ten o'clock that night everyone was fully briefed, dressed and ready to go.

"I really hope this works, Boy," Violet whispered.

"It will," he said, confidently.

"Boy," she continued, as she helped a little girl put on her jumper, "you know once this is over you can come live in my house if you like."

"Thanks, Violet." He smiled.

A few minutes later, with the room ready, lights off and shutters open, Boy addressed the crowd.

"Leave the orphanage just as you would on any normal night," he said. "Don't act strange if the nurses stop you, myself and Violet will wait just round the corner."

Boy and Violet left first and waited by the side of the orphanage for their twenty recruits. Then they split into four groups: two of the older orphans were appointed as leaders alongside Boy and Violet. Boy's group would go first with Violet's taking up the rear.

"We'll meet at the bridge into the Ghost Estate. You all know how to get there?" Boy addressed the throng in a whisper.

Everyone nodded. The orphans knew No-Man's-Land better than anyone.

The groups left one at a time until it was Violet's group's turn. The coast was clear. She beckoned her orphans forward and they headed down Forgotten Road then took the next left into a lane.

An odd atmosphere was settling over the streets. Violet shivered. She tried to shake off the worry as her pack raced past the Market Yard. Only a few stalls had set up and the market was much quieter than usual.

They stuck to the walls, travelling in the shadows as much as possible. The others, now well ahead, were nowhere to be seen. She hoped they would wait at the bridge as planned.

"We need to move faster," she whispered to the orphans.

They picked up the pace and were now jogging towards the river down Wickham Terrace.

Violet could almost hear the waters ahead. They'd just about reached the river, when a loud smack filled the street followed by a high-pitched squeal.

"She pushed me!" a little girl roared, holding her arm. "I hit my elbowww!"

"Shush, Anna," Violet whispered, rushing back to the girl's side. "You have to be quiet."

"But my elbow is sore!" she cried, tears streaming down her face.

"Please stop crying," Violet insisted, scanning the street.

"Oi! Who goes there?" a gravelly voice shouted.

Heavy footsteps approached from behind.

Violet grabbed Anna's hand and the shawl that was wrapped round her shoulders. She pulled the shawl around her own head and whispered to the others to hide in the doorway.

"You have to be brave and you have to agree with everything I say. Understand?"

Anna nodded, clinging to Violet, as more tears streamed down her face.

"What are you two doing out here?" a voice snarled.

"It was my sister," Violet replied turning slowly around.

A Watcher stood close by in the shadows. "I can see that, but it doesn't answer my question, little girl."

"We're going to the market," Violet stuttered, pulling the shawl tighter round her face.

"The market's the other way."

"We got lost."

"Where do you live?" the Watcher asked, moving closer.

Violet's heart stopped. What were the street names

in No-Man's-Land? Her cheeks burned. Her mind was blank. She couldn't think.

"Moore Lane," Anna sobbed.

Violet gasped and squeezed her hand. The Watcher looked from one to the other without uttering a word.

"Well you better be getting back there then," he said, eventually, breaking the silence. "Haven't you heard no one is to leave their homes in No-Man's-Land tonight?"

"No, I'm sorry, we didn't know, sir," Violet stuttered. "We'll go now. It won't happen again, I promise."

Slipping past the Watcher's solid frame, Violet's heart was pounding so hard she was sure he could hear it.

"Oi!" he called as they neared the Market Yard. Violet stiffened. Running away would only make things worse. Slowly she turned on the spot. "You sure you know where you're going this time?"

"Yes," she answered, almost whispering.

"Moore Lane is that way," he said, pointing.

"Oh, erm…thanks," she replied quickly following his instructions.

The Watcher stood on the spot until they had rounded the corner. They kept their heads down and walked quickly, hoping he wouldn't follow them.

After a few minutes, when they were sure they were in the clear, Violet loosened her grip on the girl's hand

and stopped. Crouching down so they were face-to-face, she let out a long slow breath.

"I'm sorry, Violet," Anna sobbed throwing her arms around her neck, "I didn't mean to get us in trouble."

"You didn't," Violet whispered. "You saved us."

The pair waited for a while longer in the shadows before doubling back to the rest of the group still huddled in the doorway to resume their journey.

By the time they reached the river, the others had gone. Violet searched the banks but there was no sign of the groups. They decided to cross anyway, sure everyone else must be ahead of them.

Violet climbed onto the footbridge, gripped the wire ropes and showed the orphans how to jump from plank to plank as Boy had shown her. Her legs wobbled but she did her best to hide her nerves. When she reached the other side, the orphans were on her heels, fearless.

Once on dry land they ran through the grass, onto the tarmac road to the pillars of the Ghost Estate.

There was still no sign of the other groups and Violet's pulse raced. Maybe they'd gone ahead? She remembered the Watcher and what he'd said about nobody being allowed to leave their homes. Maybe they'd all been caught?

Her mind was spinning when something moved just inside the entrance.

"Hide now," she whispered to her group.

Not making a sound she approached the cement pillars, her heart pounding. She'd just passed by the billboard of the happy family when a figure rushed at her from the darkness.

CHAPTER 30

RETURN TO THE ROOM OF IMAGINATIONS

"Boy!" she wheezed, trying to catch her breath. "Don't ever do that again. I thought you were another Watcher!"

"What do you mean another?"

"We met one on the street, that's why it took us so long to get here," she explained. "I don't think he suspected anything. I said we were lost and he seemed to believe me. But No-Man's-Land is so quiet tonight, did you notice? The Watcher said that no one is allowed to leave their homes."

"Really?" Boy sounded surprised. "Did he say why?"

"No." Violet shook her head. "D'you think they're onto us?"

"I don't know," Boy replied. "Maybe they're just looking for you; they'll know you're missing."

"Great." Violet pulled the shawl tighter round her head. "That makes me feel much better!"

"Come on, we can't wait around here any longer. If that Watcher was suspicious he might come looking," Boy said.

He turned and raced back to his group. One by the one the four groups slipped off into the Ghost Estate; Violet's were at the back once again.

"You have to be really brave and quiet in here," she warned the orphans. "There are Watchers sleeping in some of these houses, so we can't make a sound."

The orphans nodded, each looking a little nervous. Violet had already heard them whispering to each other about the ghosts.

"It's not haunted," she said, reassuring herself as much as the orphans. "Remember, anything you feel or think is just in your head, it's your imagination. There's no such thing as ghosts."

Everyone nodded again and Violet turned towards the estate.

"Okay," she whispered, "let's go."

The other groups had disappeared into the distance as they walked in through the cement pillars under the picture of the happy family.

As they passed the house where Violet had seen her dad, she fought the urge to break from the plan and save him, but like William had said, she couldn't be selfish. She had to focus on the bigger picture. Everything would fall into place, they'd have an army to take on the Archers and her family would finally be back together.

The estate was quiet and her group kept to the centre of the tarmac road that ran round the green.

"What are they?" Anna asked, running over to look at the eye plants.

Violet grabbed her hand jerking her back before she could touch one.

"Don't!" she warned, her stomach churning at the sight of the pulsing red stems. "They're erm…flowers. Don't touch!"

"They don't look like flowers," Anna replied as one of the eyeballs swivelled under its translucent petals to stare up at them.

Violet pulled the girl away. "Don't go near them!" she scolded remembering the eye plants' deathly screech the last time one had been disturbed.

The lonely lamp post glowed yellow through the haze ahead and she shepherded the children up the hill towards it.

A shadow moved in the distance. Violet held up her hand to halt the group. The figure stood alone by the lamp post and bent down to pick something from the ground.

"Boy?" Violet whispered.

"Yes," he replied, "hurry, everyone's in the graveyard."

"What are you doing?" she asked as she reached his side.

He held up the wooden torch that lit their way the first night they'd used the tunnel. "I hid it here in case we ever needed it again."

Violet tried to forget that night and her panic, as she turned and followed Boy down towards a turnstile that led into the graveyard.

The overgrown path led them through the centre of the cemetery. Tombstones appeared to hover in the mist, and a weight hung in the air as if the dead were watching. One of the younger orphans began to cry.

"Shush, fight back your fears," Violet whispered, ignoring the goosepimples that crept up her own arms. "They aren't real."

The orphans gasped as they witnessed Boy disappear down into the ground ahead of them. The tunnel was hidden in the grass by the back wall.

"We're going down there?" one of them shivered. "It looks like Boy's getting into a grave!"

"You'll be fine," Violet soothed, but the same thought haunted her as she climbed down after Boy.

"It's an adventure, remember?" Anna said.

The tunnel was deathly quiet. It took a moment for Violet's eyes to adjust to the blackness before small outlines appeared huddled in front of her. All the orphans were back together.

After a quick break they moved off, under Boy's instructions, towards the Archers' storeroom. The air was musty and thick with damp, making each new breath a struggle.

"I'm frightened," a small boy whispered, grabbing Violet's hand.

She smiled and squeezed his palm just like her mam would have done when she was scared. Now she had to be the adult. She didn't want to grow up – she wasn't ready. Terror hovered round her and her breath quickened. She missed having her mam and dad to protect her.

"Everybody stop," Boy suddenly whispered.

Snapped from her fears, Violet quietened the group. Her heart pounded. The orphans stood frozen, statue still, as Boy peered around the corner ahead.

"Coast clear," he whispered back and everyone exhaled.

They picked up the pace and made steady progress towards the Archers' Emporium. On reaching the Watchers' empty den, they stopped.

"Keep everyone here, Jack," Boy said to an older orphan who led one of the groups. "We're going to check and make sure we can get in. We'll come back to get you soon."

Violet took a deep breath then followed her friend out onto the dark stairwell that wound up to the Archers' storeroom. Boy was two steps ahead, and she struggled to keep his pace.

Quickly they reached the top of the stairs. Boy pulled a pack of matches from his pocket and lit the torch; the flame warmed the cold stone landing.

"Hold this near the door so I can see," he said, passing it over.

He felt around for the handle just as Violet had done from the other side the first night they'd found the tunnel. He pushed in on a loose brick and it popped out from the wall. Boy fiddled with the lever but nothing happened.

"I think it's locked," he said, looking back at her.

"What? It can't be," she said, getting a closer look. "It wasn't locked before."

She moved the torch closer to the handle. There was a small hole in the brick the right shape for a key.

"Do you have a hair clip?" Boy said, a little panic entering his voice.

Pulling one out, Violet handed it to her friend and held her breath. He played with the lock but nothing budged. It was just their luck.

"What will we do now?" she asked.

He stopped and sat back against the wall.

"We'll have to wait," he sighed, dropping the clip.

"For what?"

"For one of the Watchers to come back."

"But they'll catch us!"

"Not if we get them first."

Boy pointed to the torch in her hand.

"This?" Violet asked, surprised. "What do you want to do with it?"

Boy took the torch and stamped it out, plunging them into darkness, then hit the stone floor with it, sending a deep thump through the space.

"Knock him out!" Boy said, as if the answer was obvious.

She wasn't convinced. "What if there's more than one of them?"

"There'll only be one. I've only seen the Watchers on their own in Perfect at night."

"I hope you're right." She sighed.

Violet went down to update the others then rejoined Boy by the door. It seemed like hours passed while they waited in the dark against the cold stone. Violet's body was weak with tiredness. Her head spun. She would have slept, if her mind had let her.

Suddenly keys jangled from behind the door. Violet's nerves sparked and she scrambled up from the floor.

"Blasted lock," someone snarled.

Boy moved swiftly to the other side of the door and positioned himself with the torch held high, ready to pounce. The handle turned and slowly the door swung open.

Ghostly light filtered in from the jars in the storeroom, revealing Bungalow, bent double, fiddling with the keys. He didn't see Boy swing for his head. There was a loud clunk, a howl of pain and the Watcher fell to the floor unconscious.

"Oi! You mangy, wriggling, dirty maggot!" The fiery-haired Fists roared as he rushed through the door and grabbed Boy, who dropped the torch in the scuffle.

Violet froze. Thankfully, Fists hadn't seen her as she hid behind the door.

"I knew we'd catch you someday, ya ugly orphan. No wonder your parents didn't want ya. I'm going to rip you to shreds."

Boy kicked his captor in the shin. He tried to run but Fists grabbed him, thumping him hard against the wall. Her friend collapsed and Violet watched in horror as the Watcher threw Boy's small, limp body over his massive shoulder.

Violet picked up the torch that had settled by her feet. Boy was blocking her target; if she swung the baton now she'd hit him instead of Fists.

Fists disappeared down the stairwell forgetting the keys that hung in the lock above Bungalow's head. Violet grabbed them and quickly slipped down the stairs after him, just catching sight of Fists' large frame entering the den.

She waited with bated breath sure he'd see the orphans now. There wasn't a sound from below. She peered round the door into the den.

The room looked empty.

Fists strode across the space and flung Boy's body onto the stone floor banging his head. Violet winced.

Her mind on Boy she snuck into the room and didn't notice the Watcher turn. Fists stared straight at her.

Veins on the side of his forehead pulsed. He released an almighty roar and surged for Violet. She couldn't move. Her arms and legs were paralyzed!

Suddenly what seemed like hundreds of small bodies streamed into the room from the far tunnel and wrapped themselves round Fists' ankles. He kicked in fury but the orphans held tight.

Everyone was pointing and shouting at Violet. In a daze, she couldn't grasp what they were saying. What was it they wanted? Her hand, they were pointing at her hand?

"The torch, the torch, Violet, the torch!"

Of course, the torch! In her panic she'd forgotten she was carrying it. Violet sprung to life. She tightened her grip and steadied the baton in her hand then, with an enormous rush of energy she screamed and raced towards Fists.

The Watcher moved quickly, his pace slowed only a little by the orphans. Lifting the torch, Violet slammed the solid wood down with all her force on his flame-red hair.

Fists groaned loudly, wobbled, then crashed to the floor.

"You saved us! You saved us!" the orphans cried, hugging her as if she'd just scored a winning goal.

Violet's whole body shook, like electricity was filling her veins and she let the torch slip from her grasp. "We saved each other," she answered, weakly.

Ignoring the celebrations, she rushed to Boy. He was still unconscious but breathing. "Help!" she cried. "Someone help me!"

Gently, they lifted Boy onto one of the Watchers' hammocks. When Violet was sure he was okay, she cocooned him in a blanket in case the Watchers returned. Then she addressed the group, who were now a little calmer.

"Help me dismantle a hammock," she said, pointing to one of the beds suspended from the ceiling. "We'll use the rope to tie up the Watchers."

Two boys took the hammock apart as Violet and some of the others dragged Fists into the far corner of the den.

Then they got the rope and bound his hands and feet, covering him finally in a thick, brown, stinking blanket that had been resting on one of the beds.

"We still have a job to do," she said. "Follow me and bring another rope and blanket."

Quickly and quietly she ushered everyone up the steps. Bungalow was still unconscious on the landing in the open doorway. The orphans made quick work of tying him up, then they heaved him into the Archers' storeroom, cleared a space under one of the bottom shelves and rolled him into place, covering him with the blanket.

It was only then that they stood back and stared around the room.

"What are those?" Jack pointed to the jars of colour that cast the space in a ghostly light.

"They're what Boy was telling you about, they're the imaginations," Violet replied, loud enough for everyone to hear. "We have to take one each. But be really careful, we absolutely can't break any. There are names on the tops of the jars, so try to find a family member or a friend if you can. Make sure it doesn't look like any jars are missing when we leave. We don't want the Archers to suspect a thing."

The orphans stood back at first. Then Jack stepped forward and walked the length of the storeroom carefully inspecting the lids. He finally stopped, pulled a jar from the shelf and held it aloft.

"It's my dad's," he said to the group.

Immediately the others began scouring the shelves for their loved ones.

Violet was helping a little girl locate her granny when a jar caught her eye. Light pink and purple hues swirled inside the glass. It was labelled in tiny type: *Mrs Rose Brown. Incomplete. Last session: 12th September '17.*

"Mam," Violet whispered.

Shaking, she took the jar gently from the shelf remembering how her mother used to kiss her forehead for no reason or hold her when she was upset. Her eyes began to water and she willed them to stop; a lump rose in her throat. She wished Boy was with her.

Cradling the glass to her chest, she helped the last of the orphans with their jars. Once everyone had hold of an imagination, they checked on Bungalow then locked the door behind them. As they snuck back down the stairwell, hues of colour lit up the darkness.

"Keep the noise down." A familiar voice carried through the stairwell from the room below.

Boy was sitting up in his hammock as they entered the den. "You're alive." Violet laughed, throwing her arms around him.

"Violet, my head – it's still sore, you know!"

"Oh, I'm sorry. I was afraid—"

"No Watcher's ever going to kill me," he interrupted, struggling out of his unsteady bed.

He put a hand out to balance against the wall and Violet slipped her shoulder under his armpit.

"Lean on me," she whispered.

He smiled and steadied himself against her.

"We got them." She smiled, turning slowly so Boy could see the orphans, who stood in front of them holding their colourful jars to prove it. "We're ready for William."

"We'd better hurry then," Boy replied groggily.

Before leaving they dismantled another hammock and Violet asked Jack to carry it. Then, checking on Fists once more, they slipped along the tunnel to the graveyard and into the Ghost Estate.

Everyone carried an imagination jar except Boy and as they crept past the house where her father was captive, Violet hugged her mother's jar closer.

"There's something up," Boy whispered near the estate entrance.

"What do you mean?" Violet asked.

"It all seems a little too quiet."

There wasn't a stir from any of the houses. The silence was eerie.

"Maybe the Watchers are just asleep, Boy," she whispered, "it's pretty late."

"No, it's too quiet. We need to get back to William."

The group increased their pace, passed out of the estate and headed towards the river. They reached the bank and stopped.

"I can't bring my jar and me!" Anna said, pulling on Violet's sleeve. "I need my two hands to cross the bridge."

"It's okay," Violet said, pointing to the hammock Jack was carrying. "That's why we brought that!"

Unfolding it, Jack got everyone to place their jars inside. Then with the help of some of the older orphans, he gathered the hammock back in carefully, like a net, and tied it at the top, making sure there was a long piece of rope free at the end.

Together they carried the precious package down to the river's edge. Then Boy, still a little wobbly, climbed across the wire footbridge and slid down the riverbank on the far side.

"Throw the rope over," he said, wading into the water.

Grabbing the piece of loose rope, Jack flung it across to Boy. The first time it didn't reach. He tried again and Boy almost lost his balance and fell into the running water. The third time it worked perfectly and Boy caught the rope and pulled the hammock full of jars across the water to the other bank.

Then Jack crossed the footbridge and ran down to help Boy haul out the package. Violet was the last to cross the river into No-Man's-Land and Boy greeted her on the other side.

"That was clever!" he said.

"I know, I'm a genius," she joked, picking out her mother's imagination jar. "I think we can do this!"

A dark mood had settled over No-Man's-Land. Curtains twitched behind dirty windows as they hurried by. The streets were eerily empty now the ban on going outside was in place and not a soul walked the town. Their excitement waned and a quiet fell over the group as they made their way to the Market Yard.

A figure stood alone shadowed by the branches of the Rag Tree as they approached.

"Boy! Violet! You made it!" William sounded relieved.

"What's happened?" Boy asked.

"Not here," he whispered, before marching quickly across Market Yard into the laneway on the far side.

Violet's heart was pounding as she followed. William stopped in a low doorway and ushered them all inside.

"Quick and quiet," he whispered.

Violet was the last of the group to enter and William hurried in behind her, peering round to check the street, before shutting the door.

They were standing in a fairy tale. Miniature wooden dolls, trucks and animals dotted the floor, while tiny flying machines, hot-air balloons, broom-riding witches and winged faeries hung from hooks in the beamed ceiling.

"Where are we?" she whispered.

"Merrill's toyshop." One of the orphans smiled. "It's the best place in No-Man's-Land!"

"What's happened?" Boy asked again, his voice urgent.

William glanced over at Merrill, who was sitting on a wooden stool by his tool-strewn workbench. Neither spoke.

"Please, tell us what's going on," Violet insisted.

Merrill drew in a breath. "The Archers know there's something up," he stated avoiding her eyes. "One of the No-Man's-Landers told the Watchers there's plans for a rebellion. They've shut down No-Man's-Land; no one is allowed out of their homes."

"We know about the ban," Violet replied.

"It's not just a ban," Merrill continued, "they've moved a lot of the Watchers into Perfect, and they're patrolling the streets on both sides of the wall."

"But why would a No-Man's-Lander tell on us?" Violet cried.

"They're afraid," William replied. "Fear does funny things to folk."

"But we have the imaginations. Everything's ready."

"I know, Violet," William replied. "But we don't stand a chance now. We needed to get into Perfect to give people back their imaginations. It was a hard task before but now it's impossible. Just being out of our homes like this is putting us in terrible danger."

"But it was never about changing *everyone* in Perfect," Boy pleaded. "We can still creep in and change one or two people and bring them back here. The No-Man's-Landers will see their families can be reunited, they'll be convinced our plan can work and join us."

"Yes, but we can't leave our homes, Boy!" William snapped. "The Watchers have been by here twice already. What we're doing now is highly dangerous! And even if we could manage to sneak into Perfect we'd be seen going from house to house. There are Watchers on patrol now at all times – day and night."

"Do the Archers know the whole plan?" Violet asked. "Do they know about the imaginations?"

"No," Merrill replied. "As far as my sources are aware, the Archers think the No-Man's-Landers are preparing to revolt, that we're going to try and storm Perfect. They've no idea about the ReImaginator or the tea."

"That's a good thing then," Violet said. "At least we still have a chance."

"A chance," William laughed. "We haven't a chance in hell, Violet!"

Merrill walked away defeated as William sat down on an undersized stool. Violet looked at Boy, then back at the jar in her hands. After all they'd done, everything seemed to be crashing down around them.

"This can't be it, Boy," she pleaded.

He didn't respond and, for the first time, looked a little lost.

She slumped down to the floor while her mother's imagination floated oblivious in the jar by her feet, casting a beautiful glow over her mucky shoes.

She'd never see her mam again. Rose would probably start a new family, a perfect one with Violet wiped from her memory. And her dad, she'd probably seen the last of him too. She'd be just like Boy, William, Macula and Iris. All alone.

Iris! Suddenly she sat upright.

"But we don't need to go to every house in Perfect to change people. We just need to go to one house and get the Perfectionists to come to us. Then we can give them back their imaginations!"

"Yes, Violet," Merrill said, "but we can't leave my house let alone get into Perfect without the Watchers seeing us!"

"But, William, your mother, Iris, lives just over the wall at the bottom of Archers' Avenue. I've hardly ever seen anyone down there," Violet said.

"That's true," Boy added, his face a little brighter. "That end of Archers' Avenue is always empty; I think the Perfectionists are afraid of Iris, they never go near her house."

"It doesn't look as perfect as the rest of the town through the rose-tinted glasses for some reason," Violet said. "It seems a bit run-down."

"I'm sure my brothers are trying to keep people away from Mam." William sighed. "They'd never harm her but isolation means she can't cause them much trouble, I imagine! I don't know how any of this is relevant though?"

"Don't you see? It'd be easy to get to her without anyone noticing," Violet continued, looking straight at William.

"Leave Iris out of this, Violet," he replied sharply.

"But I know she'll help. I met her and she's not like the others in Perfect. She's different. She's like one of us just living in there."

"Violet's right," Boy said, enthusiastically. "She's taken me in sometimes when the Watchers were chasing me. She can see us."

"No," William snapped. "I won't have it. I can't put her in danger."

As William walked away, Anna stood up from the sea of dismayed orphans huddled on Merrill's floor. She was holding her jar of yellowish gas aloft.

"Erm…if you're going to your old house, Mr Archer, can I come too?" she said, nervously. "My house is on your street and I want to give this to Mammy. Boy said if she gets her imagination back she'll remember me again."

William hesitated.

"Please, William," Violet begged.

"Twenty orphans, you two, myself and Merrill – and the ReImaginator – we're not exactly a discreet bunch. There's no way we'll get into Perfect even if it is only to Iris's," he said, more to himself than to the children.

"Yes, but like Boy said, we don't need to change twenty people, just one or two, that should be enough to convince the No-Man's-Landers. They'll join us then!"

"But how do you propose we get out the gate?" William asked.

"We don't." Violet smiled. "A proper No-Man's-Lander never uses the gate anyway! Isn't that right, Boy?"

"Yeah," Boy smiled back. "There's a blind spot on the wall just by Iris's house!"

"And what about getting through the streets here, Violet?" Merrill asked. "We can't leave our houses for fear a Watcher will come round the bend and catch us."

"You said the Watchers are expecting a rebellion in No-Man's-Land, Merrill?" Boy interrupted, looking straight at him.

"Yes." Merrill nodded.

"Well wasn't that a part of our plan anyway? We'll just have to give it to them a little earlier than expected!"

CHAPTER 31

THE REUNION

"We'll be fine," Jack piped up on behalf of the orphans. He was looking straight at William. "We know how to avoid the Watchers *and* how to get them worked up. I'll go back to the orphanage and get more recruits. I bet we can cause enough trouble between us to make the Watchers believe there really is an uprising!"

"I'd love to see their faces if they realized it was only an uprising of kids!" Violet smiled.

"We'll make it look like the No-Man's-Landers are plotting something; you know, we'll run up and down the streets carrying things, breaking windows, causing mayhem and stuff. We'll keep the Watchers busy at the far end of No-Man's-Land while you lot sneak over the wall to Iris's."

"And you think you'll be okay?" William asked, looking Jack in the eye.

"We'll be fine," he said, confidently. "We'll keep them distracted for as long as we can. It'll be fun!"

They all discussed the plan at length. It was decided the orphans would start causing trouble on the streets of No-Man's-Land first. Once the Watchers had their hands full, Boy, Violet, William, Merrill and two of the orphans, Anna and Billy Junior, would set off for Perfect.

As dawn was approaching, Jack led the rest of the orphans back to the orphanage to round up more volunteers and start their revolt.

William and Merrill readied the ReImaginator for its journey, covering it with a blanket while Boy packed a pillowcase with two specific imaginations and a protection of soft stuffing. Once ready, the group of six snuck from Merrill's toyshop.

Violet's heart pounded as they turned off the lane onto Forgotten Road. She kept checking over her shoulder, sure they'd be caught, but as Jack had promised the Watchers were busy at the other end of the town. Noise was gradually filling the streets of No-Man's-Land. She could hear glass breaking and doors banging in the distance.

She relaxed a little as they reached the run-down house that Boy used to access the rooftops of No-Man's-Land. They climbed the rickety stairs until they were all squashed inside the slime green bathroom.

"We've to go out there," Boy said, pointing to the window.

"Across the rooftops?" Merrill asked warily.

Boy nodded as William played with the latch on the window.

"It's not big enough to fit the machine through," he said, turning to the group. "We'll have to knock the window out."

Violet stood back, shielding the orphans, as Boy, William and Merrill began to push hard on the frame. Eventually the wood splintered and cracked until it finally gave way under their assault.

Boy climbed out first, followed by William. Then Merrill gently guided the ReImaginator to them as they waited on the slates. He then climbed out to join them. Violet helped the orphans out and, on Boy's instructions they all clambered across the rooftops to the wall.

Boy quickly grabbed the rope, wrapped it round the pillowcase of jars and lowered them down the wall to the ground, then he nimbly jumped over the edge and climbed down. He untied the pillowcase and threw the rope back up so Violet and the two orphans could descend.

Once they were down, William and Merrill lifted the ReImaginator, secured it with the rope and slowly lowered the machine to the ground. Boy and Violet guided it to safety. Lastly, Merrill then William lowered themselves down.

All a little shaky, they rested by the wall for a moment before checking the coast was clear. Then they headed up Archers' Avenue to Iris's house.

Even in the dim dawn light it was easy to tell William was nervous. Setting down the machine, he turned his back to the group and walked to the door. The others hid in the early morning shadows by the wall. His hand shook as he raised it to knock on the painted wood.

Violet's stomach fluttered but nothing happened. William waited for a while then knocked again. The click of the latch was magnified in the quiet of the street. Light fell out onto the cobbled road and William's face was illuminated by the opened door.

A tiny heart-wrenching yelp flew from Iris and her son's tense stance softened in the swiftness of his mother's embrace. Violet's eyes filled with tears.

Iris Archer held her son for what seemed an eternity. The others eyed the road nervously hoping the Watchers would not patrol by.

"Mam," William said, eventually stepping back. "We need your help!"

"Oh, I knew something was brewing, William." Iris smiled and invited her ragged guests inside.

Surprisingly she greeted them all by name. Maybe Iris

wasn't as mad as everyone said.

"I knew you'd do something, Violet." The old woman winked, pouring her a glass of water. "I saw it in your eyes; you have a touch of mischief about you."

Violet smiled, taking the comment as a compliment.

"I want to thank all of you," Iris said, grabbing her son's hand, "for bringing William back to me."

"I'm so sorry, Mam," William stuttered, still shaken. "I should have come to see you sooner but I couldn't…"

"I know," Iris replied softly.

The room fell into a sombre silence.

"I knew you'd come back one day," the old woman spoke again, breaking the quiet. "You have the fight. A spirit can be dulled but it never fully dies."

"They have Macula," William blurted as though he couldn't hold onto the words. "They told me she was dead and it almost killed me. I couldn't bear to try and be happy again so I gave up the fight. I'm so sorry, Mam, I should have come to you. I just thought it'd be better for everyone if I stayed away."

"It's okay, William, you're back now. That's all that matters."

Iris looked out past the faces at her table into a place only she could go.

"So they took Macula," she said, moments later. "I wondered about that. They robbed my life from me –

those terrible two. I saw a little of it in them when they were young. They took after their father, but who can predict this of their sons?" She looked into William's eyes. "When you disappeared and then Macula soon after, George and Edward told me you'd both died. I tried not to believe them. I didn't feel it here, you see," she said, pointing to her heart, "but part of me died too after that." She looked down at her hands clasped tightly round a glass of water, the white of her knuckles showing strain. "I live outside your brothers' rules here, they allow me that much. I don't wear their glasses or drink their tea. Sometimes I think it might be easier if they took my imagination, at least then I wouldn't have to live with this guilt."

She looked down, ashamed.

"What guilt, Mam? This is not your fault!" William said, concerned.

"It is my fault, William. What George and Edward became, it's all my fault. I loved you too much. I protected you too fiercely when you were young. I had to but it made them jealous. It was hard on your brothers. I'm a bad mother…"

"No, you're a great mother," William said, reaching for Iris's hand and squeezing it.

They sat together in silence. Violet looked at Boy. Somehow it felt wrong to be there.

"We can stop them, Mam, that's why we're here," William continued. "We can change Perfect. We can take back our town." He pulled the blanket from the ReImaginator. "This will give people back their imaginations, Mam."

Iris stood up and she seemed stronger, like she'd come back to herself. She walked slowly around the machine asking questions of her son, questions Violet found impossible to understand. It was easy to see where the Archers got their brains.

"I used to think she was a bit loony," Violet whispered to Boy.

"You get away with a lot when people think you're mad, Violet." Iris winked.

Boy laughed as Violet blushed a deep red.

Once Iris had fully inspected the machine, they began to fill her in on their plan.

"We have Billy Bobbins' and Madeleine Nunn's imaginations here," Boy said, passing the jars to Iris to inspect. "They live at the top of this street."

"I live two doors from Billy," Anna said, stepping forward. "Well, I mean my mam does...I used to..."

"I remember you, pet," Iris replied, pulling the little girl onto her knee. "Anna Nunn. They took you about a year ago, didn't they?"

The girl nodded and began to cry.

"We're hoping their families will be able to see them now," Violet said. "We put William's potion into the Archers' tea. Everyone will be drinking it this morning and if it works, they'll be able to see again. They won't recognize No-Man's-Landers straight away, though, not until we give them back their imaginations."

"Then Mam will know me; you promised," Anna said, looking straight at Boy.

"Can you bring Madeleine and Billy here?" William asked Iris. "Then we can zap them with the ReImaginator. They'll recognize their children, they'll believe us and—"

"Join the revolution." Iris smiled.

"Exactly," William replied. "Then we'll bring them to No-Man's-Land to convince the people there and build an army."

"I'll try my best," Iris said, "but people around here think I'm mad. I haven't spoken to either of them in as long as I can remember. I can't see how they'll follow me."

"Tell them that Edward and George want to meet them," Boy said suddenly. "I bet they'll come here for that, everybody loves the Archers. And people in Perfect believe anything you tell them."

They discussed the plan as Iris made everyone breakfast. When it was decided sufficient time had passed for all of Perfect to have consumed their first brew of the new tea, Iris left her home on a mission.

"Make sure they take off their glasses, Mam," William called after her, "that way they'll be able to see us when they come in!"

William and Merrill lifted the ReImaginator so it sat on the table in the centre of the room. Boy and Violet took the jars and, gently opening the lids, eased the contents into the glass box in the middle of William's machine. The imaginations floated through the space and swirled together.

"Won't they get mixed up?" Violet asked, pulling on William's shirtsleeve.

"No, Violet. Look." He smiled, pointing at the glass. The imaginations had settled one on top of the other, like oil and water. "No two people think alike."

Suddenly there were voices in the street outside.

"Really? They want to speak to us?" a man said, obviously delighted.

"I knew Edward loved my Victoria sponge at the children's cake sale," a woman was saying. "I saw it on his face. He won't mind me calling him Edward, will he, now that we're friends?"

"No, of course not, Madeleine," Iris replied. "Now I must ask you both to take off your glasses inside my home, they don't go with the decor, you see."

"Oh," Madeleine said, "but we won't be able to see."

"Nonsense." Iris sighed. "Didn't you hear the wonderful news? That new doctor has fixed the problem with Perfect, everyone can see again without their specs."

"Oh wonderful." Madeleine smiled. "I knew he'd do great things. His wife is a gem."

"Lovely lady," Billy said, nodding his head.

The pair removed their glasses as Iris turned the key.

"Oh, you have guests," Billy said, looking around her kitchen.

"Oh yes…they are—"

"Daddy…" Billy Junior cried, running towards Billy.

Boy grabbed his shirt pulling him back and held on tightly to the struggling seven year old.

"We're, erm…Iris's cousins," William said, quickly covering the situation.

"Oh, how nice," Madeleine replied. "Where are you visiting from?"

"Timbuktu," Violet piped up.

"Don't I know you, dear?" Madeleine said, looking at Violet.

"Oh no, I look like lots of people. One of those faces—"

"I've heard Timbuktu is lovely," Billy interrupted.

"Would anyone like tea?" Iris asked, switching on the kettle.

"Oh, I'd love some, Iris," Madeleine replied. "Ours just isn't tasting the same this morning."

Boy winked at Violet.

"So where are Mr and Mr Archer?" Billy asked, looking about the room.

"Oh, they…erm…they're upstairs. They'll be down in a minute," William responded. "While we wait, would you mind terribly if we took a family portrait? It's for our holiday snaps; the kids are growing so quickly."

"Of course," Madeleine replied. "I know what that's like. My youngest is almost eight."

"No I'm not, that's my sister. I'm only six," Anna sniffled in the corner.

"Oh, you're just a little younger than mine then." Madeleine smiled.

"Okay, Billy, you sit here and Madeleine you here," William said, placing their chairs just in front of the ReImaginator.

"But we're not part of your family," Billy replied.

"Oh you are, we're all cousins. How could you forget our family reunion in Timbuktu?" Violet smiled.

"But I've never been to Timbuktu," Madeleine replied, taking a seat in front of the machine.

"Yes you have," Violet continued, "don't you remember? We went swimming with the turtles and you said you thought they were lovely and then we went for a drive on the beach and we saw a giant elephant and you said…"

Boy dug Violet with his elbow to stop her rambling. "You don't need to make up such a big story," he whispered.

"Maybe I do remember," Madeleine piped up, looking curiously at Violet. "I do love turtles…"

"So do I," Violet said, "see, we *are* cousins!"

"That's a funny-looking camera," Billy said.

"It's the latest thing," Boy replied. "Everyone has them in Timbuktu!"

"Right," William said loudly. "Everybody say 'cheese'!"

He pulled the cord on the ReImaginator and the machine sprang to life. Each of the bagpipe lungs began inflating and deflating at great speed. Suddenly the two imaginations were sucked from the glass centre into separate pipes. The machine pulled in its lungs as if taking a deep breath and, with an almighty sound, like a huge sneeze, spat out the imaginations.

The greenish one flew to Billy Bobbins' nose and the brownish one to Madeleine Nunn's. The pair sat frozen in terror, as the separate strains of coloured gas shot up their nostrils. Immediately, their eyes shut and their heads fell forward. Billy slipped right down onto the floor while Madeleine slumped to the side, resting her head on the table.

"Will Mam be okay?" Anna stuttered grabbing Violet's hand.

Suddenly, both Madeleine and Billy began to snore.

"What's happening?" Violet asked William, trying not to sound anxious.

"I'm not entirely sure, Violet," he answered with a smile. "I've never been able to test the machine properly before with real subjects. But I trust the science. Billy and Madeleine are simply readjusting. The imagination is at its strongest when we're asleep. That's why dreams are so real. Their brains are simply rebooting. It's a wondrous thing, the human body."

The snoring stopped as quickly as it had started and both Billy and Madeleine suddenly opened their eyes.

"Where am I?" Madeleine asked, sitting upright. "What happened?"

"Mam," Anna said, jumping from her seat and running to her mother's side.

"Anna? Anna, is that you?" Madeleine cried, wrapping the little girl up in her arms. "I thought, I thought… I don't know what I thought…"

Billy's son threw himself onto his father's groggy body and they shared a tearful embrace.

After a while William helped Billy up from the floor and everyone came together round the kitchen table. Both Madeleine and Billy had a world of questions.

"So it was the tea, that stuff I fed my family every day and night that made us blind?" Madeleine cried, hugging her daughter close.

"And these things, these glasses robbed our minds," Billy said, about to crush his in his palm.

"Oh, I wouldn't do that, Billy," William said, looking at his fist. "You may need those to blend in, the Watchers might notice if they see you without them."

"So, everything, *everything* we've believed for years has been a lie?" Billy stood up from the table.

William nodded and filled them in on all that had really been happening in their town. Their anger towards the Archer twins was obvious and it didn't take much to convince them both to come on board.

"So what do you need us to do?" Madeleine asked.

"Well we're trying to build an army," William said. "We need you to come with us to No-Man's-Land and show everyone that our plan works. If they know there's a way to get their families back, the people of No-Man's-Land will fight."

"And what about the Perfectionists?" Billy asked. "The more of us you can change here, the more people you'll have on your side, right?"

William looked at Boy and Violet, then over at Merrill.

"We could bring some more imaginations and change people here in Iris's," Boy said.

"Yes, it is working well," William replied, more to himself than anyone, "so maybe we should just keep going, as long as we don't arouse suspicion."

"I could get more people to come here," Madeleine spoke up. "I'm on almost every committee in town; I know everyone. The Watchers won't suspect a thing if I'm seen socializing on our streets. Some days all I ever do is drink tea and gossip!"

"And I'll go over to No-Man's-Land if you can arrange a meeting," Billy added. At least some of the No-Man's-Landers will know me and they'll see my story is true. I'm sure I can convince people to join the uprising."

"Sounds like a plan," Boy said. "I'll take you into No-Man's-Land then I'll come back here with some more orphans and their jars."

"I'm coming with you, Boy," Violet said. "I'm not standing around here doing nothing."

Merrill looked at Billy. "I'll go too. I'll be your best shot for setting up the meeting. The No-Man's-Landers think the rest of you are mad!" He laughed glancing around at his companions.

"Maybe we should start getting the rest of the imaginations from the twins' storeroom too," William added. "Can you organize some orphans to do that, Boy? Just so they're safe. If my brothers get wind of our plot they'll hide them all and we might never find the imaginations again."

Boy nodded.

Lunchtime was approaching as Madeleine Nunn left Iris Archer's house heading for Edward Street. Boy, Violet, Merrill, Billy and his son left too, heading for the wall into No-Man's-Land. Each had a task to do.

William, Iris and Anna remained behind. Anna sat on Iris's knee and as the old lady told her stories of Adequate, the town that used to be, William beat an incessant path to the window watching the avenue for signs of trouble.

CHAPTER 32

THE GIVEAWAY

"I can't believe I didn't know about this place. To think that my son was in here and I was living just a few metres away!" Billy gestured back across the rooftops to Perfect.

"It's okay, Dad," Billy Junior soothed. "Loads of parents forgot about their kids. There are lots of orphans in No-Man's-Land!"

The group slipped in through the bathroom window and headed downstairs. Distant noise reached them from the far side of No-Man's-Land. They waited hidden in the entrance of the house as a patrol of Watchers sprinted by heading in the direction of the sound. It seemed the orphans were still causing trouble.

When the coast was clear, Merrill led them quickly

through the streets back to his toyshop, beckoning them all inside. Boy ran towards the jars of imaginations, which were hidden under Merrill's stairs and with Violet's help found the four he was looking for.

"I have to go to the orphanage and tell Jack to send a group to the Archers' storeroom for the rest of the imaginations," he said, as he headed towards the door, his pillowcase bulging with glass jars and stuffing.

"I'll go with you."

"No, Violet." Boy shook his head. "You need to stay here in case anyone has questions about what we've done. You help Merrill."

"Okay, if you're sure." Violet nodded, though she didn't want to.

"I'll be fine, I promise," he said again before opening the door and disappearing into No-Man's-Land.

"Right," Merrill piped up, heading to the door in the wake of Boy's footsteps, "I'm going to make some house calls, see if I can't round up a few people who'll listen to you, Billy."

Billy nodded but didn't reply. He was sitting quietly with his son on his knee as if afraid to let him go. He hadn't spoken much since he'd gotten his imagination back and, as Merrill left, Violet searched for things to say.

"Are you okay? Do you need water or anything?" she asked to break the silence.

"How could I have let this happen?" Billy whispered, more to himself than to her.

Violet didn't know what to say and they slipped into an uneasy quiet.

"I don't blame her – my mam that is," Violet said, a while later, "it's not her fault. The Archers did this; it's them I blame."

"Thanks." Billy smiled just as the door swung open and Merrill walked in followed by a group of about ten people.

"There's not many here?" Violet whispered as Merrill joined her at the top of the room.

"Word travels fast," he replied. "If they believe Billy, it'll be around No-Man's-Land in a shot!"

Merrill put his hands up to call for attention.

"This is Billy Bobbins," he began, addressing the group, "and his son Billy Junior. Until a few hours ago one had lived as an orphan in No-Man's-Land while the other, in Perfect, had forgotten that his son even existed."

Billy bowed his head in shame and Violet winced at Merrill's choice of words. Eventually, a red-faced Billy looked up at the small crowd of people.

"I'm sorry," he said, there were tears in his eyes. "I'm sorry I didn't know, I'm sorry I deserted you all!"

"Are you telling us you're a Perfectionist?" the red-bearded man from the previous meeting shouted up from the back.

"Yes he is, that's exactly what he's saying, Sam," Merrill responded.

"I didn't ask you, Merrill," the man snapped. "I'm asking this fella. How do we know he's not lying to us all?"

"He's not lying," a woman said, stepping out from the crowd.

Billy stood with his mouth open as the dark-haired lady rushed forward, wrapping him in an embrace.

"Lucy, I didn't... I had no idea you were here," he sobbed. "I'm so sorry, I'm so sorry, Lucy!"

"It's okay Billy," she cried. "It's okay. I never believed this day would come. I'm just so happy you're here."

"Lucy?" Sam spoke again and all eyes turned towards him. "Who is this man, what's going on?"

"I wasn't sure I believed Merrill when he called to the door but I had to see him with my own eyes," she said, tears streaming down her face. "Billy is my brother."

Everyone fell silent and the pair embraced again, then as Billy spoke to the room once more, Lucy held firm to his hand.

"I want to explain but everything is so vague, I'm not sure I can. It's not that I meant to forget my son or my sister," he said, squeezing her hand. "It's like I didn't know I had them. But now I've found them again, it's as if they were never gone. I've been in a bubble but I can only see that now it's burst. This all sounds so strange, but I hope you can try to understand what has happened to your families. It's not that they don't care, it's not that they've forgotten you, it's far worse than that. The Archers, those twins," he spat, his face red to bursting, "they have a lot to answer for. They will never do this again!"

"I didn't even know your son was here," Lucy sobbed.

"He can't have been born when you were taken, Lucy," Billy said, hugging her once more. "We've got so much catching up to do."

"So it's real," Sam said, looking shocked and confused. "William's plans are working. All that stuff he talked about – the tea and his imagination machine – it's all true?" He looked round the crowd, a smile forming on his face. "We could get our families back?"

"Yes, Sam, and more – we could get our town back too!" Merrill said excitedly, standing up on his workbench. "Who's with us?"

"I'm in," Sam shouted.

"So am I." Another man stepped forward. "Now what can we do?"

As Merrill relayed the plan, telling the No-Man's-Landers to convince everyone they knew, Violet slipped cautiously out of the toyshop and back into Perfect. She was still on a high from the atmosphere in the room as she climbed down the wall and banged on Iris's door.

Boy was already in the kitchen with four more orphans who were newly reunited with their parents. Everyone was hugging and the tears flowed.

"It's working," she whispered, reaching Boy's side.

"I know, isn't it great?" he said, smiling at the scene in front of him.

"Not that. I mean Billy and his story. They believe him. We're building an army!"

"Really? You serious?" Boy smiled, wrapping his friend in a hug so tight that Violet could barely breathe.

"What is it, Violet?" William asked, only just noticing her arrival.

"Billy Bobbins, his story is working," she said, loud enough for the whole room to hear. "We're building an army in No-Man's-Land."

Everyone cheered and for the first time in ages Violet felt as if things were actually starting to happen, their plans were coming together at last.

"How many do we have?" William asked.

"Not many so far but Merrill says the news will spread."

"If we send more of the changed Perfectionists over it'll convince people faster. Will you take this group to No-Man's-Land, Boy, and bring some more imaginations back here? We're on a roll, so let's keep going!"

"How many imaginations?" Boy asked.

"The machine can take up to eight at a time. Can you round up eight more orphans and give the list of names to Madeleine so she can get their parents here while you're gone?"

"Okay." Boy nodded, sitting down to write eight more names on a piece of paper.

"Eight? Are you sure that number of people won't be noticed coming and going from here?" Madeleine said, her face looking doubtful.

"It'll be fine, Madeleine," William replied. "You're doing a brilliant job. No one will suspect you."

"Only if you're sure," she said, taking the scrap of paper from Boy's hand.

William nodded and Boy left the house with the four newly changed Perfectionists and headed for No-Man's-Land.

Madeleine left a little later and Violet was just dozing off, her head on the kitchen table, when she noticed the blonde-haired woman racing back by the window.

"I was nearly caught!" Madeleine cried, bursting in through the front door. "I'm so sorry I forgot the rules and I nodded at the Watchers."

"You did what?" William said, standing up from his seat.

"I'm sorry, William. I was so nervous about bringing that many people back that I completely forgot I wasn't meant to see the Watchers!"

"Slow down, Madeleine. What exactly happened?" William asked, pulling out a chair for her.

"Well, I was walking past a group of Watchers patrolling on Edward Street…"

"And?" William said, trying to speed up her story.

"…And well, I was just minding my own business when out of the corner of my glasses I saw one of them look up at me. I caught his eye and I nodded. I don't know why I did it. I'm so sorry."

"You're not supposed to be able to see them! Did he say anything?" Violet asked sitting upright.

"I know that, Violet!" Madeleine snapped. "I think I covered it up though. I just kept going and pretended nothing had happened."

"Did they follow you?" Iris asked.

"Well, I'm not—"

Madeleine was interrupted by a loud hammering on the front door. Every soul in the room stopped breathing. Iris Archer immediately shot up from the table beckoning everyone to hide.

Violet, William, Madeleine and Anna pushed the ReImaginator into the back room and watched through a crack in the door as Iris went to answer the knocking.

"You see, Iris, me dear, she nodded at me she did. Then pretended she hadn't seen me! How stupid does she think I am," a Watcher snarled barging past Iris into the house.

"I don't know what you mean. What are you talking about?" Iris asked, stepping away from the door as more Watchers filed inside. "It's just me here, on me own, like always. Just the walls to talk to. You want tea? I like visitors; I haven't had anyone to talk to in as long as my memory serves me."

"Come on now, don't play the fool, Iris Archer. We followed her here," the Watcher growled, grabbing her neck and forcing her frail body up against the white-washed wall. "We all know you're not as stupid as you look. I'm not neithers!"

"I'm *not* stupid?" Iris smiled. "Well that's a nice surprise."

William, his face red with anger, signalled for the others to leave. He lifted the ReImaginator through the back door and outside into the garden.

"Lads, search the house," the Watcher said.

Bangs and clatters rang from the rooms as the group huddled under the window outside hoping the Watchers wouldn't venture into the garden.

"What are you up to, Iris Archer?" the Watcher growled, rejoining her in the kitchen.

"I expect you found what you were looking for?" she asked her tone mocking.

Violet couldn't understand how she stayed so calm.

"Don't you be cheeky with me! Doesn't mean there's

nothing to be found, old woman. We'll get it out of ya, you're coming with us!" he snarled.

A chair scraped across the kitchen floor and William looked as if he was about to burst in through the back door. Madeleine grabbed his arm, holding him still.

"Don't hurt her, lads, this one's precious to the Archers. We'll see what George and Edward have to say." The Watcher's voice faded into the distance as the front door banged shut.

"What'll happen to Iris?" Violet panicked.

William shook his head.

"My brothers won't hurt her, I know that much, but we need to get back to No-Man's-Land and fast!"

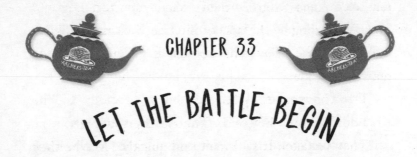

CHAPTER 33

LET THE BATTLE BEGIN

William and his ReImaginator, Violet, Madeleine and Anna hid in the entrance hall of the tall building that acted as their access into No-Man's-Land. They watched Forgotten Road in wonder as Watchers filed out through the arch heading towards the gateway into Perfect.

"They're leaving," Violet whispered. "What's going on?"

"We need to get to Merrill's," William replied.

They waited for the last of the Watchers to go, then quickly ran for the lane and down towards Merrill's. The shop was empty.

Voices were coming from the Market Yard and they ran quietly towards them. A small group of adults and loads of orphans were gathered round the Rag Tree.

Madeleine recognized some people in the crowd and ran with Anna to greet them. Violet spotted Boy and Merrill standing by the base of the tree, looking confused.

"You're here," Boy said, relieved, as Violet and William reached his side.

"What happened?" William asked.

"I don't know," Boy said. "The Watchers just left."

"They've taken Iris," Violet said quickly. "Maybe they know what we're up to?"

"But why would they leave No-Man's-Land?" Boy asked, shaking his head.

"The people of No-Man's-Land are saying they ran them out," Merrill spoke slowly.

"You don't sound like you believe them, Merrill?" William asked.

The toymaker shook his head. "Some people did join the orphans in the fight, but not enough to threaten the Watchers. We still need to convince the rest of No-Man's-Land to rise up. The Watchers may just be heading to Perfect to get reinforcements."

"I'll go into Perfect to have a look," Boy said, "and see if I can find out what's going on. Maybe we did scare them off! I won't be long."

"I'm coming with you this time," Violet said.

"Okay," William piped up. "We'll continue with the plan here and gather more support!"

Boy and Violet left William and Merrill to recruit by the Rag Tree and headed towards Forgotten Road. The gateway into Perfect hung open, the gatekeeper nowhere to be seen, so the pair slipped through unnoticed.

Darkness was falling on Perfect once more as they snuck along Rag Lane, onto Archers' Avenue then up Edward Street. The town was empty; all the Perfectionists were inside their homes.

Keeping to the shadows they ran past the Town Hall, stopping suddenly a little back from the Archers' Emporium.

A huge crowd of Watchers congregated on the street, filling it from one side to the other. Edward Archer was addressing them from the steps outside the shop door. George was just behind him, holding his mother tightly by the arm. Iris looked solemn and stern.

Violet gulped. There were so many Watchers, at least two hundred; far more than she'd ever imagined.

"The No-Man's-Landers are making fools out of you," Edward shouted angrily, "Do you realize how stupid you look! I want all units inside No-Man's-Land. Anyone who is caught on the streets is punished by any means, the more painful the better. They will remember this treachery for decades and never stand against us again! We've been too lenient on them. We will squash them tonight! Do you understand me?"

A deep roar rang out through the streets, then a few of the Watchers stepped from the crowd and began to bark orders, dividing the men up into smaller groups.

"What are they doing?" Violet whispered.

"Getting ready to invade No-Man's-Land properly," Boy replied. "We have to tell William now."

Violet tried not to panic as the pair sprinted back down Rag Lane and through the unmanned gate into No-Man's-Land.

In the Market Yard, the six changed Perfectionists were addressing a much bigger crowd, William and Merrill at their side. It seemed all of No-Man's-Land had taken to the streets. People who once rubbished their plans brandished all sorts of tools and readied to invade Perfect.

William spotted Violet and Boy and ran to meet them.

"It's happening." He smiled. "It's really happening. No-Man's-Land is rising—"

"The Watchers. They're coming now!" Boy gasped, trying to catch his breath.

"How many of them?" William asked, his tone suddenly deadly serious.

"Lots, more than we thought," Violet replied. "At least two hundred, more than us by far. Half of our army is my age!"

"I don't know if we can beat them," Boy continued. "Not yet. We need to change more people in Perfect."

"We can change more Perfectionists, I know we can!" Violet said urgently.

"How?" William asked. "The Watchers are coming. We've changed as many people as we can. Look around you, No-Man's-Land is ready to fight, our plan has worked! We've got to face my brothers. There's no more time left."

"What if we can do both?" Violet said. "Like we'd planned. But it means we'd have to face the Watchers out there in Perfect, on Edward Street, catch them before they come back to No-Man's-Land," she said, thinking on her feet. "While the Watchers are distracted fighting the No-Man's-Landers, we can take the orphans and the rest of the imaginations and change as many Perfectionists as we can. All we have to do is get them to their doorsteps and zap them with the ReImaginator. Someone can run around taking off their glasses as they sleep. Then, when they wake up and see what's happening, they'll join their families and fight."

"Brilliant, Violet! There's no time to lose," Boy said urgently. "The Watchers are on their way – we have to move everyone out of No-Man's-Land now!"

Night was setting in and an energy unlike anything Violet had ever felt filled the cool air as William Archer and his makeshift army strode down Forgotten Road. The people of No-Man's-Land had a chance, more than a chance to get back their lives.

As they approached the lane that led to Perfect, William mounted the steps and turned to address the crowd.

"This is it," he said. "When we get through the gate keep moving, we want to hold the Watchers at the Archers' Emporium end of Edward Street for as long as possible to give our young friends time and space to work unseen. They will change Perfectionists on their doorsteps and when our friends and family wake into their new reality they will join the fight, I know they will."

There were tears in the crowd as the No-Man's-Landers stood proudly, shoulder to shoulder.

"Use your pain," William shouted, "don't let these years of exile mean nothing. We will take Perfect tonight – take back our homes, our families and our pride. If this is the last thing we ever do, know that we fought hard and true for the right to be different, as free men and women, not for one, but for everyone."

The crowd let out a deep and earthy roar filled with passion. Violet looked at Boy, tears rimming her eyes.

"For you," she whispered.

"No, for them," he said, looking around at the small faces of his friends, holding firm to jars of colour. "They've lived too long without their families."

Violet glanced back up at William standing tall on the steps. "For all of us." She smiled.

Boy squeezed her hand and closed his eyes. When he opened them again his expression had changed; it was hard, determined.

William turned towards the open gate into Perfect, held up his arm and roared. Head down he raced for the exit. Behind him were the men and women of No-Man's-Land bearing axes, shovels, hatchets and pitchforks.

A group of Watchers approaching from the other side, too slow to react, were the first victims of the battle.

Violet turned to address her crew. They were the last remaining on Forgotten Road. Everyone held a jar and Madeleine was shakily trying to organize them into some kind of order.

"This group is first," she said, pointing to a row of orphans. "The owners of those jars all live near each other down the very end of Edward Street so we'll be well away from the battle as we change them and shouldn't be seen."

"We have to go," Boy interrupted, racing back through the gate. "Now!"

He ran to help Jack lift the ReImaginator and headed out towards Archers' Avenue.

Everything was happening so fast. Injured Watchers lay groaning at the side of Rag Lane and Violet winced as she stepped round a few in her path.

Boy had stopped at the top of Archers' Avenue and was peering around the corner onto Edward Street.

"What's going on?" Violet asked as they came to a halt behind him.

"It looks like a stand-off near the Town Hall. The No-Man's-Landers and the Watchers are facing each other," he whispered over his shoulder.

"Let me have a look," Violet said, pushing up beside him.

She could just see Edward Archer's head over the crowd. He was standing on a bench by the side of the Town Hall facing William's army. George lurked behind him backed up by a wall of Watchers.

"William, it's been a long time," Edward shouted. "We were just about to go meet you and your friends; isn't that a coincidence after all these years!"

"I'm sure you've missed me, Ed." William smiled.

"Not that much," Edward replied. "You and your pathetic army will regret this reunion, brother. Though I have to say I do admire your spirit."

As all eyes watched the brothers, not a soul paid heed to the band of children that snuck out of Archers' Avenue down to the opposite end of Edward Street.

They stopped near the bookshop and, quickly, Violet poured eight imaginations into the central glass canister of the ReImaginator.

"You have Macula!" William shouted angrily at his brother.

Edward looked at George. The taller twin snarled.

"Yes, George," William said. "I know about her and all this time you made me believe she was dead. You made us all believe we were dead."

"You might as well be," George spat.

The crowd behind William hissed and shouted, swelling forward. Alerted by the sound of Edward's voice, some Perfectionists began opening their front doors.

"We have an audience." William smiled.

"That lot?" Edward laughed.

"Don't underestimate your citizens, brother," William warned.

"That lot will do as I tell them!" Edward snorted. "So what's this rebellion all about? Want more food, do you? Or an hour or two of daylight?"

"Well, we'll certainly be needing more food." William smiled signalling to his army.

The first line of No-Man's-Landers stood aside and five changed Perfectionists walked forward, took off their rose-tinted glasses, dropped them on the ground and crushed them under their feet.

"You robbed years from us and ripped our families apart," Billy roared. "You won't take anything more from me. I'll die winning back these streets if I have to!"

Edward's face dropped and he looked back at George. The taller brother moved forward towards the No-Man's-Landers, his fists clenched. The Watchers were looking at each other now too and a murmur ran through their ranks.

"Billy Bobbins," Edward called, silencing the crowd. "Seems we didn't mush your brains altogether, you hadn't many to begin with, I would have thought it an easy job."

"You—"

One of the other changed Perfectionists grabbed Billy's arm, holding him back.

"Your rebellion has gotten a little out of hand, I'll give you that," Edward said, composing himself to address his younger brother, "so you kidnapped a few Perfectionists and told them what to say. Do you think that's scaring me? Go back home, take those fools with you and we'll forget this ever happened."

"Fools," Billy spat, "I may have been your fool for years, but I'm not anymore, Edward. You'll never control me or my family again, I'll see to that."

"Oh. He can think for himself! Seems our Hollower is not working as well as it should," Edward continued. "After we sort this little rebellion we'll fix the problem. Thanks for bringing it to our attention, Billy."

"You might have a bigger problem than you think

Edward." William smiled. "Have you checked your imagination stores yet? I think they've run a little low."

Edward turned to George once more, his face red with fury.

"You think you're so clever, William, you were always the same. Lording over us with all your friends and your popularity; breaking all the rules. Well you won't do it now, this is our world, these are our rules and you'll play by them. I don't know how you got those Perfectionists to say what they did, but I don't care. Soon nobody in this town will need glasses, we'll fix their eyes perfectly, permanently, and there'll be nothing you or anyone can do about it!"

As William argued with his brothers at one end of Edward Street, Perfectionists were falling asleep all over the place at the other.

Madeleine ran to the next house on her list and knocked on the door. A man answered and quickly she grabbed his glasses.

"Larry Doyle," she called over her shoulder racing ahead to the next house.

Boy, who was standing poised with the ReImaginator, pressed a button and a shot of purple gas flew from the machine up the unsuspecting man's nose. He collapsed to the ground asleep, joining the others who lay strewn all over the street.

Boy stepped round Larry's unconscious body and raced after Madeleine to his next target.

"Ellen Smoulds," Madeleine called, speedily removing the woman's glasses.

Ellen looked around confused and eyeing the sea of sleeping bodies, screamed.

"They're killing us! They're killing us!"

All eyes, Edward's and George's included, turned towards the bloody sound. Violet froze.

"What is going on?" Edward roared.

"You're not as clever as you think, boys," William said. "If you happened to ever drink your own tea, you'd have noticed it's tasting a little different today!"

"They're killing us, Mr Archer, down the bottom of the street!" Ellen Smoulds called, racing frantically through the crowd.

Edward looked around, confused. George raced from behind his brother towards the No-Man's-Landers followed by a stream of Watchers.

"Attack!" William cried, advancing forward.

The army of ragged No-Man's-Landers charged, following their fearless leader. Their years of imprisonment burned in their eyes, adding strength to their bones.

The battle had begun.

Cries and roars rose above the street as William's army threw all they had at the Watchers. Pitchforks, shovels, even planks of wood served as weapons as Violet, Boy, Jack, Madeleine and the orphans danced through the battle to change more Perfectionists.

The unchanged were not hard to spot, the only ones standing still, open-mouthed amid the chaos. Violet ran straight for a woman Madeleine had told her about just metres away.

"Sinead Cribits," she roared, pointing at the lady.

"I have her, I have her!" one of the orphans shouted, running forward to fill the ReImaginator with murky gas from his jar.

Within seconds, Boy pushed the button and Sinead was unconscious, asleep amongst the mayhem.

Violet fought her way through the sea of battling bodies to point out another Perfectionist. The jars of imagination were dwindling. Their plan was working.

One by one, the sleeping Perfectionists woke and pulled themselves from the ground to find out what was going on and join the No-Man's-Landers in battle.

Violet was just pointing at another stunned onlooker when Boy yelped and collapsed to the ground. George Archer loomed over him.

"Think you'll take Perfect?" He gave a grisly smile, a golf club hanging loosely by his side. "Not without this stupid machine you won't!" The tall twin took a swing at the ReImaginator and glass flew through the air in all directions.

Boy dragged himself furiously off the ground and jumped onto George's back, beating him with his fists. It was too late. William Archer's machine was smashed to smithereens.

George Archer wrenched Boy over his shoulder and dropped him onto the road. "You!" he spat. "You've been the bane of this place from the beginning."

He raised the golf club above his head as Boy struggled onto his feet. George brought the metal stick down with speed, smashing it against Boy's shoulder. Violet's friend roared, collapsing onto the tarmac.

"No!" she screamed, running blindly towards the giant.

Anger pulsed in her veins; she bared her teeth and bit deep into George Archer's hand. He wailed and dropped his weapon. "You vermin!"

He grabbed Violet by the hair and pulled her close enough to smell his stinking breath. "I'm going to make you watch while I pulverize his little head."

Violet squirmed, kicking wildly at George's gangly legs as he bent to pick up his club.

"Who knew my golf skills would come in so useful? Even with one hand I have a great swing." He smiled as Boy lay groaning. Violet wriggled trying to free herself from his grasp. "I've often thought it'd be much more fun if the golf ball screamed when you hit it!"

Violet shrieked as the club crashed towards Boy's head.

Suddenly she was pushed sideways and fell, hitting the ground with a painful thud. Boy was on the road a little away struggling to his feet. She hurried across to him.

"What happened?" he gasped. "I thought George would kill me for sure. I thought I was dead."

"It's William!" Violet pointed. "He saved you. He saved us."

William Archer wrestled with his older brother on the ground just metres away.

Quickly Violet helped Boy off the road to the footpath. For a moment they rested, gathering their breath amid the madness.

The struggle was in full flow, the people of Perfect battled side by side with their long-lost friends from No-Man's-Land. Woken up to their new reality, the Perfectionists fought fiercely against the Watchers for a freedom they never knew they'd lost.

"Violet," Boy said urgently. "Look!"

Edward Archer stood solemnly at the other side of the road. The stocky man watched in horror as his dreams of perfection crashed down around him. Suddenly, his gaze fell on William and George still exchanging blows. His face changed and with swift and purposeful movement, he disappeared into the crowd.

CHAPTER 34

CHOICES

"Edward's up to something," Boy said, rising gingerly to his feet. "We have to follow him."

"What do you mean?" Violet said.

"We're winning! I bet Edward's desperate to save what he can – the eyeballs, your dad and Macula. I bet he's gone to the Ghost Estate," Boy said quickly.

"But which way, Boy?" Violet asked.

Boy shrugged. "We have to split up. I'll go by the optician's; you go by No-Man's-Land. If you see him just follow behind, okay? I'll meet you at the estate entrance. Then we'll decide what to do."

Boy spoke with urgency and, though Violet didn't want him to be, he was right. They had to split up.

She waited on the footpath as Boy crossed the road heading towards the Archers' Emporium. He was still clutching his shoulder. She was just about to head off in the other direction when he turned and called her name. "Violet. Be safe, okay?"

She could only manage a nod – anything else would crack her voice and she wasn't crying in front of Boy, not now. Taking a deep breath she turned and raced towards No-Man's-Land.

The chaos of battle had taken over Edward Street and she narrowly missed being hit by a flying chair as she turned onto Archers' Avenue.

She hadn't said good luck to Boy. What if something happened to him? Lost in thought she was turning onto Rag Lane when she spotted a figure just ahead. She pulled back behind the bend and watched. A short, stout man passed through the gateway into No-Man's-Land. It was Edward.

She followed him at a distance down through the arch and onto Forgotten Road.

No-Man's-Land was empty. The streets were a mess. The insides of homes lay outside front doors where only hours before people had searched wildly for anything that could be used in battle. Violet had even seen some with cooking-pot helmets on their heads. Now the place was lonely, like a warm seat someone had just left, though the crashes and cries of the battle in Perfect seeped in over the high stone walls.

Edward moved as fast as his stout figure allowed him, up Forgotten Road towards the orphanage. Then he scuttled down to the right along one of the lanes, as if he was heading for the river. Suddenly he ducked left and came to a halt in the middle of a dimly lit, dingy back alley.

Violet had poked her head down there before but Boy had warned her never to explore it. He'd said it was a place where bad things happened. Every window on the alley was broken and rubbish was piled knee-deep against graffitied walls. Rats scampered in and out of the waste as if it was their playground.

Holding her nose to block out the stench, she crouched down behind a bin of rotting food as Edward disappeared inside a derelict building.

He vanished round the back of a battered iron door which had the words *Erebus Emporium* sprayed in red over a set of crossbones. Torn and tattered posters patterned the broken windows with headlines like *Passion for Poison?* or *Mad about Murder?* Violet's heart pounded.

A few minutes later, the door screeched on its hinges and Edward Archer returned to the alley carefully carrying a small, slim object.

"Pretty pistol." He smiled stroking the long, black

neck of the deadly weapon. "I'm sure you could cause damage, my dear."

What was he doing with a gun? Violet lost her balance and tipped against the bin, rattling it. Edward shoved the pistol into his pocket and looked around the empty street. She ducked and waited. Sweat raced down her forehead and stung her eyes. She held her breath.

A rat ran out from behind some bins and scuttled down the road. Satisfied, Edward continued out of the alleyway and turned left, heading towards the river. He was going to the Ghost Estate.

Violet needed something. She couldn't go unarmed now that he had a gun! She raced back out onto Forgotten Road. Surely she'd find something in the contents that were scattered outside homes. She was busy rifling through a cardboard box filled with small shovels when a swish of material caught her eye.

She stopped dead and turned. Rose Brown stood in the middle of the empty road. The hem of her apron swung a little as she moved nervously from foot to foot.

"Mam?" Violet whispered, her voice trembling.

Rose didn't answer.

"Mam!" she said, running to Rose's side. "Mam, what are you doing here?"

Rose looked at Violet, her eyes blank.

"Mam it's me, Violet!"

"Oh, were you speaking to me, little girl? I'm sorry I thought you were talking to your mother. I suppose I am the only one in this strange place," Rose replied, looking around in a daze.

"Mam! Mam, please, it's me," Violet choked, her voice breaking.

"I'm sorry, you must be confused."

"You can't have forgotten me already. You can't, Mam. Please! I only left a few days ago."

Her mother eased away from Violet. "I don't know how I ended up in this place," she stuttered, turning her back on her daughter. "I was walking up from the bookshop, someone bumped against me and my glasses fell off. Suddenly there were all these people around and they were fighting and it made me nervous. Then I saw children coming out from a lane; it looked quieter than the street. I'd never noticed before. Isn't that odd? So I walked down here and…"

"It's No-Man's-Land, Mam. It's where I've been. I've missed you so much…"

"Please," Rose interrupted, "I'd rather you didn't call me that – what would your real mother say! Have you hit your head, dear? Maybe it's this place. It is very confusing."

Violet searched her mother's face for some recognition, something that told her she had not been forgotten. Rose began to back away.

"Do you happen to know how to get out of here? I have to get to the shop; I ran out of eggs, you see. You can't make Madeira cake without eggs." She laughed nervously.

"I'll get William," Violet said suddenly. "That's what I'll do. I'll get William. He'll fix the ReImaginator and then he'll fix you. I have your imagination, Mam. I left it at Merrill's. We couldn't fix you then because you were on the other side of town, though I really wanted to. I'm so sorry, Mam!" Violet's eyes welled with tears.

"I think you've banged your head, dear. Anyway it was lovely to meet you, but I must be on my way."

"I can help you get out of here," Violet blurted desperately. "Please, please, follow me!"

Rose looked around cautiously and after a little hesitation followed her daughter. They were just near the arch when a loud bang shook the streets. Violet and Rose jumped in unison.

"My goodness, that sounded like a gunshot!" Rose gasped, her hands cupping her mouth.

It had to be Edward! Boy, her dad, Macula, William... their faces all flooded her mind. What was she doing? She was about to abandon them all! The only way to save Perfect, and her family, was by working together. She couldn't be selfish.

"Mam," she said firmly, "you have to stay here. There's

trouble in Perfect. I have to go but I'll be back for you. I promise."

"I'm not your mother, little girl. Please stop calling me that!"

"I'm sorry, I'm sorry," Violet stuttered. "It's, erm…it's the Archers. They asked me to find you. They said you make the best…erm…the best Madeira cake in Perfect. They want you to make some for a party they're having…"

"A party, how wonderful. Why didn't you say so sooner? We must get going then. I really need those eggs now," Rose said, walking up the steps towards Rag Lane.

"No!" Violet shouted. "No, they said to wait by the steps. They are getting the eggs delivered here. The shop is closed for Christmas."

"Closed for Christmas? But it's only September!"

"Oh, Christmas is early this year," Violet said, pulling over an abandoned crate. "Sit on this and don't move until I come back. The Archers are very excited."

"Okay, but be sure and hurry back with the eggs, won't you?"

Violet nodded then sprinted at bullet speed through the streets, slowing only to negotiate her way over the footbridge.

She stopped at the entrance to the Ghost Estate. She'd promised to meet Boy there but he was nowhere to be seen. Maybe she was too late?

CHAPTER 35

THE LAST STAND

Violet waited a few minutes in the darkness. Boy still hadn't arrived. She had to go in. She snuck by the pillars past the billboard of the happy family and round the green to her left.

Violet was nearing Macula's house when another shot ripped the air.

Suddenly the night was filled with the shrill cry of a thousand wailing babies. The eyes were awake. Goosepimples pricked her skin.

"Oh, shut up!" someone yelled.

Violet ran and ducked behind a half-built wall in the garden of Macula's house, as two figures emerged, walking across the green in her direction.

Edward Archer was pushing her dad roughly over the grass. They stopped briefly and Edward pulled two eye plants from the soil, throwing them into a plastic bag he took from his pocket. The screeches and wails grew louder and the plants shook in a mass frenzy.

Her father seemed very weak and stumbled several times trying to keep pace with Edward. What had they done to him? She looked away, plunged her fingers deep into the loose earth and squeezed the soggy soil. Her body shook; she wanted to act but she'd learned the art of timing from Boy.

"Faster, Eugene!" Edward roared. "We have to get out of here. That blasted brother William never could keep to his own business."

"I can't move any faster." Her dad coughed, tripping over a tuft of grass. "I haven't eaten in days."

"I fed you last week!"

"I'm not a plant," her father complained. "Once a week isn't enough... Where are you taking me?"

"Somewhere else," Edward sneered. "I'm going to create my own Perfect where William won't find me." He was advancing on Macula's house.

"What about my family? You promised they'd be okay."

"Oh, they are, Eugene. Well your wife is at least. She's _perfect_. As for that daughter of yours, I left her in the middle of a battle." He let out a hollow laugh. "With any luck my Watchers have sorted her out by now."

"Violet's fighting back?" Eugene said, with a hint of hope. "I knew it. She's braver than all of us."

Her father's voice was weak. He was standing on Macula's lawn just metres away from Violet – a broken man. She had to do something.

Suddenly she was on her feet.

"Dad!"

Eugene Brown turned to face his daughter. All weakness left him and he ran, wrapping her in his bony embrace. He held Violet tighter than ever before. All her bravery fled and she was his girl again as she collapsed into his arms.

Another shot cut the night.

Eugene pushed Violet behind his back and turned to face Edward. The stocky twin pointed his pistol at the pair.

"Eugene! GET. BACK. HERE!"

"You've had your day, Edward Archer. I won't let you take my family." Her father's voice was strong and steady, like the old him.

"I don't want your family. They can go to hell as far as I care. You're the only one I need!" Edward's eyes bulged ready to pop their sockets.

"You can't have me. You've taken enough! You have

348

my research, take it and leave us be. Do your sick project somewhere else!"

"I can have whatever I want. I have a whole town at my fingertips."

"Had," Violet shouted, sneaking out from behind her father. "The town isn't yours any more. William saved it!"

Violet noticed movement in the upstairs window of the house. A shadow passed by the pane and rested there for a moment then retreated back into the shadows of the room. It was Macula Archer.

"William is a better man than you'll ever be," Violet roared, drawing all attention towards her.

"Oh, William the golden boy. Everybody loves William. Well, he can take Perfect if he wants but I will have his precious Macula! She's mine." Edward laughed.

"You kept her prisoner," Violet shouted, loud enough for Macula to hear. "You told her lies, made her believe William was dead when he's not!"

"You'd better shut your mouth, little girl!" Edward's voice was full of venom.

Macula gently prised open the upstairs window. Eugene had seen her now too.

"Just go, Edward, we won't try to stop you. Perfect is gone. The game's over!" her dad shouted.

"Not without Macula!"

"She doesn't love you!" Violet roared.

"I will not leave without her! William robbed me of my mother – I didn't really want that old bat anyway. He robbed me of my friends too. Okay, so they were a bunch of idiots – but when he stole Macula, that was too much. He didn't get to keep her though, did he? She's mine now. I'm taking something from William, I'm doing it right under his nose and there's no way you Browns can stop me. Macula loves me!"

Edward Archer turned and charged for the house. The window was fully open. It was now or never. Violet raced across the lawn towards him.

"She doesn't love you. She loves William!"

The stout twin stopped, turned and glared at Violet. His eyes changed. Hatred was replaced by evil. She'd made a deadly mistake. Time slowed. He raised his arm and cocked the gun. A faint click, then BANG!

Something heavy slammed into Violet's chest and she was catapulted backwards. The air left her lungs as she smashed into the soil. Everything went hazy, foggy. She couldn't see. Slowly shadows merged. Her father's face floated in the sky above.

"Violet! Violet are you okay?" a voice echoed around her.

"I'm...erm..." she couldn't reply.

The weight. Something was sitting on her chest. Edward must have shot her. It always happened this way in films. The person took ages to realize they'd been hurt. She felt no pain – there was never any pain in the movies.

"That boy. He saved your life!" her father stammered.

"What?" Violet bolted upright and the weight seemed to shift. She wasn't dying?

Boy slumped off her chest onto the grass beside her, unconscious. He was floppy just like he'd been after he'd fought Fists.

"Boy! Boy, please wake up!" she cried, kneeling over his body.

"Let me take a look," Eugene said, pulling Violet aside.

"Will he be okay, Dad?" she sobbed. "He's my best friend."

The front door of the house opened and Macula Archer ran out across the lawn picking up the gun from where it lay by Edward's open hand. The stout twin was out cold on the grass.

"Is your friend okay?" she panted, reaching Boy's side. "He saved your life."

Violet was hysterical as Macula pulled her away from the scene. She was shaking. Pain dug into her chest, she couldn't breathe. She couldn't lose him. He couldn't be dead. Not now. Not after everything.

Edward Archer was sprawled flat across the lawn behind Macula. The thickest book ever lay open beside him: *The World's One Thousand Worst Eye Ailments*.

"I dropped it on his head." Macula smiled, glancing up at the open window as she hugged Violet closer.

Boy's lips were a faint blue now. His cheeks paled too. Time slowed and Violet stood still, frozen, as her father bent over her friend. He was gently slapping Boy's face, saying his name. Anger boiled her blood. Edward Archer couldn't get away with this. Unable to watch any longer, she broke from Macula's arms and turned to the unconscious twin. But he had disappeared.

Quickly she scanned the area. His stocky figure was wobbling up the hill towards the graveyard. Furious, she sprinted after him. Anger propelled her legs forward. Everything was his fault and now he'd killed the best friend she'd ever had. Edward Archer would suffer. He would pay.

The twin staggered past the lantern. She followed, and watched as he slipped into the graveyard. Though it was the dead of night, she wasn't afraid as she entered through the turnstile.

Gravestones lined the path that divided the cemetery. She couldn't see him. She ducked down behind a headstone and waited, listening. Her heart beat loudly as her breath formed icy clouds in front of her. The graveyard was dead still.

"I know you're in here, Edward Archer," she shouted. "You won't get away with this. My dad and William are on their way."

"You're on your own, Violet!" The twin laughed, his voice echoing around the tombstones. "Aren't you afraid?"

Something moved behind her. Quickly she turned and raced after the figure. Edward cut through the tightly packed graves. In her haste she tripped and fell onto the path, bloodying her palms. He stopped and turned; a shadow in the night.

"What's wrong, Violet?" he mocked, moving towards her.

Suddenly her dad's voice carried on the air.

"Violet! Violet, where are you?" He was at the graveyard wall.

"Seems like you're saved, this time, Violet," Edward sneered. "But we'll meet again."

A strange sound like stone crunching over stone filled the space. Violet picked herself up and raced to where Edward had stood moments before but he'd vanished behind a tombstone.

She checked nearby but saw nothing. Where could he have gone?

The tomb where he'd last stood was covered in thick moss. She scraped it away to read the inscription, but the text was too damaged by time to make any sense.

"Violet, why did you run off? Don't do that to me again!" her father panted, reaching her side.

"I'm sorry, Dad," she stammered, looking up at him. "It's just I wanted to catch Edward Archer. He can't get away with what he did to Boy. He's gone though, Dad, he's disappeared!"

"I know Violet," her father soothed, pulling her up into his arms. "Don't worry, we'll track him down. Those Archers are not as clever as they think. As for your friend Boy, he's going to be fine."

"Boy's alive?"

"And kicking." Her father laughed. "Macula dropping that book on Edward's head caused him to misfire. Your friend just knocked himself out in the fall saving you."

Happiness, relief and exhaustion flooded Violet's body. She buried her head deep into her father's shoulder and cried, not for sad things, but for Boy. Her best friend was going to be okay.

Macula was tending to Boy on the soggy grass when they reached them. Violet ran over and hugged her friend.

"What's that for?" Boy smiled groggily.

"For you being alive!"

"I told you before, it'll take a lot more to kill me," he joked, "I'm a No-Man's-Lander you know!"

Her father bent down and helped Boy up from the ground. He was too hazy to walk unaided.

"Come on." Eugene smiled. "Let's go home."

A piece of paper lay on the lawn where Boy had been.

It must have slipped from his pocket in the fall. Violet picked it up and read the short message:

So you'll never be invisible.

Suddenly, she knew what had been familiar about the note: the beautiful handwriting. She'd seen it before in Macula's room – the letter on her desk. Holding the prized paper gently in her grasp she ran to catch the others.

"I think this is yours," Violet said, tugging on Macula Archer's sleeve. "You gave it to a friend of mine a long time ago."

"Oh, thank you," she said, a little puzzled.

Macula opened the note to read it, just as someone called her name in the distance. A figure was standing shadowed at the entrance to the Ghost Estate.

"Macula," William cried again, his voice shaky.

Macula stopped dead in the road. Violet almost walked into the back of her. Macula's hands cupped her mouth and she gasped, crumbling slightly on the spot. William raced along the tarmac and on reaching her, wrapped Macula in his arms as she struggled to stand.

Moments later she grabbed his face.

"It's you, it's really you," she repeated over and over again as if the words were only true if she said them a million times.

Violet was watching the pair in silence when she noticed her dad beckoning to her.

"Leave them be, Violet," Eugene said gently.

She tiptoed round the couple and took Boy's other shoulder. The three hobbled together out of the Estate towards the bridge into No-Man's-Land.

"Dad," she said, looking up.

"Yes, pet?"

"Mam will be okay too."

"I know pet," her dad said, a quiver in his tone.

❁　　❁　　❁

Everyone waited eagerly in Iris Archer's house for a war-worn William to fix the ReImaginator.

Violet was sitting beside her dad holding tightly to his hand while he used the other one to shovel Iris's home-made stew into his mouth. Violet had never seen him eat so much before, though she'd never seen him so skinny either.

Her other hand was wrapped around Boy's. He was still a little shaken after the fall.

Macula took up a seat beside him, her eyes red rimmed. Violet looked away pretending to be engrossed in a conversation Iris was having with Madeleine.

"I believe this is your note," Macula said, passing it across to Boy. "I remember the day so vividly, forming each and every letter, knowing that this was all you'd have of me. I'm your mother, Boy."

Boy's grip tightened on Violet's hand; she looked over trying to read his expression. He was silent, his dark eyes large on his pale face.

"I'm so proud of you Boy. You've turned into everything I've ever dreamed."

"But you...but you gave me away," he stuttered, gripping Violet's hand tighter.

Macula dropped her head and Violet could see she was crying.

"The twins told me your father, William, was dead. I thought they'd killed him – they hated him, you see. I had just discovered I was pregnant, and I knew if the brothers found out I was carrying William's child they'd kill you too! After William's disappearance and not in my right senses, I started to drink the twins' tea and wear their rose-tinted specs. It was easier to play a part in their world than to resist. Resisting made me think of William and it was too much for me to bear. They weren't able to take my imagination, I suspect, when I look back now as I could still think for myself, but grief took my mind from me, for a while a least. Then one day I found the wooden glasses in the Archers' Emporium. They looked so different to the rest of the specs that I tried them on and discovered the real horror the twins had created."

She stopped for a minute. Macula was shaking as though the memories were all too much. Violet squeezed Boy's hand, longing for him to say something to ease his mother's pain.

"I went to No-Man's-Land looking for William but nobody had seen him and so I believed the twins' story, I believed he'd died." Macula wept. "So I hid myself away in Perfect hoping nobody would notice you growing inside me and when it was time, I had you in secret. The moment I held you, my life made sense, you were it, you and…" She stopped and looked into Boy's eyes. "I knew of the orphanage from my trip to No-Man's-Land. It was the only way I had to protect you from the twins. So I gave you up…" Her eyes welled again.

"…Then I surrendered to them. I knew it was the only way I could stop myself from contacting you. If they found out you existed, they'd kill you. Giving myself up to them was the only way I could ensure you were kept secret – stayed safe. I thought of you every day, I wrote to you every day…"

"She did," Violet whispered. "I saw the letters."

"I'm so sorry, Boy," Macula said, as the tears spilled down her cheeks.

She reached across to him. Boy hesitated for a minute then held out his hand. Macula took it in hers and kissed it. Then she moved closer and wrapped him in a hug.

Boy squeezed Violet's hand one last time then let it go. She watched as tears filled her friend's eyes, then he closed them and buried his head deep into his mother's embrace.

Violet looked away; she was teary now too. Her mother was in the corner of the room busy chatting to Iris and Madeleine about baking and a new recipe she'd just discovered. Violet was silently willing William to fix the ReImaginator, when suddenly the kitchen door swung open and William walked in looking tired but happy.

"Rose," he said with a smile, "would you mind following me? I've a few books I'd like to discuss with you for the next book club."

"Oh," Rose said, turning away from Iris, "that's very kind of you. We're always looking for new suggestions."

Her mam dusted off her apron then followed William from the room. Violet and her dad looked at each other. Neither spoke or moved or even took a breath. It seemed like an eternity as the sucking noises seeped in under the kitchen door. Then loud snoring filled the room and Violet's heart beat faster. After what felt like an age, there was movement in the hall outside. Violet stood up from the table as the kitchen door opened.

Rose Brown stood in the doorway, tears streaming down her face as she searched the room for her family. Violet raced to her mother as Eugene pushed back his seat and stood up.

Rose opened her arms and Violet flung herself into them. Moments later her dad was by their side, wrapping them both in a huge bear hug.

"Welcome back, Rose," Eugene said, kissing her forehead.

"I missed you Mam!" Violet choked. "I thought I'd never…"

"Shush, Violet," her mother soothed. "I'm back now and I'll never leave either of you again."

"Mam?" Violet said, pulling back from her embrace.

"Yes?" Rose whispered.

"Promise me you'll never join another book club!"

Everyone burst into laughter as if a weight had been lifted in the room. When the mood settled Macula stood up from the table.

"William," she said, still holding firm to Boy's hand, "I've someone I'd like you to meet."

He looked at Macula, then down at Boy. Violet watched as her friend blushed and pushed himself up from the table to stand beside his mother.

A sharp cry filled the room. "I knew it, I felt it in my bones," Iris exclaimed, looking from Boy to William and back again.

"Boy is our son," Macula almost whispered.

William steadied himself against the table. Then took two strides and wrapped his family in a huge embrace.

After a few moments, Iris shuffled across the room and put her hand on William's shoulder.

"Do you mind if I join in?" She smiled, poking her head into the reunion, "I've waited a long time to give my grandson a squeeze."

CHAPTER 36

OUR TOWN

Boy and Violet sprinted down Edward Street past the newly planted flower beds. They were late.

"Did you hear George is on trial this week?" Boy panted.

"What'll happen to him?" Violet asked.

"He'll probably be sentenced with Fists and Bungalow and the rest of the Watchers." Boy smiled.

"At least we won't need to worry about them turning up again, unlike Edward. I wish we knew what happened to him. Sometimes I've nightmares he'll come back." Violet shivered.

"They'll find him, Violet," Boy reassured. "Anyway he'll never dare sneak back with those watching out for him," he said, pointing to the newly erected beds of eye plants.

"Ugh." Violet shuddered. "I still think they're creepy."

"Those *creepy* eyes are keeping you safe, Violet!" Boy smirked. "Anyway you have to admit it was a pretty ingenious idea of William's...I mean Dad's to connect them to a surveillance system. Now Edward will never get back into town without being spotted!"

"Oh my dad is sooo amazing!" Violet teased. "I still can't get used to the idea of you having parents."

"Imagine how I feel!" Boy joked. "I mean it is kinda cool though," he said, his tone a little more serious. "I can see now why you were so worried about your parents, Violet. It's nice having them around."

"Wait until they give out to you for not doing your homework. We'll see who loves them then!" Violet laughed, sprinting ahead down Rag Lane.

Everyone was tightly packed near the gateway into No-Man's-Land when the pair arrived and they had to push their way through to get to the front. Iris scolded them for being late while Macula laughed and pulled Boy into a bear hug, kissing his forehead. Her friend blushed and Violet had to stop herself from laughing.

There was a small, red velvet curtain on the wall near the gateway and William Archer's hand rested on its woven gold cord as he finished his speech. He was a hero since he'd saved the town, and couldn't walk down the street without being stopped. He was movie-star famous, Boy often boasted.

"And now let us break down the boundaries that divide us," William said, proudly.

A man in a yellow hard hat picked up a huge hammer and belted the gateway wall. Violet held her ears and watched as a hole formed in the stone big enough to see through into No-Man's-Land.

The crowd cheered in celebration.

"And welcome a new future where everyone is valued not just for what we have in common but for what makes us different. Let us build a society that appreciates opinion, is open to discussion and values each and every citizen just as they are. There is a great and fierce beauty in our imperfection." He smiled, pulling tight on the cord.

The curtains glided gracefully apart, revealing a marble engraved plaque:

Welcome to Town.

The crowd erupted once more.

"'Town' – what kind of a name is that?" Boy smirked.

"You can't talk!" Violet laughed. "And anyway, it's not just any town, Boy. It's our Town."

THE END. FOR NOW...

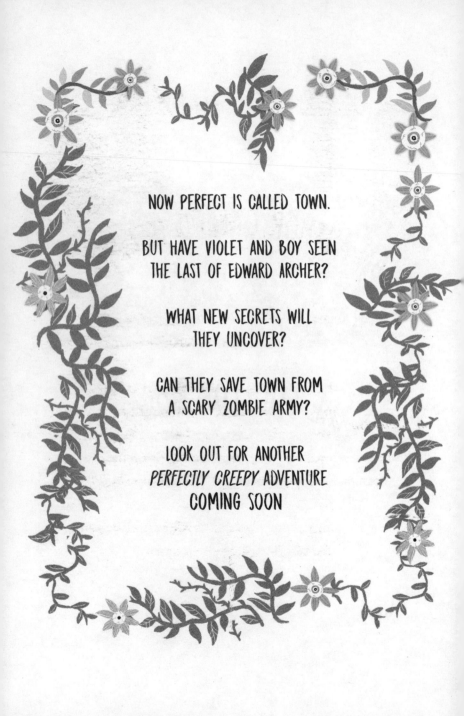

NOW PERFECT IS CALLED TOWN.

BUT HAVE VIOLET AND BOY SEEN
THE LAST OF EDWARD ARCHER?

WHAT NEW SECRETS WILL
THEY UNCOVER?

CAN THEY SAVE TOWN FROM
A SCARY ZOMBIE ARMY?

LOOK OUT FOR ANOTHER
PERFECTLY CREEPY ADVENTURE
COMING SOON

AN AUTHOR CALLED HELENA

Helena Duggan is a children's author, graphic designer and illustrator from Kilkenny, a medieval town in Ireland.

Lately, a lot of new things have happened in her life. She got a puppy – he limped out in front of her car one morning and she couldn't leave him behind. She married Robbie in her parents' hay barn, and welcomed baby Jo, born just months before the launch of her book.

She's enjoying settling down with all these things and creating lots of new memories.

IF YOU LOVE MYSTERY AND
ADVENTURE STORIES
GO TO:

WWW.USBORNE.COM/FICTION